Jennifer,

Thank you, ~~[illegible]~~

I hope you enjoy the adventure.

Take Care!

Sincerely, Ryan Oliver

M000310102

A FANTASY ADVENTURE SERIES: BOOK 1

BEASTS OF MEN AND GODS

SOLDIERS OF FIRE

Ryan M. Oliver

RYAN M. OLIVER

Soldiers of Fire, Beasts of Men and Gods: Book 1
Copyright © 2020 by Ryan Oliver. All rights reserved.

Published by:
Aviva Publishing
Lake Placid, NY
(518) 523-1320
www.AvivaPubs.com

Ryan Oliver
Ryan@Ryanmoliver.com
www.RyanMOliver.com
www.BeastsofMenandGods.com

ISBN: 978-1-944335-21-2
Library of Congress: 2020914141

Editor: Tyler Tichelaar, Superior Book Productions
Cover Designer: Shiloh Schroeder, FusionCW
Interior Book Layout: Shiloh Schroeder, FusionCW
Author Photo: Ashleigh Oliver

Every attempt has been made to properly source all quotes.

Printed in the United States of America

First Edition

4 6 8 10 12 14

DEDICATION

To my wife, Ashleigh: Thank you for all of your support, love, and guidance over the years. You are my greatest friend and my partner in life. I love you.

To my children, Lucas and Jackson: You boys motivate me every day to work as hard I can to make the best life possible for us, while having the most fun. Daddy loves you.

To my mother, Mary, and my siblings, Chris and Emily: Thank you all for the support, repeated brainstorming sessions, and hundreds of hours of evolving plot lines I bombarded you three with over the years. I love you.

To my family and friends: All of you have influenced my life. All of you have urged me forward. All of you have led me to who I am today. You know who you are. Thank you. I love you all.

ACKNOWLEDGMENTS

Everyone below has helped, supported, and inspired me to write this book. I thank them all:

To my family,

You know who you are, both blood and not. Thank you for being my sounding board, my editors, my creative inspiration, and my rock throughout this entire project. I love you all.

To my publishing coach, Patrick Snow,

Thank you for all of your guidance, knowledge, and experience. You truly helped me create my own destiny.

To my book publishing network: Mary West and The Mary West Network, Jeanne Broxton, Tyler Tichelaar, Shiloh Schroeder, Rachel Langaker, and Aviva Publishing,

Thank you for aiding me in this book's production, in networking, and for moral support. This book literally would not physically exist without you all.

To my friends, followers, and colleagues, both past and present,

The incredible support shown by all of you has truly inspired me to deliver to you and all of my readers the best story I can create. Thank you all!

To the fantasy authors before me, J. R. R. Tolkien, J. K. Rowling, Patrick Rothfuss, Christopher Paolini, and many more,

Authors inspire authors, artists inspire artists. I feel as if my vision for this story would never have begun to ruminate if it wasn't for your labors on your works.

CONTENTS

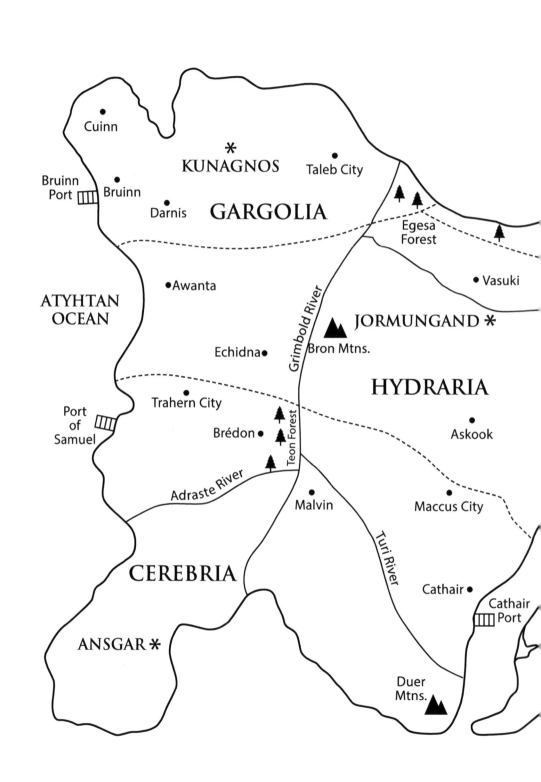

THE KINGDOMS OF RUXAR

CHAPTER 1

CHASING PREMONITIONS

Golden flames framed in silver light illuminated the dancing silhouettes. Clanging steel slashed through screams of terror in the firelight of the burning town. Young and old alike scurried as rodents from deadly serpents. An old man stood in the eye of the chaos, squinting through smoke and swirling embers. His body shook in the cold of the night and the wicked's actions.

An endless stream of hatred flowed into the engulfed hamlet. Helpless to stop it, the old man stumbled about aimlessly, being passed by soldiers—soldiers clad in armor, wielding deadly instruments, playing them for an ever-shrinking audience. As moments passed, the old man's ears flooded with shouts of fruitless rebellion and retribution. His stumbling rose no alarm, nor attention. He was invisible to those around him.

Among the choir of chaos, the old man heard raucous shouting in the distance. He advanced, shuffling slowly into the smoky curtain. A rush of wind pushed his attention toward a shadow. A towering form stood among the cyclone of fire and smoke, face illuminated by the sharp glow. The physique was of a man, chest out, proudly drinking in the sights resulting from his actions. An untainted helmet atop his head accentuated a scarred face and empty eyes.

The elder felt a deep fear strike through his chest. Shaking with dread and uncertainty, he turned away from the monster at the gate and back toward the harsh cries. Moving now like a man to the gallows, taking every step as if it were his last, he came upon several fluttering shapes emerging from the black and gray. A cluster of townsfolk huddling for safety, several soldiers out for blood, and one man, a guardian, soaring, leaping, and clawing at the attackers, came into view.

The old man became entranced by the guardian's movements. He watched intently as the young defender rolled and launched himself up and over swinging and slashing blades, striking fatal blows one after the other, and ushering mothers, fathers, and children out of the crumbling town. This deadly dance attracted more attention than that of a few passersby. He watched with great horror and desperation as the heroic guardian rapidly became overwhelmed like a bear to a beehive.

The young protector used his superior agility to parry and retreat, eliminating all he could. Inevitably, the hive of armored hornets encircled him. The protector, sensing the end, sent a war cry pulsating through the town that resonated with all who heard it. The old man quivered and fell to the ground, his senses berated and his mind hazy. In his last moments, he witnessed the soldiers as a pack of wolves, teeth gnashing and snouts snarling. Then, among the ring of howls and war cries, a final whirlwind of hatred and steel fell upon the protector, silencing him, snuffing out the bright light of a hero—a light never again to glow.

• • •

As the cries and clanging ceased, Nestor sprang from his slumber as a slingshot. Sweat poured from his bedclothes. His lungs burned as if he were there among the flames. The elderly Nestor gazed upon his beautiful wife, still asleep, and sat down to catch his breath.

"No. No. Not again," Nestor whispered to himself. "I can't. I won't."

A stirring Phaedra woke to find her husband distraught. "Are you unwell, my love?"

"It happened again. I must leave this time," said Nestor.

"Leave? Where?" asked Phaedra, startled by her husband's response.

"I don't know. I will figure that out as I move. I have to save them. I can't let this one go," Nestor said, still panting.

"Why this one and not all the others?" asked Phaedra.

"This one feels different. It feels big—bigger than any of us. I can't stay and do nothing."

"Do? What happened? What did you see?"

"A fire. But one caused by men. Not an accident like the others."

"You're going to leave your wife in the middle of the night for a fire? One that may not happen?" asked Phaedra, raising her voice.

"I'm sorry, my love. I wouldn't unless I believed it to be important." said Nestor, now getting dressed.

Phaedra stared at her husband, eyes dark with sadness. "I don't like this, Nestor. You have had visions before, but never have you reacted in this manner." She paused to calm her voice. "I fear for you. I know your gifts give you great insight, but I feel that once you leave, we will not see each other again."

Nestor stopped gathering clothes and sat down with Phaedra. When he looked into her eyes, he felt a wave of calm come over him. His pulse slowed and his breathing stilled. "I, too, am afraid. But I am more afraid of what will happen if I don't investigate."

Phaedra, sensing his genuine concern, reached over, clutched him, and pulled him in for an embrace. The two sat together in the night's silence, savoring every second. Moments later, Nestor gathered the last of his necessities, kissed his dear wife, and took off on a whim, chasing a premonition that would change their lives forever.

CHAPTER 2

FORESEEN
MISFORTUNES

Nestor limped over the threshold of yet another town. His journey to find the exact location he had seen proved to be harrowing in his old age. In his haste, he decided not to bring a horse. He figured the opportunity to gallop home might encourage his tired heart to turn back. However, now he knew that was a foolish decision. As he entered the small settlement, it seemed familiar. The buildings' facades, the village's layout, even the sturdy palisades echoed an imprint in his mind. *Could this be it?* Nestor thought.

Wide-eyed, Nestor stood in the middle of the wet road, looking for the courageous man in his vision. Minutes passed as he stood in the chilled air. Nestor approached a group of Cerebrian men enjoying a drink at a table outside the town pub, merrily talking with each other after a day of work.

"Excuse me. What town is this?"

One jubilant patron turned to Nestor. "Why, this is Brèdon of Cerebria."

"Brèdon. Thank you." Nestor nodded and began to turn away. "Cerebria…I've traveled incredibly far south."

"What was that old man?" asked the patron.

"Oh, nothing." Then a spark of inspiration hit Nestor and he turned back to address the group. "Have any of you seen a short, agile man with brown hair, traveling alone?"

"Oh, yes," slurred an inebriated man. "Look around; that describes most men in the realm."

"Oh, never mind. Go back to your drinking!" Nestor replied.

"I have! I know who you're talking about!" shouted a barmaid, approaching them. "He's staying in one of the huts back on the far side of town."

"Thank you. Enjoy your brew," Nestor said, heading toward the new location.

As Nestor arrived on the town's outskirts, he saw several huts. He had no idea which one the man resided in. So, being an elderly man with no time to spare, Nestor did the only sensible thing—he began yelling. "Hello! Is there a man traveling alone staying here?" He continued to yell until townspeople and patrons emerged, irritated. Some folks, furious with the old man's barking, yelped back even in their groggy state of consciousness. "Is anyone here traveling alone? Someone answer me!"

All of a sudden, a man ran out of the crowd. "What's going on here?" asked the man.

Nestor couldn't believe it. It was him! The man in his vision. His breath halted. Nestor staggered to the man, weary from travel and dizzy with success. "I believe you are the man I've been searching for."

"Oh? Are you sure? What does he look like?" the man asked.

"Well, son, he looks like you," said Nestor, mesmerized as if caught in a dream.

"Me? Why would you be looking for me?"

"We must talk in private," said Nestor quietly. "These people are making me nervous."

"Of course. Although, I think you made them nervous first."

The sturdy man walked Nestor to his hut where no one could interfere. As they entered, Nestor gladly fell onto the ruffled bed, to the relief of his feet and back. Long moments passed as the young man looked strangely at his elderly visitor. "So, why were you looking for me?"

"First, what is your name?" asked Nestor.

"Aedan."

"Aedan. Aedan of what?" Nestor asked.

"Of Dragonia, sir."

Nestor nodded, as if agreeing with Aedan's homeland choice.

"Sir, are you mad?" asked Aedan.

Nestor chuckled. "No, son, of course not. What would give you that idea?"

Aedan shook his head and rubbed his eyes, attempting to erase his negative thoughts of the elderly man. "Then exactly why are you here, sir?"

"I had a vision. I am one of very few people in my country who are burdened with this gift," Nestor said, now sitting up straighter on the bed. "I can sometimes see what my wife will say to me, or what one of my friends will do later in the coming days. Matters of that nature."

"So you are Gargolian?" asked Aedan.

"That is correct. You're smart. I like that. Dragonians are smart folk. Not like these Cerebrians here, large oafs. Anyway, I fell into a vision many nights ago. One of golden embers and silver coals. Men in armor slaughtering all in their path."

"What does that have to do with me?"

"I was just getting to that. Just wait. Throughout the vision, I saw you. You had picked up a sword to protect the people of this very town from being murdered."

"Murdered? I thought you said it was a fire," said Aedan.

"Yes, a fire set by soldiers. And you rose up to defend against these marauders."

"What marauders? Who did you see?"

"Then you were surrounded." Nestor paused. "And killed. Torn apart really. It was quite gruesome."

Aedan fell back and landed on his cot. "Right, and you expect me to believe this? It sounds to me like the wild nightmares of an old man. Not a vision of a prophet."

"Look here, son; I may be old, but I have been a seer nearly my entire life. I know what I saw, and you should heed my warning."

"First off," Aedan spat, irritated, "stop calling me son. We have not known each other long enough for you to call me friend. Secondly, prove it. Prove to me that you are a seer, or visionary, or whatever you call yourself."

"I can't."

"You can't?"

"I can't prove to you with physical items. But I can share stories from my past."

Aedan sat pondering for a long moment with his arms crossed. "All right, speak your stories. Change my mind."

Nestor breathed deeply, readying himself to relive his youth, and began. "Many years ago, as a young man, I was introduced to the love of my life, Phaedra. Her cherry-blossom hair and tantalizing eyes lured me to her." Nestor smiled at the memory. "Well, over time, she grew fond of me, though probably not as much as I did of her. Regardless, we were married young. During that time, we acquired a gargoyle as a gift of our union. We named him Fajer. To this day, he resides with us. Now over time, as you may know, once people cohabitate with a beast such as a gargoyle, or a dragon perhaps, they can take on certain odd attributes. In this case, Fajer was a rare gargoyle indeed. He could sense the presence of danger in our land, and would disappear at odd hours, even for a gargoyle, to investigate and frighten off anything that might threaten us. Never did we have attacks by bandits or even wolves that bothered our livestock."

"Perhaps you did not have any in your region," interrupted Aedan.

"No, my family fought off many who thought themselves entitled to what others have, at least until Fajer," Nestor replied. "Throughout Fajer's time with us, he became part of our family. Fajer would sleep in our home from time to time. I realize now that he stayed close when he felt danger looming. After several years passed, Phaedra and I decided the time was right to start a family. Around the time Phaedra announced her pregnancy to our families, I began to have premonitions. The visions that came to me were innocent at first. Scenes of conversations with Phaedra and others. Scenes of clumsy moments, and even events as silly as knowing when the chickens would escape their coop."

"That seems like nothing but knowing routines of others, lucky guesses," interjected Aedan. "Not premonitions of the future."

"Please, let me explain. It takes time for abilities to develop. You, at one point, did not know how to ask questions. First you had to learn to speak, and then later, to think for yourself, yes?" said Nestor, perturbed by the interruptions.

"I see. Continue. I apologize."

"As I was saying, small insignificant events in our lives unraveled every night when I closed my eyes. After several months of this, I finally confided in Phaedra. She told me if it were true, then I would be burdened with these visions for a lifetime. I would need to be wise in how I acted upon them. The grander the vision, the more dangerous the repercussions if I were to interfere or inform others of their futures." Nestor looked around and sighed heavily. "I am still uncertain if what I am doing here is right. But I cannot let this one go."

"What you saw was truly that terrible?" asked Aedan, compassion now in his voice.

"Yes. It shook me to my bones."

"Please continue. I must hear more."

"Soon after Phaedra warned me of my gift, I fell into a vision of a handsome man receiving a promotion into the Gargolian army as a lieutenant. At the end, I realized it was my son. In the vision, he was embracing my wife; I saw her cherry blond hair had, by then, turned to silver. I knew then I'd had a deep premonition—one that, if I informed my family of it, could potentially not occur. So I waited…for more than twenty-five years, keeping this secret until the day of my son's elevation to lieutenant. That night, I told Phaedra about the vision. She smiled at me, kissed me, and thanked me for holding onto that piece of knowledge."

Aedan nodded his head. "If what you are saying is true, then why did you not go to your son after having the vision of fire and death?"

"Being a seer is seen as a bad omen in my country. In fact, my son did not learn of my ability until recently. My wife informed him. She felt it was time for him to be included in our family secret. However, if he were to bring what he knows to his command, or even to the king, my family could be in danger."

"I see," said Aedan. "People in power would want to use you, or potentially use your family to get to you."

"That was the fear. I told my visions only to Phaedra to keep everyone safe. Keeping them to myself proved to be very difficult during several other events. One, in particular, will haunt me for the rest of my days. The vision showed a neighbor's house. In my sleep, I saw their house engulfed in red. The fire swept orange sparks and embers across the street. Smoke billowed and belched from the rooftop. I saw failed attempts at dousing fire with buckets from the wells. Nothing could quench it. My heart ached as I witnessed my friends and neighbors struggle to gain control. Once my neighbor's home sat tattered and scorched, the people of my village rummaged through the rubble, only to find the remains of the entire family. Both parents and their child had been taken by the heat and flames."

"You saw your neighbors die, and you swore to do nothing?" asked Aedan. "I couldn't do that."

"Neither could I. Until that moment, all I had seen were small mishaps and joyous events. Nothing so tragic. I had to see if I could stop it. Even if Phaedra warned me not to. For the next several nights, I waited. Staying close, I wandered about the perimeter, giving the excuse that I was searching for bothersome rodents. I slept for only a few moments at a time to ensure the family's dwelling was safe from harm. Although, it seems the world has a sense of humor. The world deeply enjoys irony." Nestor broke off. A tear swelled up in his eyes and fell down to his scraggly beard. "Perhaps moments or hours later, I could not stay awake any longer. A wave of exhaustion pushed my eyes closed, and I fell into a deep, visionless sleep—something I have not experienced since before the premonitions began. Then, as I awoke to Phaedra shaking me, I realized that not only had I missed catching the fire, and saving the family, but in my tired stupor, it appeared I had toppled a lantern that ignited the exact blaze I had set out to prevent." Nestor ended his story, looking at Aedan, his face lined with tears.

"And what makes you think this time will be different? You could not save a family from that house fire," said Aedan, though he instantly regretted his words. "I'm sorry; that was ill of me to say."

Nestor nodded his head in understanding. "Last time, I did not clue anyone in on the misfortunes I foresaw. This time, I intend to break the burden of my silence in hopes of changing what has already been set in motion. It will happen if we don't do something. Of that, I am certain."

"What do we do? Are you asking me to fight?" Aedan asked.

"No, I am asking you to become a leader. Will you?" Nestor inquired nervously.

Aedan put his hand on his eyes and sighed deeply. He stood up and looked down at the old man. "Yes, I will help. I'm not sure what it is about you, old man, but yes. To be honest, I am only agreeing because I'm interested in seeing if you are wrong, and terrified to see what happens if you are right."

Nestor drew a great sigh of relief and thanked him. "I will help you prepare."

CHAPTER 3

TRENCHES

Aedan stood up and walked out of the hut, followed closely by Nestor. "Where is the town leader's house?" Aedan asked a group of people congregating outside. All were still irked by the disturbance Nestor had made, so no one answered.

Nestor reached out, grabbed Aedan's arm, and pulled him toward the center of town. "He lives there," said Nestor, confidently pointing at a house slightly larger than the others.

"How do you know?" asked Aedan.

"Do I really have to answer that question?"

"Never mind," said Aedan, feeling foolish.

Nestor and Aedan rushed to the one-roomed house and Nestor barged right in, unannounced. A large Cerebrian man, standing eight feet tall and with bushy hair, shot up out of bed, nearly hitting his head on the ceiling. "What is this?" shouted the town leader.

"Sorry for this," said Nestor.

"Get out," ordered the town leader, "or I'll—"

"Again, I am sorry," said Nestor, "but it's important."

"I truly apologize for him, sir," said Aedan, stepping forward and grabbing Nestor. "He's quite mad."

"Mad? I thought you believed me?" said Nestor.

Aedan shrugged. "Begrudgingly. Your tales of being a seer were moving. But I still have my doubts."

"What is going on here?" asked the town leader. "Did you say a seer?"

"We need to talk to you," said Nestor.

"What about? And why so damn late? Wait; you're not one of those boys who doesn't know how to talk to the ladies, are you? Because I'm not asking them to lower themselves to—"

"No!" Aedan shouted, interrupting.

"Shut up! Both of you!" Nestor shouted.

"There's no need to be rude," the town boss said. "You've already broken into my house. I should have both of you fed to the cerberus pup outside for what you just did." Once everyone was quiet, he stood up, stepped outside briskly, saw people gossiping in the streets, and returned to the confines of his invaded home. "Well, what is it then?" he demanded.

"Nestor," Aedan said, "answer the man."

"Yes, yes. All right, boy; this mind isn't what it used to be."

"Yes. I figured that out."

Nestor shot Aedan a disapproving look, then turned back to the Cerebrian man. "What did you say your name was?"

"I didn't give it. You barged in on me so fast I didn't even have a chance to hit you, let alone give my name. It's Magnus."

"Pleasure. I'm Aedan of Dragonia. And my rude counterpart here is Nestor of Gargolia."

"Now what is so important that it couldn't wait till morning?" Magnus asked.

Nestor began his story all over, about his foresight, and particularly the vision of Brèdon on fire and under attack, hoping to convince Magnus faster than he had the young Dragonian. After his speech, Magnus seemed skeptical. "How do you know this is true? You mentioned being a seer earlier."

"Yes, I have had visions since I was a young man, and all have come true," Nestor said with conviction. "Being a seer is seen as a burden because it comes with responsibilities not to interfere, but I couldn't ignore telling someone this time."

"I don't know about this," Magnus said.

"If we do not prepare and an attack occurs, everyone here will die, including yourself," Nestor said.

Magnus gave a heavy sigh. "How long do you think we have?"

"Maybe an hour, a day, a week. I'm not sure, but in any case, being slightly prepared is better than being completely exposed," Nestor said.

"What do we need to do?" Magnus asked.

"I have a few ideas that might work," said Nestor, relieved to be listened to.

"You actually believe him?" Aedan asked Magnus. "Just like that?"

"Boy," Magnus replied, "I have heard of many strange happenings in this land, and more so of people in the north region of Ruxar. Visionaries have been put to death for conspiracy, only later to have their visions end up being true. That means mad Nestor here is risking more than just looking foolish by talking to us tonight."

Aedan's face turned red with embarrassment. "Can you send out a rider to warn your King Rordan?" asked Aedan. Nestor smiled approvingly.

"Yes, I can, but I'm not sure the king will believe us. I mean, if an attack occurs, if men from one country are being sent out to take over another, it would be the first time in the history of Ruxar," said Magnus, sounding sullen over Nestor's prediction.

"Nevertheless, send a rider to King Rordan at Ansgar," said Nestor firmly.

"All right," Magnus agreed.

"Excellent," said Nestor with a smile.

Right away, Magnus walked outside and rang a bell signaling everyone to arise. Immediately, people came out of their huts to see why the bell was ringing so early in the morning.

"Who is ringing that wretched bell?" yelled a disheveled man.

"Apologies for waking you all, but we have information of a threat," said Magnus. The annoyed and tired townspeople clamored toward Magnus.

"What threat?" shouted one man.

"A rogue cerberus?" shouted another.

"Sickness?" asked a woman.

"No," said Magnus. "However, I have on good authority that an army is coming to attack and seize this town." Everyone turned to each other, whispering and laughing to their own commentary. "I know it may sound far-fetched," Magnus added.

"Far-fetched? It's nonsense. In the whole of our lives, no army has ever marched on a settlement. What's changed?" asked another person in the crowd.

"All I know is that we must prepare for the worst," said Magnus.

"But what can we do? We're all just miners and farmers. How can we make a difference?" asked another.

"Today's scheduled work is canceled," Magnus replied. "I will be assigning embattlement tasks momentarily. In the meantime, I need to introduce the men who alerted us to this threat." At that moment, Nestor and Aedan approached the bell and stood next to Magnus for all to see. "This man here is Nestor of Gargolia. And this man is

Aedan from Dragonia. These two brave men brought me communications of the threat and will be aiding us with our preparations."

"How do we know one or both of their countries is not sending an army here?" asked another from the crowd.

"It breaks down to whether you trust me and my judgment," said Magnus. "If you don't, then you can find somewhere else to live."

"Magnus, if you are truly concerned, shouldn't we evacuate and go somewhere more fortified?" asked someone in the crowd.

"No, this is our town, and I am not leaving it for anything. We need your help if we are going to survive this attack. I am as apprehensive as all of you to accept this as truth. However, peace can't be forever, and we are lucky for the time we've had." The townspeople hesitantly agreed. "Now, if there is to be a fight, shall we be the first victims or the first heroes?"

"What do you want us to do?" asked one person.

"We will need a group to prepare the defenses, and another to be our militia. I need everyone in town to help, or we may not see tomorrow." It seemed Magnus' speech had convinced them to help. Magnus instructed folks to prepare for a hard day's labor, and to meet back as soon as the horizon glinted with light.

• • •

As the townspeople dispersed, Nestor, Aedan, and Magnus conversed. Nestor led the charge by giving defensive suggestions. Over the next several hours, the prophetic Gargolian drew up strategies and jobs for Magnus to delegate to his people. Later that morning, Magnus instructed people to work on a large trench around the three exposed walls of Brèdon. This could be used to slow down or even trap some of the invaders. At the back of Brèdon lay the

Teon forest. This forest would be their escape route if the fighting townspeople were overrun by the invading army. Anyone who did not wish to participate in the battle could hide in the forest's thick brush and tall trees.

"Do you have an armory?" Nestor asked Magnus.

"Yes. It's two buildings down past my hut," said Magnus.

"Great. I'll head there now," said Aedan eagerly.

"Hold on, Aedan!" called out Nestor. "You said you have a cerberus pup on the premises?"

Magnus smiled wide. "I wouldn't call him a puppy. That was more a term of endearment. He's more of an ornery three-headed teenager that could consume you thrice as fast as any other beast."

"So he is an adult then? Fully grown?" asked Aedan.

"Oh, yes. Kaustos is mature. However, he is dangerous."

"Dangerous enough to be used in a fight?" asked Nestor.

"No. Not reliably. He would attack everyone. He has lost the sentiment between friend and enemy."

"Where is he?" asked Aedan, curious.

"In the back of town. I had him caged. The last time he was out, he killed and ate a whole horse, rider included," said Magnus.

Nestor and Aedan's eyes widened. "Well, then, perhaps we will be leaving Kaustos alone," said Nestor.

"May I see him?" asked Aedan.

"I have no problem with it. Just don't stand too close to the cage," said Magnus nervously. "I'm certain that cage won't hold if he gets too excited."

"On second thought, I will just visit the armory then."

· · ·

Aedan walked toward the building, through the door, and lit the lantern inside the armory with a match on the windowsill. The building was old and dusty. Inside hung cobwebs, thick as thread. Its one window had accumulated enough dust to render the glass' transparency useless. In the past, an armory's purpose in any settlement would be to defend against a rogue creature—a beast on the loose who was maiming folks, damaging property, or killing livestock. Surprisingly, Brèdon's armory contained chainmail vests, dozens of axes, bows, an abundance of arrows, and several swords, some, including giant-sized ones, only found in Cerebria due to the unique strength and size of its people in regards to the other kingdoms.

Aedan began collecting weapons to bring to the front wall. He would allow Magnus the honor of assigning others to move more. After removing dozens of items from the rustic building, he was confused by the sight of many barrels of oil. *I wonder if we could use these,* he thought. He quickly dismissed the idea and continued to unload the weapons from the dusty refuge. As he proceeded, inspiration hit Aedan like a rock to the head. He realized the oil's usefulness.

Scrambling about, Aedan ran over to see how construction on the large trenches was progressing. To his amazement, the workers had come together and nearly completed the front portion of the trenches. Magnus, with forty men, their spouses, and older children, was digging the trench rapidly.

"Nestor!" Aedan called when he spotted him. Nestor stood on top of the front wall of the town, supervising the digging of the trench. Aedan ran over to him. "How are we doing?" asked Aedan, panting.

"Oh, we are moving along well," said Nestor.

"Great. How long do you think it will take to finish?"

"At the rate they're digging, by evening's end, the front and portions of the sides should be complete."

"Impressive," said Aedan. "By the way, I found oil in the armory. I thought we could use it to fill the trenches as a last resort."

"That's a great find," said Nestor. "Once Magnus calls the workers down, we need to think about assembling a defense force. In the meantime, go work with Magnus. Help him dig, and then the two of you can make an announcement to the people about volunteers."

Aedan nodded, climbed down, and joined the digging party next to Magnus. "It appears your people work quickly."

"The Cerebrian work ethic is legendary," boasted Magnus.

"Then why have I never heard of it until now?" Aedan asked.

"Perhaps you were too busy running through visions of being a hero," said Magnus, smiling.

Aedan grinned. "You're right. I need to find other hobbies."

"We Cerebrians have few hobbies because we are experts at everything we do in our country."

"Yes. It seems as though many of you have a bit of a physical advantage on others."

Magnus grinned. "Why, yes, the gift of the cerberus is most useful."

"Then, why does it seem that not all Cerebrians possess the same size and strength?" asked Aedan.

"Your lack of knowledge amuses me," said Magnus.

"But seriously, why is that?"

"No one truly knows why. All I know is it has to do with your bond with the beast. For example, I have had many cerberus as friends. Many I have raised as pups, and their children and so on. If one is raised with the great beasts and they believe you worthy of their friendship, somehow you benefit. In my people's case, we grow to mirror the brute power of the mighty cerberus."

"Okay, that makes sense, I guess. Then why haven't more of my people developed abilities because of our close association with dragons? And why is it that everyone seems to have different proportions of the same ability?"

Magnus grinned wide. "Perhaps they were too busy asking questions and not working. The beasts don't like talkative ones."

Aedan chuckled at Magnus' bantering. "If you are so well-equipped to handle anything, then we ought to think about assembling the fighting force. I'd say it's time to split the group in two now. Half continue to work, while the others prepare for bloodier endeavors."

Magnus' smile quickly faded to a serious scowl. "I understand." The large town boss turned to face his people, "Attention!" he announced. All work ceased and eyes turned to face their leader. "They're all yours, young Dragonian," Magnus told Aedan.

Surprised at being put on the spot, Aedan stammered a moment until he found his voice. "We need volunteers who wish to fight alongside myself, Nestor, and Magnus. Please come immediately to the armory to be suited with the proper-sized chainmail and weapons," said Aedan, feeling a bit foolish.

Aedan began walking from the trenches and toward the armory. To his surprise, people followed him and Magnus to receive their armor and weapons. Everyone stood in a cluster of nervous apprehension. With guidance from Magnus, Aedan began distributing swords, bows, and such to the people he hoped would be alive in the morning.

As preparations continued, Aedan counted the number of people he gave weapons to who would serve as soldiers in the possible onslaught. After several minutes, he had counted seventy-five warriors, including Nestor, Magnus, and himself. Brèdon's defenders consisted of mostly men, plus several women and a handful of adolescents.

While enlisting the new soldiers, Aedan discovered two like himself who were not from Cerebria. The first was Aloysius, a young man of eighteen from the Islands of Manticoria; he was much smaller, both in muscle and height, compared to the massive Cerebrians. Aedan recalled, however, hearing of the Manticorians' prowess in shows of accuracy, coordination, and balance. It was said that a person imbued with the manticore skill could hit a target with any object, weapon or not. The second was a woman from Hydraria named Turia. She had dark brown hair that came to her shoulders and framed her brown eyes and eloquent face. Hydrarians were people of great creativity, and some, as it was told, were blessed with the gift of long life. Although, seeing that no hydra had roamed the central mainland in decades, no Hydrarians had benefited from the beasts' proximity and, consequently, their energy.

After Aedan and Magnus completed their tasks, they wandered over to check the trench's progress.

"Wow!" said Aedan, astonished.

"Oh, yes," said Nestor when Aedan and Magnus approached him. "I, too, am quite impressed with their productivity."

The townspeople had completed the front trench, and they had nearly completed the two sides. The only task left was to pour in the oil Aedan had found in the armory.

"Nestor, are you ready to fight?" asked Aedan.

"Of course! Even in my sixties, I can still bout with you young men," said Nestor.

Aedan smiled. "I hope you are wrong about this attack, Nestor."

Nestor breathed heavily. "So do I, boy. So do I."

Day turned into dusk with many defensive tasks having been accomplished. The trench was dug. It was as deep as Aedan was tall, wrapping around the front and two side walls of Brèdon. Oil had been poured into all parts of the trench; in some parts, the thick black liquid would have come up to a soldier's ankles. Magnus had completed handing out weapons to the soldiers and encouraging the others to prepare their belongings so they could retreat to the Teon Forest.

After all was organized, the soldiers were instructed to return home to sleep. A lot had been accomplished in a short time. Now they had to wait and hope no one would come. Once the town had settled in for the night, Aedan, Nestor, and Magnus stood on top of the wall and watched for any movement in the distance.

"Anything?" asked Magnus.

"No, nothing yet," said Nestor calmly.

"All I see is darkness," said Aedan, becoming anxious. "Didn't you say the battle occurred at night, Nestor?"

"Yes," Nestor replied. "We need someone on watch. Magnus, could you arrange that?" Magnus nodded and moved away to locate newly anointed soldiers for yet another task.

"If it happens, we'll be ready for them…whoever they are," said Aedan.

"I hope so," Nestor replied. "This will be dangerous, Aedan— something most have never seen."

"Most? Have you seen combat before?" asked Aedan.

"Stories for another time, perhaps. Now go rest. We need to be ready."

CHAPTER 4

DRAGON'S BREATH

Aedan was awake but had not yet been called for a shift on the wall. He felt refreshed, despite a twinge of guilt for not taking watch. Perhaps the old man was wrong; wouldn't that be a relief? The night had not yet given way to the sun's morning rays; a few more hours and it would be bright enough to investigate the surrounding areas for trouble.

Without warning, Aedan found himself in the presence of an uneasy Magnus. "Aedan, wake up!" he shouted, while grasping Aedan and shaking him vigorously.

Aedan sat up hurriedly to see what the commotion was about. "What is it?"

"Look! On the horizon! An army!" exclaimed Magnus.

Aedan sprinted to the front wall and climbed the stairs. The force inched upward from the dim horizon line. Blocks of warriors marched in synchronous formation. Glinting steel winked at Brèdon as the day's light grew brighter.

"What do we do?" Aedan asked.

"Sound the bell. Wake everyone. We must get them all to their positions," said Magnus.

The large town boss sounded the bell once again. Everyone began running out of their homes, scrambling for their chainmail vests and weapons. In just moments, every soldier was suiting up, stringing his bow, and strapping a sword and ax to his hips.

The sun had not yet fully risen; the morning dew had already made its claim upon roofs, so Aedan's breath was visible even in the dimly lit town. Aedan and Magnus began giving directions to their soldiers. The task was demanding, like herding livestock into a barn after being spotted by a larger creature. After many moments of confusion, the two leaders had finally sorted the soldiers and placed them in positions where they could each fire arrows at the advancing army.

"Is everything in place?" asked Aedan.

"Yes. Except Nestor," Magnus replied. "Where is he?"

"He should be here. We need everyone," said Aedan, beginning to worry.

"After I relieved him from his shift, he said he was going to make something to help us," said Magnus.

"Where did he go?" asked Aedan.

"Try the armory," suggested Magnus.

"All right. Make sure no one moves from their position," said Aedan as he walked toward the middle of town. Magnus gave an affirmative nod and turned to fulfill his duty.

Aedan ran to the armory—empty. Next, he tried the pub. He found Nestor sitting at a table stuffing old cloth into bottles that were filled to the neck with the remaining oil.

"Ah! Aedan, my boy!" exclaimed Nestor.

"What are you doing?" asked Aedan. "Didn't you hear the bell? You were right; the army is within minutes of the front wall."

"Oh, yes, I heard it."

"Then why aren't you out with the rest of us? What are you making?" asked Aedan, sounding like an agitated father speaking to his child.

Nestor looked up at Aedan. "Dragon's breath," he said in the most honest and casual voice.

Aedan looked at him curiously; then he knelt next to Nestor, picking up one of the oil-filled bottles with a piece of cloth sticking out of the top. "Dragon's breath? What exactly does it do?"

"Oh, these are brilliant. Quite useful for clearing brush and scaring off wolves and such," said Nestor, shoving more cloth into another wine bottle full of oil. "You light the top cloth on fire and simply throw it at anything you want to burn or scare away."

"Where did you get this idea?" asked Aedan.

Nestor stood up and began to load bottles into boxes. "Now is not the time for prying questions about one's past. We've got an army to fight."

Aedan nodded and grinned. The two men commenced loading the bottles into boxes. Once they had finished, they carried the volatile concoction carefully out of the pub and back to the front wall, placing the loaded boxes out of harm's way until needed. Aedan's mood was steady until he ascended the stairs to rejoin the force. He stopped abruptly because he now could truly see the opposing force, now in full view, and getting much closer to the town. He could estimate just how many of the enemy he and his fellow soldiers were up against—five hundred had been sent to take Brèdon.

With this army were ladders to scale walls and a battering ram. Aedan found himself frozen in thought about what would soon happen. The volunteer soldiers, and Magnus, Nestor, and possibly himself, would be killed before the morning sun rose over the horizon. Aedan thought of the dozens of innocent children, women, and men in hiding who were just waiting to be found and slaughtered.

Magnus joined Aedan, looking perturbed and even more nervous. "What took so long?" he whispered.

"Making dragon's breath," Aedan replied.

Magnus eyed Aedan oddly. "What?"

"Come help me with these boxes, you two," ordered Nestor. "Put them by the stairs, carefully." The two men obeyed without question.

"What are these for?" asked Magnus.

"You'll find out soon. Right now, we have to focus on what lies outside these walls," said Nestor. Aedan, Magnus, and Nestor strapped weapons to each of their waists, and gathering a bow and a quiver of arrows, they joined their improvised fighting force for the first battle in Ruxar's history.

CHAPTER 5

FIRESTORM

Aedan's breath was heavy, as if someone were standing on his chest. His legs shook nervously. His only option was to glare at the army of hundreds ready to attack. Immediately, Aedan's gratitude grew for Nestor and his uncanny abilities. He was thankful for the time spent preparing, but he couldn't help thinking the townspeople would be better off far away from Brèdon.

"Everyone get ready to fire!" Magnus ordered. Apprehension grew steadily within the small ranks. To fire upon others was, for the most part, unheard of.

"Fire on my command!" shouted Aedan, taking ownership. The enemies' flags were now in sight, revealing the attacking kingdom's identity. The Hydrarian flag waved gracefully in the wind. The symbol of a shield and a sword between two hydra heads dotted the field in front of the town. The army began to spread around the three walls of the keep, several horse-lengths away from the trench.

"Hold!" shouted Aedan. He could see moving fingers anxious to release.

Men were now bringing up ladders to the front of the columns from a wagon train following the army. Their intention appeared to be to scale the walls. "Aedan, look here. There are no catapults, nor archers in the army," Nestor pointed out.

"What does that mean? That's good for us, yes?"

"Most assuredly."

Magnus interjected, "They didn't plan on us being here to defend it."

"Right you are, Magnus. Perhaps your people are not as daft as I had previously assumed," said Nestor.

Magnus smiled. "And it appears that you, old man, are not as mad as we originally thought."

The Hydrarian soldiers looked surprised to see people on the wall, armed with bows at the ready. Every soldier appeared apprehensive to proceed with the siege. Aedan looked to see how their own force was reacting. Similar expressions matched the soldiers of the army in front of them. One, however, stood out of the crowd. The only Hydrarian among them. Terror and betrayal showed in Turia's eyes. Aedan could see she was holding back tears. She stared intently at her nation's flag. The people she called her kin, her country, her king had decided to thrust everyone into a fight, possibly more.

Aedan walked over to her, bow drawn and arrow taut in the string. "You don't have to fight," he said.

No words passed her lips. A trance enveloped her, making her oblivious to Aedan's presence. She stared at her kin. "Why are they doing this? Betraying their allies. For what?" Turia asked, her voice quivering.

"I'm not sure," said Aedan. "Do you still want to fight?"

"I will be here for you all," Turia said firmly. "They may be kin, but I will take them down the same as any wild animal." Aedan grinned at her strength.

The Hydrarian army halted and looked into the eyes of Brèdon's defenders. To Aedan, many of the men appeared discontented at the thought of assaulting a town full of people. However, others seemed eager. Regardless of how each man felt, all were slaves to their commanders' wills. The tension grew with every passing moment of silence; apprehension flooded hundreds of minds. Eyes shifted in all directions, as if no one desired to witness the aftermath, nor its making. How could anyone escape this tribulation alive? Silence shrouded the misty land. Daylight was coming; everyone could sense it. The quiet engulfed everything and everyone. The stillness could not mask the heavy storms in people's minds, beginning to recall the weighty memories of people and places they loved. Oh, how all wished they could be there one more time to say their goodbyes.

Without cause, the heavy silence was broken by a flood of roars from the Hydrarian army. A loud horn bellowed its deep note, signaling the siege to commence. Despite their earnest silence, none of the townspeople faltered from their defense positions.

"Be ready!" shouted Aedan. All tightened their strings and aimed true. The horn trumpeted once more, and the large Hydrarian army lurched forward into a fast-paced march.

"Steady!" ordered Nestor, bow ready.

"Take aim!" called Magnus.

"Fire!" shouted Aedan. The small Brèdon force let loose their arrows, sending forth bolts of pain and death that whistled a lethal lullaby. Instantly, the volley hit the enemy with the force of a tidal wave. Men collapsed to the ground, dead. Those who survived screamed their last notes. A scared and rampaging force pushed forward, regardless of the injured. Aedan could hear the injured's shouts. He felt responsible for their agony. But guilt at this moment would be a dangerous thing. He could not linger on such thoughts.

"Fire at will!" shouted Aedan, now drawing his own bow to commence firing. He reached for an arrow, drew back, and released. Arrow, draw, release. Without realizing it, he had released his third, fourth, and fifth arrows. The effects seemed only to slow the force slightly from reaching the trench. Some men jumped over it and began thrashing at the gate, in futility. The constant rain of arrows from overhead thwarted enemy progress. Most would fall before landing a second hit on the reinforced gate. Others who tried leaping across fell into the pit and were overcome by oil fumes. Some were rendered unconscious while trying to escape from the now accumulating mass grave filling the protective trench.

Aedan quickly took account of his men. None had yet been struck or wounded. This fact fed his confidence in their defenses, but the fight had just begun. Next, Aedan spotted the moving of ladders. The enemy initiated construction of makeshift bridges to cross the trench.

It's almost time, Aedan thought. All he had to do was yell a few words to eradicate the threat. *Am I doing the right thing? Should I take more life? Yes, I have killed already, but should I continue?* thought Aedan, fighting himself.

As remorseful thoughts festered in Aedan's mind, the Hydrarians had already successfully maneuvered dozens of soldiers over the obstacle and were now hacking at the gate. Aedan's time to act had come. He had prolonged his judgment for long enough. He stood up straight, swung his bow over his shoulder, drew his sword, and announced the fatal word, "Firestorm!"

"Firestorm!" shouted Nestor, echoing the order.

"Firestorm!" cried Magnus.

Almost instantaneously, the men closest to the gate, accompanied by Nestor, lobbed the bottles of oil and cloth to the men on the wall, with Magnus by their side. Soldiers caught the bottles, lit the cloth, and threw the dragon's breath at the oil-filled trench. The bottles broke open and fire spilled upon them like sunlight on the earth, engulfing them in rays of gold. As the small fires consumed a few soldiers, one at a time, Aedan grew concerned, for not one bottle of dragon's breath had hit its true mark. The defenders needed one good throw that would hit the bottom of the trench, ignite the oil, and turn the battlefield into an inferno.

"Nestor!" Aedan shouted.

Nestor looked up at him from below.

"How many more bottles do we have?" asked Aedan.

"Two!" Nestor yelled.

"Toss me up one!"

Nestor tossed one of the two bottles. Aedan grabbed a torch from a stand on the wall and lit the cloth. He needed to find an uncongested spot to ignite the trap. He commenced the quick search for the open area, but he was having difficulty pinpointing one particular spot open to interception. The bottle grew warmer by the second. Aedan had to locate the key area for his weapon or risk burning himself alive if he dropped it suddenly. Then he spotted it, over by the far right side. The opposing army had clustered to the front wall to gain cover from archers. The trench on either side had sparsely been touched by clamoring soldiers.

"Nestor, throw the last bottle in the trench on the other side of town!" commanded Aedan.

He received affirmation from the old man and ran to his target, tossing it. The glass container flew like a bird directly over the trench and quickly dropped like a boulder into the pit. It lit the oil, and not a moment too soon. The Hydrarian force pulled some ladders off the trench to begin ascension. As Aedan turned to face the invading army, he was greeted with a scorching roar that speared through the trench, colliding with the mass of invaders. The melody of cacophonous screams and wails echoed in the ears of Brèdon's fighters. Aedan, Nestor, and Magnus found each other on the wall once more. They were helpless to look away from the horror they had unleashed. The fire's mighty force was gorgeous, yet terrifying.

"It's working," said Magnus, astonished.

Nestor gazed, revolted by his part in the chaos. "What have I done?"

Aedan said nothing. He merely stared at the roaring inferno he had helped create.

. . .

Over the next long hour, the defenders sat as their trap ensnared their attackers. One by one, each member of the enemy either fled or was burnt into submission. Soon, a black toxic cloud wreathed the town. Smog closed in and blurred the line of sight. Screams had ceased. The insanity seemed to have halted. The air was thick with the smell of smoke and the dead. The men in the trench were nothing more than charcoaled-skinned corpses. Aedan and the rest of the Cerebrian army stared blankly into the abyss. No one could avert their eyes from the horrific scene.

Then the small, petrified defenders began to see movement. The soldiers who had escaped the firestorm had not run away as they had assumed. Instead, the Hydrarians had waited for the right moment to strike again, hiding behind the cloud of smoke. The enemy soldiers appeared like wild animals stricken with fear, fueled by hatred. Revenge seemed present in their hearts as they now fought to avenge their burned comrades.

Loud roars were unleashed from the invaders' bellies. Their war cries reverberated through the ears of everyone on the wall. Aedan felt a cold shiver run down his spine as the rallying continued. Suddenly, the horn joined battle cries as an ominous crescendo. Once more, the Hydrarians began their second charge at the gate.

The last few arrows rained down upon the attackers to little avail. The furious force was too determined to back down now. This time, their approach upon the wall met little resistance. Most either leaped across without worrying about archers, or climbed across the trench, using their dead comrades as bridges to the other side. As men reached the gate, they began hacking at it with everything they had—swords, axes, shields—with the full weight of the remaining force pushing against the barrier.

"Brace the gate!" Aedan shouted to the fighters below. Dozens of defenders gave all of their might to hold the gate together.

"Draw your weapons! Prepare to fight for your lives!" shouted Magnus.

Only moments passed. The gate was becoming more and more damaged. Soon, only splinters would remain. Brèdon's forces had been fortunate. No lives lost. That would change rapidly once that gate fell. Finally, they could hold it no more. The men bracing the gate became the only obstacle. Holes in the gate allowed deadly blows against the defenders. Spears thrusting inward struck down all in their path. After four of their own fell to their enemy advances, the townspeople backed away. Aedan, Magnus, and Nestor all drew their weapons and ushered the men off the walls to fight on the ground.

"Go! Defend!" shouted Aedan.

"Keep them in a tight formation," ordered Nestor.

The next moment, the enemy army was flooding into the town like water upon a sinking vessel. Men began to crash to the ground against the onslaught. Furious steel met frightened hearts. Aedan, with his two short swords, ran to an oncoming soldier. Deflecting an overhead swing, he spun around and sliced the man's back. His men were being killed mercilessly.

Aedan called out to his two companions, "We have to push them back!" The two men nodded.

They ran toward the enemy. Magnus commenced swinging his oversized sword at the Hydrarians, striking many and frightening more. Nestor grabbed a dagger out of one of his pockets and threw it at an enemy soldier, pinning it in his neck. Then he began swinging his ax around with a surprising fluidity. Aedan's confidence grew that Brèdon might be saved. He left Nestor and Magnus so he could assist others.

Aedan sprinted to reach the other defenders in need. He found a cluster of them fighting with all of their will and strength to stay alive. He joined in the fight, cutting down one, two, and then three Hydrarians. As they fought on, he noticed some of the Hydrarians were beginning to flee. But still more men pushed into the town.

At that moment, Aedan wished he had more dragon's breath. More fire for the brutes. Then it struck him. Kaustos! That terribly angry cerberus. "Magnus! Magnus!" Aedan looked for the large man, without success. He needed to act or they would be finished. He sprinted for the pen many street-lengths back. He needed to be quick to save his friends from being surrounded and killed. Aedan dashed to Kaustos' enormous pen. Thankfully, no one paid any attention to him. All were focused on the fighting, everyone locked in mad combat; the defenders' numbers were dwindling. Kaustos, sensing the calamity, thrashed violently against the steel. All three of his heads stared at Aedan, perhaps thinking him a light snack. Hopefully, the screams and smoke would draw him there rather than consume Aedan first.

"Good Kaustos. We need you, Kaustos," said Aedan calmly. The three-headed beast jumped forward and barked. Its sound stung Aedan's ears more than the fighters' screams. "It's all right, boy. No need to eat me. You will have plenty to devour out there." Aedan hesitantly snatched free one of the latches. Then the second. With still one lock on the cage, Kaustos erupted out of confinement, bursting forth to the unwelcome guests invading his home and, to Aedan's relief away, from him.

The three-headed savior leaped into combat, unleashing an onslaught of claws, teeth, and ferocity. Brèdon's fighters' screams were now replaced with Hydrarian cries for mercy. The wild, three-headed beast gnashed, smashed, clawed, and ripped into the forces inside the town. Kaustos let out a smooth howl—his trio-voiced chorus renewed Magnus and Nestor's spirits, and those of the rest of the force. Those who ran were falling back into formation. Several wounded even gathered what strength they had to venture forth to aid their new furry companion.

Kaustos met little resistance. Men were tossed about as a child tosses dolls. Several attempted to flank the beast, meeting its hind claws instead.

When Aedan rejoined the battle, he was quickly discovered by several Hydrarians. They chose to follow him rather than risk their chances with a deranged cerberus. Three men came at him, swinging violently. Aedan did not perform any sort of counterattack. Instead, he did like any sensible man would do who was staring down the blades of three enemy swords—he ran. He ran to the stairs to his right. He climbed them while being followed by the soldiers. His pursuers seemed to be faster than him. Fear and anger surely fueled them.

Halfway up the stairs, Aedan turned around, swiping at one of his pursuers' necks. The body fell down the stairs. Two remained. As Aedan reached the top, he turned once more and sunk his sword into the second man's chest, then retrieved it rapidly, only to have his left leg slashed by the third pursuer, who had just reached the summit of the staircase. Aedan fell to his knees, bleeding. His sword was out of reach, thrown as he fell.

"I'm going to die. Everyone is dying." Dark thoughts raced through Aedan's mind.

The final pursuer drew back his arm to make the final blow. Aedan closed his eyes, waiting for the inevitable, still hearing Kaustos gnashing. Then, out of the fog, he heard a whistle and a thud. An arrow struck the man's temple. The assailant fell backwards, midswing. Aedan opened his eyes wide, stood up slowly, and looked around to where the shot had come from. At last, his sight landed on the small Manticorian, Aloysius. He could not believe his luck! There was no time to waste. He had to return to the fight.

As Aedan rose to his feet, he peered down at the mighty beast. At that moment, he witnessed a devastating sight. The opposing force had found its fervor once more and stuck Kaustos with a spear to the side. Then another, and another. Soon spears stuck out of Kaustos as if he were a porcupine. Even as Kaustos felt the cold sting sweep over him, he continued to swipe, but now the beast only pawed at ghosts and shadows. At last, the grand, three-headed savior fell to the ground, joining the many other casualties.

Aedan's head dropped. He could see the townspeople's numbers falling more and more, yet hundreds of foes remained. It was useless. Nestor had been right. Why had they fought if everyone was to die anyway? There had to be some reason Nestor had had that vision. Or had it just been some big joke orchestrated by other-worldly forces no one would ever understand. With little energy and hope remaining, Aedan returned to the battle, knowing his fate had already been written that he would end here upon the blood-soaked ground of Brèdon.

"Dragonian!" someone cried out.

Aedan did not recognize the voice. His eyesight was blurring from his energy draining. Hope was oozing out of him faster than any blood from wounds could. Yet the instinct to stay alive was stronger than his momentary depression. Another attacker swiped at Aedan, parrying and slashing, dispatching his foe.

"Damn you, Dragonian! Over here!" cried the voice again.

Aedan caught sight of the small Manticorian. He was rolling a barrel. A barrel of oil! "What! Where?"

Aloysius unsheathed his dagger and popped open the barrel, spilling its contents upon the earth. "Light it!" he told Aedan. "I'll take care of the rest!"

Aedan desperately searched for an open flame. He thought all had been extinguished after the firestorm. No! There were torches still on the wall. Daylight had now spread across the land, so the small flames were hidden in morning light. With a last burst of energy, Aedan strained to reach the wall once more, jumping over and crashing into men still fighting for their lives. His body was truly feeling the battle's effects now. "Just a little farther," he told himself.

Aloysius, too, was battling his way to the wall. His small stature gave him an advantage against the Hydrarians. A quick slash to the legs brought down many. As he rolled the barrel to the wooden wall drenched with the dead and the dying, he proceeded to add to the degradation. A quick strike allowed oil to gush out onto the ground, spilling the barrel's contents. Aedan, at last, had reached a torch. He and Aloysius, however, were on opposite parts of the small town.

"Throw it! Throw it or we are done!" cried Aloysius.

Aedan gauged the distance; it was a far toss. He again had a bird's eye view of the carnage. At this point, Nestor and Magnus were nowhere to be seen. Possibly dead. The last few defenders strained themselves against their foes. The enemy, sensing victory, pushed hard against them.

"Damn it! Throw it!" shouted Aloysius again.

With that command, Aedan launched the embered torch high in the air. It flew like a red-breasted hawk over the settlement, then dove down to snatch its prey, or in this case, make its mark on the blood-and-oil-doused earth, igniting the substance. The fire struck the wall, sending a cluster of Hydrarian soldiers, who had gone through the trench to get across, into a panic. As more and more people were bathed in flame, the soldiers ran frantically to extinguish the liquid fire. In the process, they spread the flames to other Hydrarian soldiers who were contaminated with oil from the trench. Meanwhile, Aedan and his remaining men continued the fight against those who were now running, collapsing, and dying right in front of them.

Indeed, the flames would rid them of these foul people, but it would not rid the world of violence. In fact, it would fan the fire. As the battle raged on within the settlement, Aedan was witnessing another, grander conflict developing—a fight he had helped fuel, just like the fire that raged on in front of him. As the remainder of Brèdon watched, they mentally prepared themselves for what was to come after the blazing firestorm was extinguished. For now, the siege of Brèdon was over.

CHAPTER 6

SOLDIERS OF FIRE

As the acrid smoke cleared once again, the town found itself in complete silence. The Hydrarian soldiers had gone. They had either died or become frightened of the second firestorm unleashed upon them. The crooked army was running back to Hydraria, ashamed and defeated.

Aedan emerged from hiding. At last, he could lay his eyes upon the true scene of their close victory. Hydrarians and Brèdon defenders alike lay dead, charred and scorched. Aedan felt forlorn. He had not wished for this to happen. He had been told he would save the villagers, and he had. But he could not have foreseen the cost of saving them. He could have pushed harder for everyone to evacuate, instead of assembling an army to fight.

As flames turned to coals, survivors began rising. People had started to stand just as Aedan had. The remaining defenders were stunned. A large sigh of relief engulfed their faces. The grateful living closed their heavy eyes in thanks for their luck, and their bodies showcased exhaustion through lumbering movements as many staggered about the aftermath.

Then, collectively, the soldiers caught Aedan's attention. He looked at all of them and grinned weakly. The few remaining rang out a roar of victory. Their voices echoed through the town. Birds and other animals scattered, fleeing from Brédon as though from a predator. The soldiers' victory cry could be heard by the villagers in the forest, who now began to emerge. Aedan was pleased to see the people who had decided to sequester themselves during the battle.

"Where are Nestor and Magnus?" Aedan asked himself. "Did they get struck down by the enemy?" This fear fell through his mind like an arrow falling from the sky. "Nestor! Magnus!" Hysteria rushed over him like an overflowing river. His breathing grew heavy, a cold sweat hit him, and he began to feel sick with grief.

"Over here, Aedan!" shouted Nestor weakly. Aedan scanned the grounds, trying to locate the origin of Nestor's voice. Then he saw him. Nestor raised his arm. He was by the gate. Aedan limped over to him, stepping over corpses and trying not to trip.

As Nestor's face came into view, Aedan knew the old man was injured. That did not stop him from breathing a sigh of relief. Nestor was pale, his eyes gray—more so than usual. His breathing was labored, and blood blotches had formed on his skin and clothes.

"You're hurt!" exclaimed Aedan.

"I'll be all right, but I'm afraid Magnus is not faring as well," Nestor said.

"Where is he?" asked Aedan.

"He is to your left, about ten steps. That's where I last saw him."

Aedan stood up and followed Nestor's directions. He began turning over the dead in search of their large Cerebrian ally, but he could not find any trace of him.

"Nestor, I don't see him. Are you sure he is over here?"

"I'm sure of it. But in the meantime, I could really use some assistance." said Nestor, starting to become a bit impatient.

Aedan yelled for help to the survivors and returning townspeople. "I need all who are able to assist in the disposal of the deceased, but first we must move the wounded so they can be cared for."

At that time, out of the seventy-five they had started, Aedan counted only six who were still standing. The rest were either dead or waiting for medical help. So began the difficult job of separating the dead from the living. After hours of searching and separating, only seven others were found alive. Two of them would be lucky to live through the night.

After sunset, the deceased were tallied. The Hydrarians had lost an astounding three hundred thirty-six soldiers, while Brédon had lost sixty-three, including Kaustos. Though this was a hard loss for the town, it was an even more astounding victory. A town with no military training, only basic fighting skills, and full of miners and hunters, had fought off an army composed of hundreds of soldiers. Nestor and the other wounded had been brought into various homes and buildings, including the pub. The pub was big enough for the five who stood the best chance to live. Sadly, the two who were wounded severely died before any real assistance could save them.

Aedan was exhausted. The past few days had been life-changing for him. Being recruited by a vision-manifesting man had led to the defensive victory of a town he was passing through. He had helped to lead the first battle in Ruxar's history. Cerebria's first victory.

· · ·

The next morning, in the pub turned into an improvised medical ward, Aedan sat next to Nestor's bedside as Nestor slept. Nestor had been cut on his forearms and sustained lacerations on his legs. Luckily, all he needed were stitches, bandages, and rest. On the other hand, Magnus' body had still not been found. Aedan's fear of Magnus being consumed by fire may have been correct. But maybe he could learn more from Nestor when he woke. In the meantime, Aedan joined the cleanup of the town.

As Aedan exited the pub, he reflected on the battle. He thought of the men who had died, of Magnus' disappearance, and of the repercussions of yesterday's events on the world. As he pondered these things, Aloysius, the Manticorian, joined him. Aloysius seemed tired from the last few long nights. The pair walked to the front gate to investigate the battle's aftermath and search for any traces of Magnus.

Once they arrived at the gate, Aedan began to scour the fighting grounds. The once light-brown earth was now stained black and red and stamped with the footsteps of fallen soldiers. Weapons lay upon the scorched earth. Aedan could still hear the haunting chorus of screams that had filled the air. He stumbled upon one of the large swords he believed to be Magnus' weapon. He knelt down to examine it. The blade was dirtied with blood, and chips of the sword had been hacked away by its use.

"I wonder if Magnus ran after them," said Aedan. "I'm certain he was not among the dead. I examined them myself, and nobody came close to resembling him."

"I saw him, you know," said Aloysius behind him.

Aedan stood up quickly. "You saw him?"

"Yes, before I saved you on the wall, I witnessed him fighting valiantly. He was doing well until a slash landed across his back, and then he was bludgeoned with the hilt of a sword."

Aedan eyes fixed on Aloysius, saddened. "So you watched him die then?"

"Oh, he did not die. The man who struck him did not end his life; instead, Magnus was dragged out of town and back to the open field."

Aedan was shocked. "Why Magnus? Why not end him if given the opportunity?"

"It was their leader who took him," Aloysius stated. "A man with a large scar on his face." Aloysius turned back toward town. "You need to make a decision, Dragonian. Stay here and fortify, or spread the word of this attack."

Aedan looked down, sighed, and lifted his head back to Aloysius. "Help me then."

"Which do you choose?" asked Aloysius. "Stay and fight, and probably die, or spread the word, and probably die—but for a cause more important than being a thin piece of armor for this small town."

Aedan's face contorted with confliction. "You think I need to go warn the masses? Who would believe me? We sent a rider out to the King of Cerebria the day before last."

Aloysius chuckled. "That rider is not coming back. Nor did he make it to Ansgar. Others still need to be warned about this, and if many join us, we can convince them to take up arms and prepare for more attacks."

"We?" asked Aedan.

Aloysius bowed his head. "I would be thrilled to accompany you. I mean, you'd be dead without my sharp eye."

"Excellent. We must go visit someone."

"Your elderly friend? Nestor I believe you called him. Will he be joining us as well?"

Aedan said nothing. He merely nodded towards the pub where Nestor had been recovering. They turned in that direction. When Aedan and Aloysius arrived inside the makeshift hospital, Nestor was sitting up comfortably in his bed, drinking a cup of tea.

"Ah, there you are! I have asked everyone where you were!" Nestor exclaimed, still spry despite his injuries.

Aedan smiled. He was glad to see his friend's condition was improving. "Nestor, I want you to meet someone. This is Aloy—"

"Aloysius of Manticoria," Nestor interrupted.

"Have you two met?" asked Aedan.

"No," said Aloysius, befuddled.

"I know him the same way I found you, Aedan," said Nestor.

"I'll explain," Aedan told Aloysius.

After Aedan explained Nestor's visionary abilities, the three men discussed Magnus' capture, Aloysius' actions during the battle, the second fire, and finally, how to move forward with a plan to combat retaliation from the Hydrarian kingdom.

"Well, Aedan, we must act!" said Nestor, leaning forward excitedly.

Aedan sat at the foot of Nestor's bed and put his head in his hands. He sighed deeply, pondering. Stay and defend or venture out? Maybe he was meant to do more than protect a small town from destruction. Perhaps he could still protect the people without being at Brèdon. At last, he took his head out of his hands and stood up to face the two men. With absolute certainty in his voice, Aedan said, "We must go. We have to do more."

"You've made the right decision," said Nestor, beaming. "Now we have much to talk about and not much time to do so. By early tomorrow morning, the three of us must be outside those walls heading to our first destination."

"You are coming with us?" asked Aedan, surprised. "But what of your injuries?"

"Don't worry about such things. I can take care of myself. Plus, did you honestly think I would let you go by yourselves?"

"All right, where to first then?" asked Aloysius. "What's the plan? It's got to be better than the last one. It nearly got you both killed."

"We will speak more in depth," said Nestor, "but we must move to someplace more private. Magnus' house will do for now, but first I need you two to help me out of bed."

Aedan and Aloysius got on either side of Nestor, helped him out of bed, and guided the old man to Magnus' home. There, they would begin to plan for a journey that could eventually destroy them all. Inside the small building, the three plotted their route to Ansgar, Cerebria's capital. Unfortunately, something slowed down their plans—deciding between a northern or southern route. The southern route included a river. This infamously treacherous river contained fast-moving rapids, large rocks, and small boats that had sunk to its bottom between its banks. However, by taking the southern route, they could reach Ansgar in two or three days. The northern route promised to be a safer, yet lengthier road. This safer trip would require them to travel northeast around the Teon Forest to cross a bridge, then south to cross two more bridges over two more rivers, completing the trek many days later.

"If we want to get to the capital to tell King Rordan quickly of what happened here, we must bear south," Aedan said sternly.

"Yes, but how will we get across the river?" asked Nestor. "It is the most dangerous body of water in Ruxar, second only to the Trahern Channel."

"I agree with Aedan," said Aloysius. "I think we should go south."

"Nestor, are you sure you're strong enough to travel?" asked Aedan.

"Yes, of course I am. What kind of question is that? I still have enough strength to take on the two of you if I need to," Nestor replied.

"I'm sorry to ask," said Aedan, "but you were injured in battle. I want to ensure your intentions for taking the long way round are not due to your wounds, old man."

Nestor looked at Aedan with irritation, as if Aedan had just taken his pride and stuck a knife into it. Nestor stood up slowly, jilted from the insult, and walked over to a pitcher of water. Picking up a glass, he set it in front of him, and poured himself a cup. After he finished pouring, he put the glass up against his lips and began to drink. He did not stop drinking until the glass was empty. Finally, he set the cup on the table and gave a great sigh. "Fine, we will take the southern route, but I assure you it will not be easy. That river will make you wish you were taken by those Hydrarians." Nestor grinned.

"Only if we fall in," said Aloysius. Everyone smiled at the dark humor.

Aedan and Aloysius were relieved to have ended the frustratingly long debate with their elderly companion. At last, after many hours, they had a route to Ansgar. The question remained how to get across the treacherous river. The three decided to discuss the matter later. Now all that was left to do was to catch a couple of hours of sleep before sunrise. The three weary men parted ways and found beds to their likings.

As he lay down to nap, Aedan's thoughts ceased. Images of what they would endure in the short time to come and his uncertainty about his companions drifted away and made way for a dreamless sleep.

• • •

The sun had begun to peek out from under the horizon. Its bright-orange and dark-yellow color clashed with the light-blue sky. The light bounced off the dew on the grass to display a silver earth, filled with mighty trees swaying in the morning's cool breeze. It seemed like the land itself was granting them a safe journey with gorgeous weather.

Aedan awoke slowly. Thankfully, the few hours he had slept were sufficient for the journey ahead. As he stood, he stretched and proceeded outside to welcome the beautiful morning. He tried to relax the banter in his mind, questioning the adventure he would undertake.

Luckily, the onslaught of Aedan's own mind was short-lived, for Nestor had woken just moments after and was now approaching him, grinning joyously.

"Good morning, Aedan. How did you sleep?" asked Nestor, appearing to have his color back.

"I slept well, and you?"

"Like a dead man," Nestor said proudly.

"That's good to hear. Where's Aloysius?" asked Aedan.

"I haven't yet seen him," said Nestor. "Perhaps he went to fetch us some supplies with some of the brutes in the town."

As Nestor finished speaking, Aloysius himself, accompanied by two Cerebrian men, appeared from around a corner and ambled over to the pair. "Morning all! Look what I have procured," Aloysius said. The men held swords, bows, arrows, chainmail, axes, daggers, and even food prepared for the journey.

"Now all we need to do is pack up and start walking," Nestor said.

The two Cerebrian men set the items down on the ground. Aedan walked slowly over to the weapons and picked up some chainmail. The sparkling armor gleamed in the bright sunlight. He quickly put it on, pleased to find it fit him well.

"This feels very surreal," Aedan said. "For some reason, it did not hit me until now that we may not survive this journey."

"Yes, that is possible," said Nestor, "but that feeling should not stop us from doing our very best to end the sinister time fallen upon us."

Aedan looked at him, grinned slightly, and nodded. He did not say anything, for he did not want to upset anyone with his doubts of the future. He walked back to Magnus' hut, where he had left his weapons—a bow, a quiver, a dagger, and his two short swords. Aedan was now ready to begin his quest to Ansgar where they would request an audience with King Rordan. To speak with him was the next step in ridding Ruxar of this rising plague.

As Aedan stepped outside the hut, he saw something quite astonishing. The townspeople he had helped save from annihilation had come to wish them a safe journey. Almost one hundred people stood in front of them, chanting praises to the heroes of Brédon. Aedan graciously bowed his head. Nestor and Aloysius joined him.

"They are calling us the Soldiers of Fire," said Aloysius proudly. "Though it really should just be soldier instead of soldiers since I did most of the work."

"What do you mean?" asked Aedan.

"Well," said Aloysius. "I guess it was a team effort. I believe we owe it to them and all who were lost to become bigger than messengers."

"It's a well-deserved name," said Nestor. "We are the first resistance fighters in history."

"Soldiers of Fire—a resistance force?" said Aedan, letting the name roll off his tongue.

"We'll make certain the Hydrarians know of us. Our presence will catch the wind and spread as flames to dried tinder," said Nestor.

Aedan said nothing more. He, along with his two fellow resistance fighters, smiled. They held their heads high while walking toward the gate. As they reached the small town's exit, the three warriors turned back to wave one final farewell to their new allies, hoping that one day they could return in peace.

CHAPTER 7

A KING AND A DOG

All was quiet in the dark hall of the Hydrarian castle. A king sat upon a throne of stone. Darkness shrouded the dimly lit chamber, and a twinge of anxiety lingered in the king's heart. The room was deathly quiet. Absent were scurrying rodents and footsteps; only the king's sighs could be heard as he grew more restless with every passing second. A distant clatter of a door opening and slamming was heard, followed by steady footsteps that grew closer with the king's every restless breath. At last, the pattering stopped. Three raps were made at the door of King Ulysses' chamber.

"Enter," ordered Ulysses.

The door opened with a shrill creak. A broad man entered, head high, his scar shimmering in the torchlight. Something was wrong. His eyes told a story, not of confidence and victory, but of anger and failure. His steady walk to the foot of the king's throne reminded Ulysses of a predator approaching prey. A great anticipation filled Ulysses, whose heartbeat was now in sync with each clap of falling feet. As the man approached the throne, he kneeled, no words muttered.

"Well, General, were you successful?" Ulysses asked. The general's dead eyes met Ulysses'. With one look, the king knew his answer. The silence was incriminating. "General, were you successful?" Ulysses repeated.

"No, I was not."

"How is this possible?" shouted Ulysses, jumping to his feet.

"I'm uncertain, my king," said the general. His stoic sensibility irked Ulysses.

"How did this happen?" asked the king. "You promised me Brèdon, Anwar!"

"I promised you Brèdon on the assumption that my men would be adequately armed!" barked Anwar. "You want to know how we failed? Your arrogance lost us that settlement, sire!"

"My arrogance! You are my general and advisor! Damn you for failing me, for failing Jormungand!" yelled Ulysses, teeth gnashing against his lips. "I want Brèdon, General."

Anwar stood up to meet the king's eye. "And it will be yours, my liege. I'm developing a plan. But, sire, they knew we were coming."

"How can that be? Were you followed?"

"No."

"Then how do you explain this?"

"There were others."

"Others? Who?"

"People not of Cerebria. Travelers."

"You think a few travelers had something to do with this?" asked Ulysses, mockingly.

"Yes," said Anwar, nodding. "Two of them were at the helm of their leadership. Possibly more."

"Did you get a good look at them?"

"No. The battle's chaos was too egregious to focus on small details," said Anwar. His instincts told him the king did not understand the impact a few could make upon a group. "The few travelers—their knowledge of the world—turned what was supposed to be a simple takeover into a fiery slaughter."

"Explain. I want to hear the details."

"Aye, sir," said Anwar, gruesomely describing in detail his warriors' demise.

"Out of all that occurred, you have no good news for me?" asked Ulysses.

The general looked up at his king and said with great confidence, "In fact, I do."

Ulysses looked perplexed, but intrigued. "Well, spit it out. I should have you whipped for not sharing this with me sooner?"

Anwar ignored the threat. "I have brought you someone. One who was there."

"Why? How?"

"As the second stage of the battle began, I witnessed this person taking down men like a sickle to grain, so I decided to act."

"You brought him here?" asked the king, now grinning a bit.

The general smiled and nodded. "He is a hard man to handle."

"Oh?"

"The man has not said a word, nor has he admitted to pain," said Anwar.

"Cerebrian then?"

"Yes, this one is strong. He is most assuredly hiding something."

"I see. I wish to see him now."

"Yes, my lord."

Anwar bowed and began walking toward the chamber doors. Once there, he opened them quickly and barked a few orders to waiting soldiers standing outside the room. Like a wild boar, the large Magnus trampled in, being led by twelve soldiers, chains and ropes in their hands, tied to his boulder-like physique. Rapidly, Magnus was guided and shoved to the king's feet.

"In light of failure, this is a good find," said Ulysses.

"Thank you, my king," said Anwar.

Magnus had been forced to his knees, having previously been beaten to encourage proper behavior. The king approached the mammoth Cerebrian.

"You are in a great deal of misfortune, Cerebrian. Terrible, in fact. I am a merciful king, but even I have my limits, so I expect answers." Ulysses grinned at the bleeding Magnus. "Who led Brèdon to victory?" Magnus did not speak. Instead, he fired a stare through Ulysses. Ulysses looked up to gaze at the tall ceiling, then back down at the haggard prisoner. "What is your leader's name?" Ulysses repeated. Once again, Magnus did not speak, nor did he move. He maintained the same look—the same menacing stare that could knock the chamber down, if not properly contained.

"Speak fool!" yelled Ulysses, now frustrated. Ulysses knelt to Magnus' level, leaned in close, and whispered one more question. "Do you want to die? I will gleefully put you and the rest of your people down like the dogs you are. You dog people disgust me. Allowing your bodies to be tainted by mutts. To let them stain you with grotesque traits of beastly size and strength is truly unfair. Your people should really be rid of the animals and their unnatural effect."

"Perhaps if the three-headed mongrels gifted them with traits as invaluable as our hydra," said Anwar.

"Yes. If only. Sadly, we Hydrarians are not as fortunate. Our beasts were forced to migrate many years ago to prevent catastrophe; it is incredible what one rogue beast like the hydra can do to a city. It appears that somewhere in our history, we, as a people, forgot how to control them. Perhaps that will change," said Ulysses, turning his attention again to Magnus.

The great Cerebrian leered again at Ulysses and greeted the royal man with a large ball of spit seen by all in the room. Ulysses rose to his feet, wiped the glob of saliva off his cheek, and kicked Magnus in the face. Breathing heavily, Ulysses knelt down to Magnus' level and whispered, "You will tell us everything you know, or I will see to it that your head, and that of the other survivors, will be on a pike in my quarters," said the king, now smiling. "Take him away!" As the king's order fell, the men began to drag, hit, and shove Magnus back out the door. "Ah, General," said Ulysses as they departed, "see to it that the prisoner be seen by my daughter. She has a way of getting stubborn jaws loose."

"I will relay the order," said Anwar, quickly. "But first, we must continue our discussion."

"Oh?"

Anwar waited until his men and the prisoner had vanished from earshot. "Turning plans into action. Next steps," answered Anwar sternly.

"Well, with the defeat at Brèdon, we must move ahead on our invasion sooner," said Ulysses.

"Agreed."

"I am leaving for the capital tomorrow morning. From there, I will send further instructions."

"I am to remain here?" asked Anwar, sounding disappointed.

"Yes. For my daughter. Watch over her. Continue her training."

"I am not a babysitter, sire. I can move forward on our plans to capture Brèdon."

"No!" belted Ulysses. "Do as I command, General."

"Is my council not required of you anymore? If I recall, you appointed me your advisor as well as your general. My aid has—"

"Greatly expanded my horizons. Yes," said Ulysses. "But I am still king. I rule. My hand, my word is supreme."

Anwar, abashed, replied, "Yes, sire. I will do as you require of me."

"You're a good man, Anwar. A loyal one at that. Be patient and you will be rewarded."

"I am an old man. What could I possibly desire that you have not given me?"

"Power, my friend, more power," Ulysses said. 'Now please, let me be. I must prepare for tomorrow."

Anwar thanked the king and glided out of the room, his eyes forward, aiming toward the future.

CHAPTER 8

THE THREATENING CAULDRON

The stone walls were laced with frost, and icicles formed from droplets by way of cracks in the ceiling. Puddles of the same origin grew ever wider. The dingy, hay-filled mattress was much too petite for Magnus' massive body. The cage's bars reminded Magnus of freshly lit charcoal among flames. Red-hued rust permeated the iron. The prisoners before him had appeared to damage the metal rods to little benefit. Their efforts had yielded only small shards of metal, which had left bars themselves full of miniscule daggers.

The dungeon hall was as well-lit as murky water during a storm, pitch black with the chance for flashes of blinding light. Torchlight replaced lightning as guards passed on watch. The floor itself maintained two distinct parts: a dry side with a few rodent residents, and a wet side pooling with what Magnus hoped was mostly rain water. Guards' occasional shouts and prisoners' occasional cries during interrogations resounded in the stone tomb. In an odd way, the echoing cries made Magnus' dark, dank, pest-infested cell feel like a safe haven. A sudden flash of light sparked into the prison's darkness. A slender-bearded man in uniform approached the cell. Behind him was General Anwar.

"Are you ready to talk?" asked Anwar.

Magnus did not reply. Instead, he maintained the same glare he had given King Ulysses.

"Well," said Anwar, "since your jaw still appears to be inoperable, I think it's due time to crack it open for you!"

Magnus' glowering stare burned through the slender man's confidence, transforming the general's sinister smile into a facade of fear. Anwar ordered his soldiers to restrain Magnus and move him to a room he liked to call "The Cauldron." It was a room of wounded screams and frightened tears.

I must go. I must get back to Brèdon, Magnus thought.

As the bearded soldier drew his keys to unlock the barred refuge, Magnus tightened all of his muscles, ready to pounce. As Magnus fixated on the bearded man, time slowed; he could feel every second skip by. He had to do this correctly the first time. With his last thought cemented, the cage door swung open toward the band of newly arrived soldiers, and with it came the massive, irate Cerebrian.

No one predicted his advance. Magnus lunged across the cell, grabbing the bearded man, throwing him back into the cold, unforgiving cell. The soldiers, swords drawn, had not realized the sheer power their prisoner possessed. A furious man, his size matched his ferocity. Magnus' surprising agility swiftly disarmed the first two soldiers. Thrusting forward, he grasped arms and catapulted men over his shoulders. For a moment, Magnus felt the sheer pain of an arrow pierce his left thigh. Unfortunately for the Hydrarians, the shot elevated Magnus' tirade into a rampage. Once Magnus noticed the long wood jutting from his leg, a rush of energy pushed him to victory.

Acknowledging the painful savior, Magnus fearlessly ran through the remaining soldiers to reach the archer who had shot him. Upon arrival, Magnus elegantly disposed of him by means of air travel, landing him atop his bloodied kin. Anwar appeared to have run off like a coward. Magnus' hopes were lifted at once. The remaining men ran at him, swords and knives drawn. Magnus eyed and snatched a fallen torch with his large muscular fingers. As he grasped the torch, he rose from his knees to deflect an overhead strike, which sent yet another motionless to the dungeon floor. The remaining soldiers had managed to deflect the continual rampant swings, and now surrounded Magnus with all swords pointing at the massive man's torso. Seeing himself surrounded, Magnus halted movement, frantically looking for an escape. As he realized he had few options to consider, an arrow blew in front of his nose, missing it by less than a feather. Magnus' attention turned to seek the arrow's origin. To Magnus' dismay, his maladjusting eyes landed upon Anwar setting yet another arrow into his bow.

"If you give up now, I won't put this arrow in your neck!" barked Anwar.

Magnus' eyes widened as the pain of his injury began to zap away his energy. His victory had been fleeting.

I'm so close! Magnus thought.

"Put your weapon down!" ordered Anwar again.

Magnus put his chin to his chest. The Cerebrian gave a great sigh, one that could be felt by all who occupied the dungeon. As calm swept the room, the wave of serenity opened Magnus' mind. He knew what to do! Magnus slowly brought himself out of his trance. He awoke to Anwar and his soldiers' demands for him to yield. Then, as if thunder itself had arrived, Magnus belted a deafening roar that reverberated like knives in their ears.

Capitalizing on the moment, Magnus threw the torch directly at Anwar, who at the same instant released his bolt, which hit the torch and ricocheted. The torch continued at Anwar like a boulder down a mountain. Magnus grabbed two of the swords by the blades, jarring them loose from their wielders' hands. His palms now dripping blood, he flipped the swords over. The two unarmed men dropped to the floor, fearful, while the remaining soldiers lunged forward, meeting the deadly power of Magnus' swing.

After the rest of the soldiers fled from the chaos, Magnus turned to an unconscious Anwar. He approached cautiously, as one to a rattlesnake, readying his swords. He focused on the man who moments ago had been ready to place him into The Cauldron—the room of torture. He gazed upon the man who had led an army to destroy Brèdon. He saw in this man nothing but ignorance and misguided hatred; still, Magnus wondered what fueled the Hydrarian's actions.

Then came the sound of hurried footsteps, and a large bell clanged deep in the dungeon. Magnus needed to escape, but he had no clue where to go. He needed to start running, taking down anybody he could. Within those few moments of wondering, he had not realized a dark figure now stood at the end of the hall outside the dungeon. He stared at the outline in the shadows. Hypnotized, his mind sprinted from thought to thought. Magnus began to sweat, his movements restricted. His breathing had now jumped from gasp to gasp. In a blink, darkness consumed him.

CHAPTER 9

INVINCIBLE RIVER

The morning of their departure could not have been more pleasant. The late morning's light-blue sky flirted with silvery clouds that danced in circles, morphing to the playful wind's will. The long golden strands of wheat grass waved at Nestor, Aedan, and Aloysius as they passed, and the mighty trees of the Teon Forest bellowed and swayed in the refreshing cool breeze. The birds even seemed to be in a lighthearted mood. Several of them would dive and flip within the enormous trees until they found a nice, shaded branch to perch on, singing their unique songs to the three travelers. By now, Aedan, Nestor, and Aloysius had traveled long enough to completely lose sight of Brèdon.

"Aedan, what ideas do you have for crossing the Adraste?" asked Nestor.

"At the moment, none. I'm waiting until we arrive to better understand what we are up against," said Aedan.

"The Adraste," said Nestor, "is known as the Invincible River. It has a reputation for taking lives and being impossible to cross. People have tried to build bridges to cross, but during construction, the river destroys pilings and the people who attempt the valiant but futile task only fall and are swallowed by the white, swirling waters."

"Here I thought we were going to have a really big issue in our path," said Aloysius.

"Between the three of us, I'm certain we will find a way," said Aedan.

"I suppose you are right," said Nestor. "But there's no harm in a little concern for our general safety."

"Yes, of course," said Aedan, grinning.

"Nestor, why don't you just manifest a solution for us?" said Aloysius. "Close those seer eyes of yours and let your mind tell us how to cross this invincible river?"

"My visions don't manifest on demand, young Manticorian."

Aedan smirked and asked, "How far to the banks?"

"In Manticore, you only travel a short distance and you run into a whole ocean," said Aloysius.

"This is not Manticore. This is Cerebria," said Nestor. "A much wider landscape surrounds us. Besides, the edge of the forest is very close to the river."

"And how would you know this?" asked Aloysius.

"As a young man, I traveled. I learned the lay of the land and other tricks, as well as how to defend myself from dangerous creatures," Nestor replied.

"What creatures?" asked Aloysius.

"Cerberuses and gargoyles, of course," said Nestor. "Don't worry, Aloysius, cerberuses are good friends of people; they rarely attack humans."

"Until they're hungry," Aloysius replied.

"I'm sorry," said Aedan. "I have seen firsthand what a cerberus can do to people. I will remain cautious."

"I was there too, Aedan," said Aloysius.

The three continued until they reached the edge of the woods. The sight before them was so beautiful it could be watched for a lifetime. Beyond the Teon Forest lay a vast ocean of golden thread. The men's faces were warmed by the sun's rays as if by a lover's hands. The wind was no longer barricaded by massive trees, but as free to run as the wildest creature. The wind manipulated the blond grass, pushing an airy current through the valley that, if left adrift, could take you anywhere you desired. Then, in the distance, the blare of white water grew like the sound of thousands of footsteps.

When the three companions heard the distinct noise of the Adraste, they began to chase it, in hopes of soon seeing the invincible river's great and awesome power. Their pace quickened to a gentle jog. As they approached the crashing water, their ears felt overwhelmed, as if by an avalanche, until the mighty roar of the river was all the three could hear. At last, the three men had the obstacle in their sights. They could now feel the beating heart of Ruxar itself. With hesitation, Aedan, Nestor, and Aloysius inched toward the river's edge.

"The stories do not exaggerate. This must be the most ferocious river in all of Ruxar," said Nestor, "if not all of the world."

"Ruxar is the only world we know. So, for now, the Adraste takes that title," said Aedan.

The riverbank was itself a cliff twenty feet above the water on either side. The sheer width of the river was more than the height of a full-grown tree. With that, the rapids seemed endless. The water could churn, flip, spin, and drag anything and everything that got in its path. The house-sized rocks possessed razor-sharp edges, pointing out from the belly of thick, voluminous, rushing water. Even the sun itself had difficulty lighting the few plants that lived next to the fast-paced water.

"So, what do we do?" asked Nestor trepidatiously.

"I didn't expect the tales to be so accurate. We must deliberate. Perhaps we can find a way," Aedan replied.

"What if we turn back—go north, then come back south once past the river?" asked Aloysius.

"I don't want to lose the time," said Aedan.

"What choices do we have? If we attempt a crossing, we won't live long enough for a rescue," said Aloysius.

"Boys," said Nestor. "Let's move away from here. The river's presence is only agitating our discussion."

Once some distance was placed between them and the river, the small troop made camp, each silently thinking of their next steps. Among a small grove of trees, Nestor lit a campfire and settled in to reflect. Aedan gathered firewood and paced the forest's ridgeline, also contemplating. Aloysius, the youngest of the three, darted into the wood to procure a small meal for the group. Shortly after, a small quail joined the three for dinner.

"My, you are quite the hunter, Aloysius," said Nestor.

Aloysius smiled, boyishly. "Oh, this is nothing. On Manticore, we fish and hunt much larger game."

"What big game is on the islands? I've never been," said Aedan, overhearing the conversation as he returned with an armful of logs and branches.

"The deer and boar are abundant, but not on the island I'm from," said Aloysius, beginning to clean the fresh kill. "Twice a year, my family travels to the main island of Manticore where we all venture out, set traps, and take home enough meat to last us the half year."

"Very interesting," said Nestor. "And here I thought you folk only ate fish."

"That would explain the smell," joked Aedan.

Aloysius smiled tightly. "No. We eat all sorts of foods—red meat, fruit, herbs, bread. But yes, we do eat our fair share of fish. We will go out for days on end casting and netting until we have enough to feed us for the month. In fact, fishing is what brought me out here."

"What does a fisherman from Manticore need for a life on the water that you cannot obtain at home?" asked Aedan.

"Hooks," said Aloysius.

"The bones of the Cerberus are incredibly strong," said Nestor. "I imagine, one Cerberus skeleton would make enough bone hooks to last ten or twenty years for an island like yours."

"Yes," said Aloysius. "In fact, the last supply came from a cerberus many times larger than the one at Brèdon."

"Wait. They kill the cerberus to be used for fishing hooks?" asked Aedan.

"Oh, no," said Aloysius. "Actually, I never thought about it until you said anything."

"No, boys," said Nestor. "The cerberus lives a long life. Much shorter than dragons and hydra, mind you. But in my lifetime alone, I have heard of many who have died from old age. The cerberus are sacred, but the people here, like anywhere, need to make a living." His answer seemed to quell the pair.

"So how does one pay for things, such as a whole cerberus?" asked Aedan. "Not to mention, transport one all the way to the islands?"

"My father told me to meet a group of settlers who live inland several miles from the coast of Cerebria. He gave me this bow." Aloysius pulled the weapon forward. "We trade them this bow, made from yew trees that grow on our lands. It is made with the hair of the manticore, and we give them shaved quills from the manticore's tail. Those quills can pierce the thickest wood; some even say they can pierce stone."

"So you were just passing through then? Like me?" asked Aedan.

"Why, yes. I was only to be there one night. That's when I heard all of the noise and decided to see what the trouble was."

Nestor laughed. "You wanted to be a part of something big, didn't you?"

"I was only curious at first, but yes. My life is rather boring. The seas can be treacherous, but I have longed to travel the continent," said Aloysius.

"And now you are here, on an adventure most dangerous," said Nestor.

"Yes. I hope my father will understand."

"He won't have much of a choice, young lad."

Aloysius grinned sullenly and continued cleaning the quail. By this time, the fire had burnt down enough for searing coals to be cooked over. The quail's meat dripped juice that sizzled. The grizzled meat called to the travelers, and the three enjoyed a hearty dinner as the sun began to crest behind the trees. Night was approaching once more.

"I had hoped we'd reached Ansgar by now," said Aedan.

"Give it time. We will," Nestor soothed.

"But what of the Hydrarians? Won't they attack again?"

"Yes, most definitely," said Nestor. "But it will take time. They must reform. Resupply, find their routed troops, and make another plan of attack. A force like that will not blindly attack. Not yet, at least."

"How do you know so much about the ways of the military mind?" asked Aloysius.

"Yes, and the dragon's breath in the trenches—where did you learn that?" asked Aedan.

"Ah," said Nestor. "Isn't it obvious?"

"No."

"Not to us."

"I was in the army. The Gargolian Army."

Aloysius and Aedan both sat mouths agape. After gesturing bewilderment to one another, Aedan asked, "Why did you not mention that at Brèdon, when we first met?"

"It didn't seem important at the time."

"Important! I would have believed you right away," said Aedan.

"Oh?" Nestor replied. "You made your mind up about me the moment you saw me. If I would have claimed to have once been a soldier from a different land, you would have disregarded me just the same."

Aedan thought for a long moment. "Perhaps. We will never know."

"Perhaps," said Nestor. "However, there has been one subject I've been meaning to discuss. With you most of all, Aedan."

"And what would that be?"

"Well, it is quite curious," said Nestor. "In my vision, it seemed as though, during the battle, your fighting ability was grander than that of our actual encounter at Brèdon."

Aedan cocked his head. "How so?"

"I thought he fought well," added Aloysius.

"As did I; however, there was something missing—a certain flair, if you will."

"Flair? Was it not showy enough for you?" asked Aedan.

"Perhaps flair is not the right word. No. Finesse, grace, agility. It was like you could leap over men, snatch arrows mid-flight, and dodge the swiftest slash," said Nestor, stroking his chin.

"Ah. Well, I can't do any of that."

"Shame," said Nestor. "I was sure, being from Dragonia, that you would display the traits gifted by the dragon."

"Traits?" asked Aloysius.

"Yes. Oh, Aloysius you should know," explained Nestor. "It is said through legend and lore that people who have close ties and proximity to the great beasts of Ruxar will be gifted with inhuman strengths or abilities."

"Wait. Slow down. Magnus mentioned this earlier, while we were digging the trench," said Aedan.

Nestor turned, placed his plate down, and faced the two. "These traits or gifts are something similar to being in a relationship or a lifelong friendship. During these long years, a person or persons would learn the other's mannerisms, word choices, tone, inflection, and maybe even the other's opinions and feelings on topics others would not be privy to. Over time, the individuals complement one another, all benefiting in some fashion."

"Exactly how should I know this?" asked Aloysius.

"Surely, you have heard the tale of the Beast's Gift. You are even blessed with the manticore's gifts," said Nestor. "The gift of accuracy. I assume you and your family live near manticore on your island, yes?"

"Yes. In fact, one rides with us on our vessels as we fish. We use its quills as arrows. The beasts have been used for generations as fishermen's aides."

"That explains it," said Nestor.

"Wait," said Aedan. "What tale?"

"You mean you haven't heard of the Beast's Gift?" asked Aloysius. "My parents told me that story many times when I was little."

"Yes, I, too, was told it as a young boy," said Nestor. "How curious."

"I don't know what to tell you. My mother didn't like telling stories. It made her sad. It reminded her too much of my father," said Aedan.

Nestor heard sadness in Aedan's voice. "Do you remember him? Your father."

"Only flashes of him. But I do recall him at my bedside telling me tales of wonder and sorrow. When I confronted my mother about him, she would only tell me that he could spin a story better than any other she had met." Aedan stared into the fire, as if searching for detail from his past. "I couldn't help but wonder if any of his stories were true." A long pause hung in the air. A moment and a loud crackle snapped Aedan out of his trance. "But please, enlighten me. Tell the story, Nestor."

"Yes, I want to hear it too. I wonder if there are any differences from my family's version," said Aloysius.

Nestor grinned. "Of course. It begins many centuries ago. At the very infancy of Ruxar. A child wandered the forest on a warm summer day. The young one enjoyed the shade of trees and the birds singing their songs. But at the forest's end, the child came upon a curious scene. For what the little one saw was a great and powerful beast. It stood upon a ridge overlooking the landscape. The child approached the beast carefully, trying not to startle it.

"'Go away, little one,' the beast said, sensing the child.

"Undeterred, the child asked, 'What are you doing there so close to the edge?'

"The beast turned to face its small visitor. 'I have decided to leave this land, and to never return.'

"'But why? What happened to you that makes you want to leave?' asked the child.

"The beast stared into the child's eyes, pondering whether to trust it with its motives, 'This world does not understand me. This world and its people fear and hate me. I have nothing here. So I must leave. To find another home to call mine.'

"Saddened by the beast's words, the child said, 'Not all people are bad. There are many that would love to know you, even to be your friend.'

"'How do I know you are telling the truth?' asked the beast.

"'Let's make a deal,' said the child. 'You come with me back to my family, and every morning, I will ask you if you still want to leave. Then if you do, I will not stop you again.'

"The beast stewed on the idea. He was apprehensive to accept the little one's gesture, but something about this child assured the beast's safety, so it reluctantly accepted. 'I will come with you.'

"Over the next several days, the child showed kindness to the beast. Giving it food and water. The two talked, and listened, and laughed, and even learned about each other's ways of living. And every day, the child would ask, 'Are you ready to leave?'

"And the beast would say, 'Not today.'

"Their friendship continued for many years. Each learning and growing with the other by their side, lasting all through the child's adolescence, to adulthood, and even to parenthood. The child was no child anymore but still shared a life of kindness and love with the beast, and still at the end of every day, the question would be asked, 'Are you ready to leave?'

"And the beast always replied, 'Not today.'

"Until one day, a day like any other day. The now-grown child asked, once again, 'Are you ready to leave?'

"But this time the beast replied, 'Yes. Today is the day.'

"The response astonished the beast's friend. 'How could you want to leave after all of this time? Have I not shown you kindness? Have I not shared my family with you? Have we not become great friends?'

"The beast approached its longtime friend with a soft grin and a nudge. 'It is not that you haven't shown me kindness, friendship, and love that I must leave. It is because you have opened yourself up to me, and restored my faith in humanity that I must leave you. I must take what I have learned from you and make a life of my own, with my own kind. That way I can teach them what you have taught me. You saved me that day on the ridge. I want to spread to others that same energy you shared with me on that day.'

"The grown child began to tear up, eyes filled with sadness. 'I don't want to lose you.'

"The beast smiled wide. 'Then I will give you something to always remember me by. To protect you and your family from dangers seen and unseen. This way we will always be connected.'

"'I don't understand. How?'

"'Come closer. Let me give you a gift,' said the beast. The beast raised its giant head and placed it softly on its friend's head. The warmth of the beast was a comfort. Then, as if a star had appeared out of nothing, a blinding light illuminated the two friends. The wondrous luminescence shined on for many minutes until it finally dimmed to barely a twinkle.

"Once the light had vanished, the beast spoke again, 'I have left you a gift, my dear friend. A part of me now lives inside you. You will forever be protected by my power. Safe from all things dark, and your children, too, will gain its benevolence.' The grown child thanked the beast for its gift and long friendship. Then, with a leap and a bound, the beast was gone.

"Dozens of years passed on. The now elderly human wandered the forest. The same forest that led to the ridge. This time, however, the human discovered something beyond imagining. A great group. Hundreds of beasts. Small, large, winged, four-legged, and more had just arrived to the land of Ruxar.

"'Oh my,' said the old one.

"A familiar beast stepped forward. It, too, had aged. 'Hello, old friend.' The two friends embraced tightly, and they watched as the many new inhabitants found their way onto the land and into our everyday lives. These beasts, as you may know, are the beasts that live among us. The beasts that we idolize in our way within our own separate countries. Friendship brought them here to Ruxar, and friendship shall make us all stronger for it."

"Wow. That's quite a story," said Aedan. "Thank you for sharing."

"Yes, indeed it is. Children particularly enjoy it," said Aloysius.

"Very true. To add to the story, these traits are particularly strong when families are exposed to their beasts through their lineage. For instance, my family owned, trained, and bred gargoyles throughout most of their history. Over time, many of my kin possessed one of the three gifts of the gargoyle."

"One of those gifts is visions, but what are the other two?" asked Aedan.

Nestor coughed lightly and took a drink of water from his pouch. "One of the last two traits is being blessed with dreams—dreams of beauty and times of love and joy, spectacles yet to be imagined. The person who possesses this gift is hopeful, positive, and quite creative. Creativity comes from solace, and these people thrive on it."

"And the other?"

"The third trait is to be cursed with nightmares—nightmares of cruel creatures in the dark. Terrors from the deep corners of a man's mind, feeding fear with fear. Many have been driven mad by these, a terrible fate indeed."

"Well," said Aedan, "it's a grand thing, indeed, that you were blessed with visions."

"Burdened," corrected Nestor. His eyes dropped to his plate of quail, lingering on the small bones. "Anyhow, Aedan, have you spent any time with dragons?"

Aedan studied Nestor a moment. "Yes. In fact, my town finds the abandoned eggs and raises them. The last time I was there, we had seven hatchlings. Many were still learning how to control their breath."

"Very curious," said Nestor. "Do you know anyone who has the traits of the dragons' gift?"

"No. No one I know."

"Pity. Perhaps it takes time, or an incident to resonate."

"After what we have been through," said Aedan, "if any abilities were to transpire, they would have already."

"Perhaps you are right," said Nestor. "Dragons are fascinating creatures. Living much longer than most. These abilities may take many more generations to show up."

"So, Aedan, what brought you to Brèdon?" asked Aloysius, changing topics.

Aedan stirred. "It was a personal matter. Nothing to get into."

"Come now," said Nestor. "We have been through a great ordeal with much left to experience."

"Yeah, Aedan. Share with the group," Aloysius said, grinning with wide eyes.

Aedan's silence broke at their insistence. "Fine, as long Aloysius stops making faces."

"No promises."

"I was there searching for someone," Aedan said heavily. "Someone I am not even sure is alive. Someone I didn't even know existed until a few weeks ago."

"Who? Who were you searching for?" asked Aloysius.

Aedan rose to his feet and stepped away from the campfire. "We should probably get some sleep."

"Well then," said Aloysius, taken aback, "I guess I'll take the first watch."

· · ·

The three settled in for the night. While trying to fall asleep, Aedan pondered the mighty river. He reviewed the dozen or so poor crossing methods in his mind. He thought of turning around and going north, but then it would take several days to reach the capital of Cerebria. By that time, it might be too late. Another attack might have taken place by then. Aedan ruminated on the responsibility he had undertaken. Whether he liked it or not, he had been sought out to help save a town, and he had accepted his new role. The past few days weighed heavily on his already buzzing conscience.

After several hours passed, Nestor's shift began. Aedan could not sleep. His mind was still active, full of dreams of him and his friends falling to their deaths in the raging rapids. After another sleepless hour, Aedan decided to rise and take his shift early.

"Nestor," Aedan whispered.

Nestor turned, startled. "Can't sleep?"

"Yeah, I haven't slept at all," said Aedan. "If you'd like, I can take the rest of your watch."

"That would be nice, but I wouldn't be able to sleep either. This river has a way about it. The rolling waters lull us into a state of self-doubt. Anytime I come close to it, my fear and anxieties rise to an almost irrational level. Perhaps that is why it is said to be impassable. A certain magic, perhaps—something older than anything we can understand," said Nestor, smirking. "So, instead, I think I will stay up with you. Keep you company."

Aedan nodded appreciatively. "You said this river opens you up to your doubts, right?"

"Yes."

"Then, why is our young Manticorian friend sleeping so soundly?"

Nestor chuckled deeply. "Hubris and youth would be my diagnosis."

Aedan joined Nestor in a belly laugh. "He sure is confident. Were we all like that once?"

"Oh, of course," said Nestor, coming out of his chuckle. "My son was the same way at his age."

"You have a son?"

"Oh, yes. He is a little older than you, I'd say." Nestor quieted. "He's strong, like you. Sure of himself as a young boy. The older he got, the more affirmation he required. Humility and discipline earned him a high honor in our army."

"Sounds like a good man."

"Thank you. Sometimes, I feel he got his modesty from his mother more than me."

"How do you mean?"

"Service has a way of taking your prime years, and if you're not careful, a decade or more can slip past you, becoming barely a memory."

"I'm sure you did as well as you could," said Aedan. "My father died, many years ago."

"I'm sorry."

Aedan nodded in thanks. "He died on a hunt. I never got to know him well enough to truly know or resent him."

"Is that what you were doing in Brèdon?" asked Nestor. "Searching for your father's past?"

"In a manner of speaking," said Aedan, turning his head and his attention from their conversation.

In the dense forest, the sound of crashing trees and profound thudding approached. It overwhelmed even the throb of the distant rumbling rapids. A monstrous, piercing howl echoed in the dark. The noise immediately woke Aloysius. Both Aedan and Nestor stood up, drawing bows and axes, ready to fire.

"What was that?" shouted Aloysius, also jumping to his feet to grab his weapons.

"A wild cerberus? Wolves?" inquired Aedan, looking to Nestor.

"Not any cerberus I've ever heard," said Nestor. "It was too loud even for a pack of wolves."

Just then, a tremendous shadow leaped out of the distant wood. The men flinched, nearly releasing their ammunition. Their breathing quickened as they steadied their weapons. Then out of the darkness lunged a beast of great stature. It stood nearly nine-feet tall on its four tree-trunk legs, connected to which were paws the width of a man's chest. Even in the darkness, the men could see the creature's three massive heads, with six eyes that glared like full moons. As if the size of the beast were not enough to intimidate the fiercest warrior, its dagger-like teeth and sword-like claws added to its fierce stature.

"It's a cerberus!" shouted Aedan, stunned by how considerably taller this one stood compared to Kaustos. The large beast's behavior seemed peculiar. *If this creature truly is wild*, thought Aedan, *why hasn't it attacked yet?* Then came the answer. Following the giant was a man!

"Phelan, leave those people alone!" demanded the man.

The mammoth beast promptly stepped back, on command transforming its demeanor to that of a playful child. The cerberus jumped humorously, joyfully nudging its master, seeking approval.

"My apologies," said the burly master. "He is still young and still easily excitable when he seeks."

"If that one is still young, then perhaps Magnus was not joking about Kaustos being a pup, aye fellas?" said Aedan.

"No doubt. If we would've had him, we never would have needed that second blaze," whispered Aloysius.

The three perplexed companions continued to stare at the man and his beast. "Who are you? What do you want?" asked Nestor, sternly.

"Ah, how rude of me," said the stranger. "I am Kratus, and my eager beast here is Phelan."

The men, at last, lowered their weapons, still stunned.

"I am Aedan of Dragonia. This is Nestor of Gargolia, and Aloysius from the Islands of Manticore. We were on our way to your capital, Ansgar."

"Ansgar? What takes you three there?" asked Kratus. "You are not of this kingdom."

"A competition," Aedan lied. "We are going to an archery competition."

"A competition?" Kratus said, incredulously. "I don't think so. Three men from three separate lands traveling together. What is your true purpose?"

"Honestly, we are off to the capital to compete," Aloysius insisted.

"Don't lie to me," said Kratus. "I am one of the king's scouts. I do not handle liars well, nor does my king. Those who have crossed me have quickly regretted their decision. Now, tell me your true purpose in traveling to my master's city."

Silence swept the three companions. The large beast, sensing his master's agitation, snarled a low grumble, further eating at the group's nerves. "Phelan does not believe you either."

Eyes and queer looks shot back and forth from the three travelers. Aedan began again. "Yes, sir, we are—"

"No," Nestor interrupted. "Boys, this is exactly the man we need to talk to. Lying to him will only make our journey harder."

"Can we trust him?" whispered Aloysius.

"This isn't safe," added Aedan.

"I have lived my life behaving myself," Nestor exclaimed proudly. "Always cautious, always safe. For the last few days, I have at last decided to act boldly, and all that will await me now is to find out which of the two methods will define me. The fool or the savior. So I, for one, am taking the bold move to trust this man."

Kratus smirked, impressed with the old man's candor and honesty. "So then, what will it be, old man?"

Nestor blinked rapidly, hoping to still be breathing with every flutter of his lashes. Feeling his heartbeat thud inside his chest, he took hold of boldness and spoke to the stranger. "We have dire news from the town of Brèdon."

From that moment on, Kratus and Phelan listened to the story of the three travelers unfold. They told of the great fires, the heroic acts, and the devastating losses caused for unknown reasons. Lastly, the mention of the Soldiers of Fire fell upon Kratus' ears.

"Soldiers of Fire?"

"The townspeople named us that as we left," said Aloysius.

"I can see why. Are you really a resistance group?" Kratus asked.

"Uh, well, yes. We fought back the army on our own," said Aedan.

"It's brilliant," said Kratus. Everyone smiled. "I must join you," Kratus added.

"Truly?" asked Aedan, stunned. "Then you should come with us to Ansgar. Take us right to your king!"

"I can't. If what you say is true, I must scout farther north as swiftly as Phelan can carry me."

"The river then!" said Nestor. "At least help us cross this river."

Kratus smirked and patted his noble beast. "Now, that I can do."

• • •

The sun had peeked over the horizon. The morning light illuminated the landscape. Kratus led Aedan, Nestor, and Aloysius to Phelan's side for a proper introduction. After many questions were answered about Phelan, all were reassured that he was one of the strongest cerberuses in all the kingdom.

The first to take the leap over the river was Aloysius. Kratus would accompany each of the men. This reassured Aloysius, for he was not keen on trusting an animal to jump over such a grand expanse, even one as mighty as Phelan. Kratus started Phelan hundreds of feet from the ledge. When in position, Kratus shouted a command and the large, three-headed beast launched itself as quick as an arrow leaving a bow. The massive cerberus reached the edge and leaped into the air. It seemed as if Phelan had sprouted wings as he floated effortlessly across like a bird from a treetop. Luckily for Aloysius, they landed on the other side with several feet to spare. Kratus and Phelan repeated the same effortless jump three more times, until it was Aedan's turn. When Phelan landed on the north side again, Aedan did not hesitate to mount the majestic creature.

"Are you ready?" asked Kratus.

Aedan's chest tightened and his stomach churned. He was caught by surprise because while watching the other two take their ride across, he had felt only excitement. Now that he was actually sitting on the creature, he had a sinking feeling about the next few moments. Without warning, Kratus yelled out his command. They were off! Phelan dug into the soft earth, accelerating, then reached the edge as quick as a wasp. The great cerberus jumped, sliding on takeoff, the slick ground causing his giant paws to lose their grasp and him to lose his momentum. Aedan and Kratus both realized the error and knew this last jump would not be the same smooth landing as before. As Phelan quickly approached the slanted cliff, the two passengers grabbed onto Phelan's dense coat.

A grave emotion washed over them. Phelan reached the cliff, slamming into the riverbank on the other side with only his front paws making purchase. His hind legs and two passengers dangled above the infamous Adraste's churning waters. In a flash, Nestor and Aloysius ran over to the cliff to assist in the rescue. The giant cerberus growled. He was too heavy for the moist cliff, which was starting to give way.

"Throw us something!" yelled Aedan, desperately hanging onto the thick coat.

With those words, Nestor and Aloysius intently rummaged through the travel sack for anything useful as a line to pull the dangling trio up out of danger.

"Phelan, claw up!" yelled Kratus, desperately holding onto his beloved companion. It was no use; the large creature could not exert enough force to pull itself up without taking down the side of the cliff. Then, with a loud roar, the mighty cerberus began to sway left and right, clutching its back paws onto the cliff. With that movement, Aedan and Kratus were able to climb up Phelan's fire red mane, pushing off of the great creature's back and onto the solid rock of the cliff.

They were not done yet. Kratus began yelling encouraging words to their colossal compatriot. With the help of Aedan, Nestor, and Aloysius, they managed to cast strong reeds to Phelan, who took them in his gigantic jowls; then with the combined aid of all four men, Phelan pulled himself onto the solid bank. The giant creature crawled several paces away from the riverside to lie down. Kratus followed, going to him, and with a heavy hand, he gave him an encouraging pat, caressing his muddy coat.

"Good work, boy. That was a close one," said Kratus. Then, turning to the others, he said wholeheartedly, "Thank you for what you did for Phelan."

"And you for helping us across," said Aedan, relieved.

"Ah, before I forget," Kratus said, removing a palm-sized coin from his pocket, "take this. It's the currency of the scout. We pass it from messenger to messenger for important matters over long distances. Show it to the right people and you will get your time with King Rordan."

"Thank you, Kratus," said Nestor.

Kratus simply smiled, and Aedan, Nestor, and Aloysius returned the same.

For several hours, the four men sat and talked about little items that meant nothing and everything to them. At last, Aedan stood up and thanked Kratus once again for his kind gesture. The rest stood up and said goodbye with hearty handshakes. Kratus saw them off to Ansgar, where they hoped the king would be as generous, understanding, and willing to fight against nefarious forces as their first recruit of the Soldiers of Fire.

CHAPTER 10

FOOLISH SAVIOR

The heat of day was at its peak as Aedan, Aloysius, and Nestor arrived at Ansgar's outskirts. The city's high stone walls and dark-wood archways greeted them. A road bordered by tree boughs and stone towers led to the city's entrance. Along the path, the troop were eyed queerly by farmers and cows alike. The three men kept their eyes forward, focused on reaching the impressive stone gates.

As the men approached, the stone doors lurched open, slowly revealing the metropolis' inner beauties and bustling population. Remaining standing at the gate, their eyes enlarged at the sight of more buildings made from combinations of rock and wood. The people commuting to and fro stood tall and stocky, much like the sturdy buildings around them. Smells of rotisserie meats filled the travelers' noses, alerting them to their empty bellies' hunger. Finally, their ears were bombarded by the sounds of truly young cerberus pups. The little ones chased children in a joyful game of tag. The three-headed hounds bayed happily as they worked their muscles to catch their two-legged friends.

"Ay there!" sounded a guard, gaining the three's attention.

"Oh, yes," replied Aedan, stunned. "My apologies."

"Right, right. State your business," said the second guard.

Aedan looked to Nestor. "Well."

"Fool or savior, son?" asked Nestor.

"Yes, of course," said Aedan, flustered. "We have come to gain an audience with your king."

The two guards shared a look. "I beg your pardon? The king?" said one.

Aedan gestured to Nestor, who fumbled in his pocket for Kratus' scout coin. "On our travels here," said Nestor, "we met a scout named Kratus. We alerted him to a terrible situation, and he gave us this coin as proof of its urgency."

Again the two guards exchanged a look, perplexed. "Who are you?"

"I am Nestor of Gargolia. These two are my wards." Nestor closed the distance to whispering distance. "A terrible force has made an indelible imprint on the countryside. We must speak to your king at once."

"It truly must not be postponed," warned Aedan.

The two guards scanned the men, and one clutched the coin. "Give us a moment. I must go fetch the captain."

The three agreed, stepped aside, and allowed the gates to close once more. Worry enveloped them as they stood looking out at the fields of onlookers and cattle. "What now?" asked Aloysius.

"We stand here and await the captain of the guard," Nestor replied.

"I don't like this," said Aloysius. "They don't believe us. I can feel it."

"Is that one of your passive traits, eh?" joked Aedan.

Aloysius scoffed. "I thought we would have—"

"Waltzed on into the king's own bedchambers, being greeted like heroes for returning a coin?" interrupted Nestor. "The world as they know it may be at peace, but the role and title of a king comes with many dangers, and even more enemies."

"We must be patient," said Aedan, attempting to calm the restless Manticorian. "Kratus said it himself; he would investigate the north sector. I am sure he and Phelan can handle things."

Again, the gates opened, crackling and yawning as they slid on the dry earth. This time they revealed a band of guards, armed with blades and bows tucked on their shoulders. "All right, you three," said the guard who had taken the coin. "We are taking you into custody by order of Captain Inge."

Nestor and Aedan were stunned into silence. Aloysius felt a jolt of fear—not of violence, but imprisonment. A small cage would not be his fate. Not for anything. "We are here to help!" he cried.

"Calm down, boy," said Nestor.

"They can't do this," said Aloysius as they were surrounded. His voice cracked as he attempted to hide his fear. "I won't be put into a cage, damn it. Not after what we did to get here."

"I'm sure there's a reason for this, Aloysius," said Aedan, attempting to pacify his nervous friend.

The guards tugged chain cuffs from their pockets. "I'm sorry, son," said one, "but we have been ordered by the captain."

Upon seeing the metallic bracelets, Aloysius' angst tore away his logic and sent him into action, in the form of flight. The young Manticorian darted between the sentries with the agility of a jackrabbit bounding away from a fox. "I'm not going to prison!" Aloysius shrieked as he flew past.

"Damn you, boy," Nestor groaned.

"No, Aloysius!" yelled Aedan.

It was too late. The guards launched into pursuit. "Stop!" they shouted.

"Don't hurt him. He's just frightened," said Aedan.

"Aedan, quiet!" ordered Nestor.

"Take the boy down if you have to!" shouted the guard who had taken the coin.

Aedan shot a worried glance at Nestor as Nestor was cuffed and then led into a dark tunnel inside the gate. "Fool or savior, Nestor?" Aedan yelled, backing away from advancing soldiers. "I guess I'll be a bit of both today." Aedan analyzed his options, then decided to act. His dive to the left confused the men. He rolled and hopped up effortlessly. His movement was met by sturdy guards, cuffs in hand. Aedan's hands grasped their wrists, guiding them up and away from his own, allowing him to flee up the city street into a crowd of bystanders.

"Come back!" yelled one guard.

"After him! Sound the alarm!" yelled another.

Aedan's pulse quickened as his eyes scanned between the crowds. Sharp shrieks of people being pushed to make way told him the guards were gaining on him. Groups of onlookers parted to make way for Aedan's pursuers. He continued his trajectory along the brick paths snaking through the city. A clang and oof came into earshot; it was Aloysius! Two wide guards gained on him in an adjacent alley. Aedan sprinted to Aloysius' aid, turning sharply as a deer, and into the narrow channel of stone walls and armed men.

"Aloy—" started Aedan as he collided with the small, frightened Manticorian and careened onto the hardened clay of the street.

"Aedan, what are you doing?" shouted Aloysius, tripping over his feet.

"You need to stop!" demanded Aedan, feeling the impact of a full-speed fool landing on his chest.

"Hey! You two, stop!" ordered one of the approaching guards—there were five in all.

Aedan held Aloysius' arms to still him as the two rose. Guards on either side of the alley arrived, drawing their swords now. "Come on, gents! Take 'em!" cried one guard.

Aedan's initial hope of a peaceful getaway fell apart as quick as a hummingbird's flap. "Disarm; don't kill," Aedan quickly told his friend.

Every guard rushed the two men. Aedan released Aloysius, who scurried up and around one man like a squirrel up a tree, bending the guard's sword arm like a tree branch, causing the arm to release the sword like an acorn. Aedan squatted, missing the sharp blade by a hair's length. A sturdy swipe at a leg brought the mighty tree trunk of a man down to the brick pavement. Aedan jumped back, again just being missed by slashing blades. Another incoming attack met air as Aedan instinctively guided the slash down, knocking the man off balance with a strong shove and a gentle kick in the back side that rolled the guard to the hard ground. The two met again, this time back to back. The guards closed in slowly, their swords low and at the ready. A series of shouts and purposeful movements followed the current stalemate.

The remainder of the guards arrived, all armed with bows, this time loaded, their strings taut and their arrows aimed at the two. "Get down! Now!" yelled one man, whose complexion was changing into an ever-darkening shade of red.

"Ay, you've done it now, Aedan!" said Aloysius, holding his hands up.

"Me?" Aedan exclaimed, following orders. "You ran off like a scared pup. I was trying to save your life."

"Yeah, but if you hadn't followed me—"

"Shut it!" shouted a guard. "Cuff 'em. If they try anything, put arrows in 'em."

The archers kept their aim steady at the two. Two guards on either side of Aedan and Aloysius cuffed and guided them down the brick street back to the gate. All the while, they were eyed by smirking and concerned citizens. The sentries returned to the gate, prisoners in hand. Aedan and Aloysius were thrown together into a small cell just to the right of the watch post. The cramped cell's door was visible to passersby, adding embarrassment to the terrible setback for Aedan and Aloysius' mission.

"You two have made quite a mess of things," said the chief guard. "Stay still, keep it quiet, and we won't feed ya to the dogs!"

"Hey, where is our friend?" asked Aedan.

"I said 'Shut it'!" shouted the guard, grinning. "The old man? He's probably being interrogated by the captain as we speak. Now shut up, sit down, and behave."

Aedan sat down next to Aloysius. "You idiot!" he told Aloysius. "You definitely chose the fool."

"Me? The fool? I'm not the one who ran into me, ruining my escape plan," Aloysius replied.

"I was trying to save you."

"You see yourself as the savior? More like a foolish savior."

"You arrogant little boy," said Aedan.

"Little boy! Who was it who saved your ass at Brèdon?"

"Yeah. Him. That guy? I'd like to have him with me right now. But all of a sudden, you turned into a halfwit and took off."

"I would have gotten away!" Aloysius insisted.

"You are the largest buffoon I have ever met, and now we have lost Nestor because of you!"

"You son of a—"

"I said shut it!" screamed the guard, banging on the cell bars. "One more word and the dogs get to eat a nice meal tonight! You understand?"

Both nodded at the guard, quiet now.

Once the guard moved away, Aedan said, "Boy, these Cerebrians sure like to threaten people with being eaten by their beasts."

Aloysius shook his head. Unamused, he turned to face the dark cold wall of the cell. Aedan turned his gaze to the many people going about their business, completely oblivious to the ever-approaching danger.

CHAPTER 11

STONE DOORS

Hours slid by. Aedan watched the sun glide across the sky and tumble behind the horizon. Sparkling colors coalesced among the clouds. He sat, mesmerized by the dancing hues, letting time slip around him. For the first time in days, Aedan's mind stilled, drinking in the beauty of the world. He strengthened his resolve to prepare for what lay ahead. Until their release, patience was the strength to live by. No doubt, the king would be furious over their actions. If allowed, Aedan would like to explain his and his misguided friend's actions.

An intrusive screech, followed by heavy footsteps, jolted Aedan and Aloysius upright in their cramped cell. "You two! On your feet," called a guard.

The two restricted prisoners stood up, wincing from confinement. Muscles stretching, body parts aching. The cell's door swung open to reveal, once again, archers at the ready, and several guards armed with swords. Without words, only a head nod, Aedan and Aloysius exited their prison. Torchlight greeted them as they were guided into the same tunnel Nestor had been taken into many hours ago. Its tightness was reminiscent of the cell they had just parted from. The long chasm twisted and curled until it arrived at a set of stone stairs.

"Move on," ordered the guard, still ensuring protection for himself and his men with arrows tautly nestled in their bow strings.

Aedan and Aloysius complied, ascending the stone steps. The first flight led to another, and another, and another. No windows to let in the moon's glow; barely even a flicker of torches aided them onward. No, just a simple spark illuminated their way. Then Aedan saw it. The crack in a wall ahead of him. The wall's stony surface was interlaced with chips, broken pieces, and strings of light that streamed into the dark passage. At last, the two could not walk any farther. The wall blocked their way.

"What's the hold up?" barked a guard in the rear.

"There's a wall. I can't walk through walls, now can I?" said Aedan.

"What, you can't save us from this too?" snapped Aloysius.

"You're being childish," Aedan replied.

"Shut it and push, will you? It's a door, not a wall," demanded the guard.

The two bickering friends obeyed and leaned against the door, throwing their weight into it. The stone door crunched open, slowly at first, then faster and wider, until it revealed the source of the helpful light. The door opened to a room as wide as two city streets, and perhaps just as long. The entire floor was decorated with intertwined, ornate woodworkings. Aedan and Aloysius scanned the room, noting the oaken archways attached to granite pillars. Finally, their eyes fell upon the absent king's robust throne.

Aedan and Aloysius were led to the center of the throne room, the guards still holding their positions. "Stay here. Don't leave. I can't promise your life if you disobey," said the guard leading them.

"Understood," replied Aedan.

"Yes, sir," said Aloysius.

With that confirmation of understanding, the guards retraced their position to the stone door, slinking back into the dark tunnel. Aedan and Aloysius, standing alone in the center of the throne room, swiveled their heads, taking in the room's beauty while wondering about the absence of anyone else in the castle.

"Where is everyone?" asked Aloysius.

"I don't know," said Aedan. "I don't like this. Something seems off."

"Well, at least we made it to the king's throne room. That's a step in the right direction."

"Yes, but what of Nestor?"

A powerful crunch of stone sounded to their right. Laughter followed. Then Nestor and a woman in soldier garb appeared. Nestor and the woman glanced at each other fondly, parting ways with a bow and a smile. Then Nestor jovially joined his companions as the woman vanished into more hidden caverns.

"Good evening, boys," said Nestor. "How has your stay been?"

"Nestor, what is going on?" blurted out Aloysius.

"We thought you were being interrogated," said Aedan.

"Interrogated? Me? No. I was chatting with the captain," said Nestor. "Captain Igne and I have known each other since before you two were bumps on your mother's bellies."

"Wait! You know the captain personally?" asked Aloysius, feeling jilted. "You didn't think to bring that up at the gate?"

"That would have been helpful to know," added Aedan.

"You're right; it probably would have been," said Nestor. "Perhaps next time I will remember. And perhaps next time, the two of you will trust an old man." Aloysius and Aedan turned their eyes away, ashamed of their actions, and embarrassed for misunderstanding their companion's intentions at the gate.

Before a proper apology could pass the young men's lips, doors on all sides boomed open. Out marched several members of the king's guard, trailed closely by women warriors, who aptly surrounded the room, taking up their stations in front of the pillars. One per granite block, each armed with a sword and a shield of oak.

A robust and poised man, dressed in robes, stepped into the center before the three companions. "Presenting their majesties, King Rordan and Queen Salome."

The guards and warriors knelt for their majesties' entrance. Aedan and Nestor followed suit; Aloysius shortly after joined them, being tugged down by his partners. Just as Aloysius' knee fell to the floor, thudding inappropriately, both royal figures emerged, arm in arm. The two looked elegant and strong. Their strides emphasized their burly forms. Both king and queen stood nearly a head taller than any of the guard. As brawny as the couple were, the two seemed to float along the floor as easily as birds in flight and gracefully perched themselves upon their thrones.

"All rise," said the queen. Unanimously, all stood, eyes fixated on the pair. The three travelers rose, awaiting judgment and their time to speak.

Silence engulfed the room. Aedan could feel eyes analyzing his inferior form. The women warriors stood as statues, nearly becoming one with the granite to their backs. The king's guard held their positions in similar statuesque fashion.

"Present yourselves," said the king.

"Nestor of Gargolia."

"Aloysius of the Islands of Manticore."

"Aedan of Dragonia."

Their hearts quickened with anticipation.

King Rordan rose from his seat, his eyes fixed on the young men. "I must start by thanking you, General Nestor, for returning my scout's coin with such an urgent message."

Nestor bowed. "It was my duty and honor, sire."

"General?" Aedan and Aloysius whispered to each other.

"You two," said the king, "have, unfortunately, left me troubled. Assaulting my guards, disturbing the peace, resisting arrest, and you, young Manticorian, ruined several bowls at the local potter's shop."

"Our deepest apologies, King Rordan," said Aedan.

"My deepest regrets. I misunderstood the circumstances, sire," explained Aloysius.

The king stepped aside, making way for Queen Salome.

"Normally," said the queen, stepping forward, "we would imprison and flog the likes of you for the disturbance and insult against the guard."

"We are truly sorry—" started Aloysius, quickly being quieted by his two comrades.

"Silence!" ordered the queen. "However, given the circumstances, and Captain Igne's vouching for General Nestor and you as his guests, I will forgo punishment."

"Thank you, Queen Salome," said Nestor. "That is incredibly gracious of you. I will ensure good behavior from my guests throughout our stay."

"I can't imagine you will be staying long," said the king, "You have much to accomplish in the near future."

"As do we, my king," added Salome.

King Rordan agreed. "However, we now require details of your journey here."

"Sire, what did the captain tell you?" asked Nestor.

"Captain Igne summarized the message, very plainly: War is coming."

"I beg your pardon, but war is here," said Aedan. "We fought off the Hydrarians at the small settlement of Brèdon, only days ago."

Rordan squinted, mouth sharpened. "Ulysses."

"We have always worked well together," said the queen. "Why would he attack now? After all this time."

"We are in the dark concerning their motives," said Nestor. "But I believe they will do more than merely assault another settlement."

"Explain," said Rordan.

"You see, I am a seer," said Nestor. "I have been burdened with the gift of foresight. My visions have only grown stronger, more vivid, darker."

"I have never met a seer," said the queen. "I have only heard of them in stories. How do we know this Gargolian is truly here to warn us? Perhaps he means to trick us."

"No," Aedan exclaimed. "Nestor, is a man of truth. He traveled hundreds of leagues south to find me and saved so many from death."

The queen was silent, but her face disagreed. Her eyes blazed with frustration over Aedan's outburst. "Must I revoke withholding punishment, young Dragonian?"

"Salome," said Rordan, "he meant no harm. He's simply defending his friend. Captain Igne has vouched for General Nestor, and I am inclined to believe her."

"Of course. I worry about our kingdom. Especially when foreigners bring word of death and violence to our doorstep."

"I mean no disrespect, nor harm. In fact, quite the contrary," said Aedan.

"Yes. My lady," said Aloysius, finding confidence once more, "we wish to help, in any way we are able."

"You have helped a great deal already by meeting with our scout," said the king. "I assume Kratus is looking further into the matter?"

"Yes, sir. He told us he would look north by the border you share with the Hydrarians and report what he saw on his return," said Nestor.

"Excellent. Then we are already ahead of the issue," said the king. "On his return, the queen and I, along with our generals and advisors, will devise means to repel the force, if needed."

"If needed?" said Aedan.

"As much as I would love to completely believe the words of a seer, I need to hear from the lips of a trusted ally on the happenings of the world," the king replied.

"We shall prepare you three for separate journeys home," announced the queen.

"For what purpose?" asked Aloysius, confused.

"To act as our royal messengers and emissaries to your own lands," said the queen. "What better way to alert our allies in Ruxar than sending one of their own with this vital communication?"

The three men glanced with concern at one another, unsure of the queen's plan to split them up. "When will we depart, madame?" asked Nestor.

"The day after tomorrow. We will give you time to rest, eat, and gather the necessary materials for your return journeys."

"Then it's settled," said the king. "I will have the captain's guard escort you to your quarters, and the queen and I will retire for the night."

"Thank you for your time," said Nestor.

"Yes, thank you," said Aedan.

Aloysius nodded and added, "And thank you for not flogging us."

The queen and king smirked at the comment, then briskly exited the throne room followed by their warriors. Captain Igne's guards emerged and collected the three men, marching them to a lit corridor that led through yet another maze of stone and torches. On their arrival, the three were welcomed by feather beds and fine linens. This luxury distracted the two younger men enough to fill their minds with drowsiness; soon they were resting happily upon the pillows, careening into much-needed sleep. Nestor, however, lay in waiting in the silence and darkness for another view into Ruxar's future.

CHAPTER 12

RATS AMONG HAWKS

Two days had passed since King Ulysses had left the small town of Echidna. He had traveled by horseback across the great Bron Plains to Jormungand, Hydraria's capital. His purpose in returning home was not to rest, nor see his family; he returned for one purpose: to assemble an army to eclipse the force sent to Brèdon. As King Ulysses and his royal escorts approached the almighty city, they were greeted by an ominous cloud that made Ulysses grin. He would need the cover of darkness to march his army to Cerebria, finish what he had started, and make his impact on the rest of Ruxar.

As the carriage approached Jormungand's gates, King Ulysses grew eager to commence the launch. When he, at last, entered the city, he dismounted his horse and walked swiftly to the military yard on the capital's far west side. His presence was immediately noticed by his soldiers. All promptly stood at attention in unison and said, "Hail, Jormungand!" This pleased Ulysses. Flashing his soldiers a wicked grin, he ascended a flight of stairs onto a platform overlooking his city. Rising into view, his force of thousands stood like single blades of grass in a field, upright and ready to be molded to their supreme ruler's will.

"Today, we have assembled the first great army that has been seen in Ruxar. We are the first to send soldiers to a neighboring nation," King Ulysses announced. "We will not stop. We will grow strong and strike fast at the hearts of these kingdoms that are unworthy to exist. We will rise up against their inferiority, ignorance, and self-righteousness. So tonight, my great Hydrarian brothers and sisters, we must bring Ruxar into the light by casting our shadow over their lands. To wash away their imperfections, we must use blood to cleanse Ruxar's soul. For Jormungand! For your king! And for Ruxar!"

In response, the soldiers shouted their hatred for their enemies. Ulysses smiled at his creation. He smiled at their conviction and the loyalty being shown to him and Jormungand. "Tonight is your night!" he shouted back at them. "Tonight you will join together and set in motion the purification of our kingdoms. A new start of our reign over these lands! For Hydraria! For Jormungand!"

With those final words, the men could no longer contain themselves and began chanting their king's name. Even as Ulysses stepped off the platform and descended the staircase, his smile remained. He would unleash a force greater than any flooding river, volcanic eruption, or earthquake ever seen.

Ulysses returned to his castle and found his study. There he would write a letter to his general about the upcoming sequence of events. He had just sat down and picked up his pen when slipping out of the darkness emerged a woman, whose black hair and slender body nearly made her invisible in the inky light. Her eyes glistened in the golden orange candlelight. She hovered like a ghost watching over him.

"Hello, Mara, my queen," said Ulysses.

"Hello, darling," Mara replied. "I heard you had arrived. Then once the shouting began, I knew it to be true."

"Yes, my apologies. I was unsure if I would have time to see you. I depart in the morning."

"Leaving? You've just—" But she was interrupted by an embrace. "Are you certain you must leave? Surely, Anwar is trustworthy."

"Mostly, yes."

"So, you will march with the army to ensure victory?"

"No. No. Instead I am to pursue other matters," said Ulysses.

"Other matters? What is more important than seeing this crusade through? And what about your wife and daughter?" asked Mara with great unease.

"I'm afraid I cannot say at the moment. Unfortunately, I must keep this to myself," Ulysses replied. "I do regret being away for so long, but this is bigger than both of us."

"Even bigger than your family?" asked Mara.

"Yes," said Ulysses, pushing away from his wife. "You must understand that we have to do this. This will better all our lives."

"We already have a good life!" exclaimed Mara.

"No! We have lived as rats among hawks. It has become clear to me that we, the Hydrarians, must be in control. We have the power, the knowledge, and divine right. We will be respected and feared for it."

Mara stepped back. "I want this as much as you. But I also want you to be here for Morrigan and me."

"Agreed," said Ulysses. "I will be here for you throughout our conquest, but for now, I need you to remain hidden until the path is safe. Do this for me, please."

Mara thought for a long moment. "Of course, my love."

"Thank you, my queen."

"By the way," said Mara, "where is Morrigan?"

"She is still in Echidna with Anwar," Ulysses replied. "She has proven to be quite useful. Anwar claims she is a quick study."

"Do you truly trust him with her?" asked Mara.

"Morrigan can handle herself. She is learning combat—blades mostly."

"Wonderful, but I have seen how he looks at her, Ulysses. I don't care for him."

Ulysses eyed her queerly. "He is my general and my royal advisor. I trust him above all others in my court. I wish you would as well."

"I'm sorry, dear. It's just that his age concerns me. He is much older than Morrigan, and I don't want our daughter ending up with a man who intends to use her."

"Rest assured, she is safe. Trust me," said Ulysses. "Trust is not something I ever thought I would have to reassure you to do."

Mara's face sunk. "Shall we retire, my king?"

"You go up. I must finish a letter."

With a flick of her heel, she stepped closer and kissed him. Then she slowly walked out of the study toward the stairs to their chambers. Once she was gone, King Ulysses ambled to his desk, scribbled the final sentences on the piece of parchment, snatched twine, and rolled the parchment tightly. From there, he hastily exited the study and walked down the stairs to the entrance. Outside, the weather had turned gruesome. Rain and wind blustered, and the clouds thundered. This did not delay him. Ulysses ran to the stables, where he found a messenger grooming his horse.

"My king!" shouted the man, startled to see him.

"I need you to deliver this to General Anwar," ordered Ulysses, handing him the parchment.

"Yes, my king."

"This is for his eyes only."

The messenger's eyes widened, but without further questioning, he saddled up the fastest horse, mounted it, and rode off across the Bron Plains. Ulysses watched his messenger gallop off into the dark violence of the storm. Then he made his way back to the palace and his bedchamber. There, Mara lay awaiting his arrival. That night, they would lie in intimacy together throughout the turbulent storm.

. . .

The next morning, Ulysses woke with great anticipation. The day of the great departure had begun. He rose from bed gently so as to not wake his sleeping queen. He donned his robes and walked to Mara's side of the bed, leaned over, and kissed her cheek. Then he descended the long staircase. Once out of the palace, he beheld a scene of bustling, armored soldiers, preparing for the long march. Their movement excited the king. He breathed in the energy of the storm overhead, still pounding the land, and exhaled his desire for victory. It seemed his desires were not just his own. Someone or something greater than all of Ruxar longed for their fruition as well.

CHAPTER 13

STEEDS AND INSTINCTS

The morning of their departures had arrived. Aedan felt both excitement and anxiety—excitement to return to his home country, but anxiety that he would have to journey there alone, across a nation growing with hostility. As Aedan rose from his slumber, he peered out the window of his sleeping quarters. What he saw was grand. Skies filled with white, bloated clouds dotting light blue heavens. Below was the bustling city full of people living completely oblivious to the transforming world. In a way, Aedan envied their ignorance.

After his gaze outside the window, he made his way down the lengthy staircase to the throne room. There he was greeted by one of the guards from the day before. To Aedan's surprise, the guard smiled and happily opened the door for him. Once giving the guard a pleasant nod of thanks, Aedan entered the room and was greeted by Nestor and Captain Igne.

"Ah, Aedan!" shouted Nestor. "I'm glad to see you're finally awake."

"Good morning. How long have I been out?"

"Long enough for the captain and I to make bets on who would wake first," Nestor said with a chuckle.

"Aloysius isn't up yet?" asked Aedan.

"He may be, but I will not go searching," said Captain Igne, smirking.

"My apologies, Captain," replied Aedan. "We haven't been properly introduced."

The captain made a slight bow as Nestor introduced them. "Aedan of Dragonia, Captain Igne. Captain Igne, Aedan."

Aedan smiled at the gesture. "Thank you, Nestor. And thank you, Captain, for vouching for us."

Her smirk tightened. "Oh, I didn't vouch for you. Nestor did. I wanted to throw you in a cell for a month for attacking my guards."

Aedan's head sunk low, his eyes leading the way. "I am truly sorry for my part, Captain. Have you been waiting long?"

"Yes. Many hours," said Igne. Her broad build and short answers spoke of a disciplined woman.

"Be easy on him, Captain. Aedan here is not a military man," said Nestor. "However, I believe he will be as close to one as one can be after all of this has found its end."

"Again. My sincere apologies," said Aedan.

"What are we apologizing for?" mumbled a groggy Aloysius, entering the room.

"Excellent," said Nestor, upon seeing him.

"Now that all three of you are awake, I can show you to our armory," said Captain Igne.

"What? No breakfast?" asked Aloysius.

Ignoring Aloysius, Captain Igne stood up and walked toward the doors, waving her hand to signal to three soldiers to follow her. They hurriedly trailed behind their captain until reaching a locked door.

As Captain Igne opened the aged wooden door, Aedan, Nestor, and Aloysius' mouths fell. Inside, stored on racks, were hundreds of blades, ranging in size from small daggers to grand swords that stood five feet tall. A wall was filled with helmets and armor. Next to them, bows hung from the racks, and below them were tens of thousands of arrows inside several hundred quivers, just waiting to be used. Among the arsenal were axes of all sizes, spears, hammers, and even paint to complete the Cerebrian armory.

"This seems extensive for a nation that has never seen war," said Aedan.

"During times of peace, prepare for war, young Dragonian," Captain Igne replied.

"Well said, Captain," added Nestor.

"Where to begin?" asked Aloysius, excitedly.

"Stock up on what we have; start with what you are most comfortable with," said Aedan, answering the eager Manticorian.

"I will leave you three to stock yourselves for your quests," finished Igne, stepping outside the room.

Aedan, Nestor, and Aloysius did as the captain recommended. They found quivers and filled them with arrows. Then they inspected the smaller swords, axes, and daggers, thinking of long distance travel, until they decided what would be most suitable. When they had finished, Captain Igne escorted the three to the stables. The slotted stables ran dozens of pens deep. The structure resounded with neighing and clopping hooves. Heavy odors of manure and leather invaded the travelers' nostrils.

"Horses?" said Aloysius. "The king is giving us horses?"

"No," said Captain Igne. "I am giving you these horses. The king and queen have given me free rein over those who transport his scouts."

"You're sure no one will need them?" asked Aedan.

"No. Several of these animals have no riders now. Lately, horses have been found outside the city walls, riderless," said Igne. "The situation's suspicious nature only recently occurred to me. We lose one scout yearly. But we have lost four in a span of a few months."

"Hydrarians," stated Nestor.

"Yes. Once you three showed up with Kratus' coin, and we had a chance to discuss the happenings in the northern territories, I knew the two were related."

"How far north do the scouts venture?" asked Nestor.

"As far north and east as our lands lay. Rarely do scouts journey into Hydrarian territory," Igne replied.

"Why? We have been at peace for ages," said Aedan.

"It is a courtesy," said Nestor. "Trust is difficult to earn, and easy to lose. I hope we did not send Kratus into trouble."

"He is our fiercest scout," said Igne, "and is one of the only ones who travel by cerberus. Most find them to be too much to handle."

"He seemed to have Phelan under control," said Aedan.

"No doubt." Igne sighed. "Now, I must get you three on your way. Nestor, you will be given the mighty mare Aislin." Aislin stood short for a steed. Its coat was red in color. The red reminded Nestor of a rose that had seen too much darkness. She seemed to be calm and agile, ideal for an older rider. "I believe she possesses a gift very similar to yours, Nestor. I have observed this horse throughout her life, and I have witnessed many curious things. This horse has a tendency to protect those around her. Intuition perhaps." Nestor happily accepted the noble captain's gift.

"For the reckless young Manticorian, I have selected the great stallion Eber." The horse glowed of pure white; its hue showed similarities to the clouds that are always at the wind's mercy. "This horse has been known to be a great friends with his riders." Aloysius, too, accepted his gift.

"For you, Dragonian, I give the swiftest and brightest of our horses. I present to you the mighty stallion Niul," said Captain Igne, handing the black horse's reins to Aedan. Aedan was in awe of the animal's sleek beauty and strength. Every muscle protruded from his massive body. Niul's coat shared the color of the oil that had created the walls of fire at Brèdon. Aedan felt that with this horse, he would be able to make it to his homeland quickly and safely.

"Now that you all have your weapons and means of travel," said Igne. "I must give three more items. The first is the king's seal on three letters, one for each of your kings. The second is a supply of food. It should last each of you through your journey. Finally, I give you three my best wishes and my thanks. If you hadn't delivered the message of violence, we could very well be in dire straits."

With those final words, they all mounted their steeds, thanked Captain Igne, and trotted out of her sight.

• • •

Riding away from Ansgar, the small band passed the fields of workers and livestock, who no longer eyed them as strangers. It appeared commonplace for them to see riders scurry out from the gates and on to more important tasks. The three rode quietly along, reflecting on the recent events, and they pondered those that still lay ahead. At last, Nestor, leading them, stopped. "Before we part ways," he said, "I must tell you two something."

"What is it?" asked Aedan.

"I've had more visions," Nestor replied.

"What did you see?" asked Aedan worriedly.

Nestor paused, collecting his thoughts. "This time I saw the three of us on our separate journeys."

"Well?" asked Aloysius.

"The vision showed little," said Nestor. "Darkness, an abyss, overwhelmed my senses. A fear crept into my chest as I slept. This journey will test us in ways Brèdon never could."

"What if we travel together, as one unit?" said Aedan. "That would be safer."

"I don't think so," said Nestor.

"Why not?" asked Aloysius.

"These trials we're about to face, these quests we are about to set out on, will mold us into the men Ruxar and its people need," Nestor claimed. "My instinct is driving me to follow the king and queen's plan. It feels as if I am being directed by a force I do not understand."

"And we are supposed to trust this force?" asked Aloysius, skeptically.

"Yes," said Aedan. "I told you, Nestor, when we met that there was something about you—an instinct that made me follow you into battle. Made me believe you. And I will continue to follow your lead, even apart."

Nestor and Aedan shook hands, exchanging gratitude for one another. The three continued speaking as they rode along the path. They discussed themselves as the Soldiers of Fire and the many strategies to be used to delay the enemy. They spoke cheerfully about family, plans, and whimsical thoughts to brighten their moods until they reached the bridge over the Grimbold River. Here, they said their goodbyes, splitting off onto their own paths, uncertain whether they would ever see each other again before this dangerous saga was over.

CHAPTER 14

OLD SAMUEL'S PORT

Trees shook gracefully in the wind. Leaves dropped and fluttered away like butterflies in the breeze. Nestor had ridden his hooved companion north from Ansgar for several days. His destination: Gargolia. The king's necessary help would bring forth insurance. Aligning the four nations against the Hydrarians was the best way to stop the war from spreading.

Nestor's journey had taken him northward, over the Invincible River once more. This time he crossed by way of a small, hidden bridge made known by Captain Igne. Then he rode to embattled Brèdon. Nestor stopped in the town to glance at where his perilous journey had begun. He saw only a handful of villagers repairing walls and clearing debris, while many more were mourning at graves of their fallen. Nestor could still see where the fire had left bruises of black and char on stones and cindered wood. The old man did not stop to help; he merely nodded in appreciation for their work and pressed onward toward his destination.

Over the next day, Nestor and his steed Aislin galloped and tramped over hills and through forests. Nestor could smell smoldering fire and hoped it came from a benevolent source. Eventually, the sunlight began to dim, and his steed to tire. Nestor spotted a grove of trees among a small lake and steered Aislin toward it. There, Nestor dismounted and showered the animal with comforting pats. Then he tied her to a tree and let her rest, eat, and drink.

Nestor, now letting himself relax after a hard day's ride, sat beside the animal at the base of a sturdy trunk. His body felt heavy, his legs stiff as logs, and his back as tight as knotted rope. He could feel his breathing slow to a steady pace, and his eyes grew heavy. The strain had found his head. His eyes shut. Nestor began to fall, slowly at first; then with every passing moment, he could feel the air rushing past his ears, as if he were meteoring toward the ground. A hard thump and startling heat brought him into the light of a familiar scene. His mind, fuzzy with exhaustion and stress, showed him a town burning—Brèdon on fire. Nestor was confused. His face was flush from flame; the air rushing past his ears, created by updrafts of embers, stung him mercilessly. At last, a shadow formed. A young man rose from darkness, charging, running into the flame.

Nestor could hear the sounds of arrows loosening, the sudden stutters of swords being drawn, the shouts of frightened people. An order rang out: "Kill them all!" Nestor's heart sank like a pebble in water. His eyes teared from both the blaze and the dying songs of those being executed. In the last effort of a man's breath, he could see the foolish hero being surrounded, overwhelmed by steel, fire, and hatred. The last scene Nestor witnessed was a form of stark black slicing, cutting down the very air of the failed rescuer.

Nestor startled awake. Gasping for relief from the heat and sights, he found his clothes were soaked with sweat and his breathing labored. The steed beside him jolted and neighed, surprised by the old man's movements. Nestor stood, grabbing at the elder tree besides him for support. Then he grasped his knees and continued to breathe heavily. "Not again. I don't understand," Nestor said aloud. He stepped closer to the horse, patted the beast on the nose, and stroked him calmly. "If what I saw was true, we need to hurry. No time to rest tonight," he whispered to Aislin.

Nestor quickly gathered up loose belongings, untied the horse, mounted, and continued on. The light of day had not yet disappeared. Shimmering pinks competed with the remaining blue and red hues of the sunset. His memory was being jostled by the sights around him. Something seemed familiar about this landscape. He had been here before, but why was this so important now? He slowed his ride to a walk. Looking about, he decided to turn west toward the ocean. Something about the coast called to him like a songbird.

As the pair traveled west, Nestor could smell the sweet breeze of air over water. Gulls circled overhead. The cawing of chatting birds irked him, but it was leading Nestor in the direction his instinct inspired. He found himself climbing a sharply sloped hill, and he could hear the sounds of displacing waves crashing on land. The two travelers landed on top of the hill and could see a vast ocean in front. Nestor let out a deep sigh of relief. The sight of such a wide area comforted Nestor. He could see for miles. There was peace in being able to see what was coming. Nestor wished he felt that way about his visions. Lately, his insight into the future only filled him with fear and dread.

In the blue distance, Nestor could see the sparkling spear of sunlight glinting on the ocean's surface. His eyes scanned the landscape. He recalled many years ago a small port on the waters. "Maybe we can hitch a ride farther north. What do you say, girl?" Nestor asked, patting the beast. Aislin swooped her head down and up in agreement. "All right, let's go then." Nestor lightly nudged the horse and the two began trotting closer to the water. With the sunlight being swept away by the night sky, Nestor worried they would not see the port—if it still existed. It had been small and barely used in his youth. The chances were low that it would still be in commission.

Nestor and Aislin pushed forward. The long scenery began to dull Nestor's mind. He felt his eyes fluttering from a desire to sleep. The horse was slowing, rocking Nestor in a lull of liminal consciousness. The night sky displayed millions of twinkling stars in a background of vast darkness. Moonlight shrouded the beaches in a cool, silver glow. Nestor felt his body slip, falling fast into slumber. His companion, reaching the end of her abilities, halted close to a patch of grass near the beach.

As the hypnotic swaying stopped, Nestor woke from his doze. He sat up in the saddle, rubbed his fuzzy eyes, and took a deep breath of cold ocean air. The chill filled his lungs and brought the world into focus. In the distance, he could see a small light, flickering like that of a star in the sky. Dancing on the air, at the mercy of ocean gusts, shone a small firelight. It lay just ahead on the beach. Nestor could make out the shape of a building to the torch's right. "Well, I guess we found it," said Nestor, petting Aislin's mane. "I wonder if anybody's home." Nestor picked up the reins and encouraged the lumbering horse a little farther toward the small structure.

• • •

Nestor's discovery rejuvenated his energy. A surge of adrenaline fueled his labored body. Stopping a few feet from the front door, Nestor dismounted and tied up Aislin. Conveniently, a small trough full of water sat just to the door's left. The exhausted old Gargolian approached the door. The building stood sturdy on the beachfront, but when Nestor saw it was held up by rotting pilings and barnacles, he questioned its integrity. He gave the door a hearty knock. The clang of metal on wood chimed in the night. Then, silence.

The hinges creaked. The door parted an inch. "Who's there?" shrieked a scratchy voice.

"Hello. I apologize for the late hour, but I have been riding a long while, and I stumbled on your home," said Nestor.

"So, you're looking for lodging?" asked the man.

"Yes, si—"

"Not here. There's an inn thirty or forty miles north. Just keep going until you run into it."

"You don't seem to understand. If I travel any farther north, I will be in Hydraria," said Nestor, beginning to feel his body ache now.

"So what! They will take care of you."

"I don't trust them," Nestor said in a low, serious tone.

"Not my problem," interjected the man. He moved away from the cracked door. Nestor, overwhelmed with frustration and exhaustion, pushed in the door to the small building. He saw a small man, nearly eighty, stumbling backward and falling to the floor. Nestor immediately regretted his emotional outburst.

"I'm so sorry, sir," Nestor said, reaching down to help the man up. The old man, shaking, drew a small blade from his shoe.

"Don't come any closer. Try to rob me. I might be old, but I'll cause you damage before you get away with my things," the old man threatened, still lying on the floor and as intimidating as a wounded fish to circling sharks.

"Listen, I'm not here to rob you. I simply need a place to stay for the night. This place used to be a trading post, yes?"

"Yes, many years ago. What does that matter? You need to leave!" The old man, either giving up or forgetting he had been upset, dropped his knife and started to climb the wall for support to stand up.

"I can't leave," said Nestor. "I want to avoid the Hydrarian countryside. We are at war with them!"

The old man looked up at him, mouth agape. "What craziness are you spitting, son? The Hydrarian folk have been good to me."

"Well, something has changed," Nestor said, taking a deep breath. It felt good to say that to an actual person instead of a horse. "We were attacked at the small town of Brèdon."

The old man, still attempting to stand, looked suspicious. Nestor finally overcame his fear of being lightly stabbed and aided the old man to his feet.

"How? Why? I don't understand," said the old man.

"They besieged the place. We fought them back. Many died. I have no idea why they attacked. That is what I, and some others, are trying to find out," Nestor said. "My name is Nestor. I'm a former general of the Gargolian army. I am traveling to meet with my king, Xenos. I must warn him of the Hydrarians' actions."

The old man's expression was blank. His eyes vacant. He was searching for the logic in Nestor's words.

"Please, son, come in." The old man gestured to the back of the structure. "Come take a seat. I have some more questions for you."

"Thank you," said Nestor tiredly. The old man guided Nestor to a padded chair and then sat across from him in its twin. The house's interior was made up of old gray boards. A small fire in the middle created a soft orange glow. The heat was a welcome comfort for Nestor.

"All right," said the man. "I know the hour is late and you are tired. But please, explain how we are at war. The Hydrarians to the north have been our allies for as long as my family has lived here. In fact, in the last year, they have begun using my port occasionally."

"They have? What have they been doing?"

"Well, I don't rightly know. They would always come under the cover of night and a gentleman would knock on the door. A polite man. Soldier type, I think. He would inform me of their doings and hand me coins and supplies for my understanding."

"Well," said Nestor, keeping his reaction minimal, "that is truly kind of them."

"Now tell me. What is it you believe is leading the continent to calamity?" asked the man.

Nestor briefly retold the story of his visions, meeting Aedan, the battle at Brèdon, and the people who had helped fight. He told of his meeting with King Rordan of Cerebria, and of the Soldiers of Fire.

"That is quite a tale, General," said the old man.

"Please, call me Nestor. I haven't been a general in many years."

"All right, Nestor. I am Samuel, the keeper of this port."

"Good to meet you, Samuel, minus the near stabbing," Nestor joked.

"I'm sorry for that, but you can never be too careful. I have had a few ruffians come around here in the past. It's different, though, now that I'm alone…." said Samuel, his voice trailing off.

"You had family here?" asked Nestor.

"Yes, my wife just recently passed, and my daughters are away raising their own families. I seldom see them. Been contemplating leaving this place, but my age makes it more difficult to travel on foot."

"Can you ride?" asked Nestor.

"Of course," said Samuel, nodding fervently.

"You said this place was a port. Does that mean you still have a travel-worthy vessel?" asked Nestor.

"Yes. I still have one ol' maid that is seaworthy."

"Perhaps we can make a deal. I will help you pack your things and load up. You can take my horse. Go meet up with your family. Go. Live the last of your days beside loved ones."

"And what do you want in return?" asked Samuel.

"Well, I am trying to avoid Hydraria. Doing that by sea seems to be the safest route," said Nestor. "I'd like to take your last boat to the Gargolian port of Broinn. From there, I am going to see my family and then the king."

Samuel thought for a long moment. He looked around at the opaque walls of his home, smiled, and said, "Yes, I'd like that. We can prepare in the morning. For now, let's get settled for the night. We will both need our rest if we are to make our journeys."

Nestor smiled and nodded. He stood up, helped his new friend stand, and then the two shook hands. Over the next hour, Samuel prepared a cot for Nestor and gathered food for Aislin. By the time Nestor had removed the saddle and quickly brushed the strong beast down, Samuel had walked outside to retrieve Nestor.

"Your cot is all ready for you," said Samuel.

"Thank you. I am in your debt."

"No, we are helping each other. No payment required," Samuel said, smiling.

As the two aged men walked indoors, Nestor could see the stars fading to make way for the sun. He had been awake for nearly two days. Nestor's mind was still moving, but his body needed rest.

"Good night, Samuel," said Nestor once they were inside.

"Good night. Oh, one last thing before we sleep."

"Yes? What is it?" asked Nestor lazily.

"It's not a question. More of a memory that just lodged its way out of my mind. I remember a name. The name was spoken to me by my grandfather, who said he had learned it from his grandparents." Samuel stopped for a moment. "Solomon. Solomon of Hydraria. Supposedly, he was not a good man; he led his country into turmoil. Does that name mean anything to you?"

Nestor thought for a long moment, but his mind felt as thick as molasses in winter. "No, that name doesn't sound familiar to me."

"All right. It's just that my granddad told me to be wary of the Hydrarians. I can't remember the story now, but the name has stuck with me all these years." Samuel paused again in thought. "His name came jumping back at me when you said we were at war with them—almost as if my grandfather were telling me that story again. He always said the name with such hatred. I can't even remember why now."

Nestor shook off the conversation as an old man reclaiming his memory, trying to relive his youth. Both men found their beds and quickly slipped into a deep sleep. Nestor, however, went to sleep with the name Solomon of Hydraria drifting in his mind, searching for any relevance it might have to their current predicament.

CHAPTER 15

SWOLLEN HEADS AND EMPTY BELLIES

With Ansgar behind him, Aloysius rode east, onward to Manticore. His home island of Atwater would not see him yet on this journey. His destination was Archere, the capital of Manticore. He, like his companions, had a message to deliver. The Hydrarian incursion had been stopped for a moment, thanks to his great shooting, he thought. Aloysius had developed a keen eye for accuracy while fishing on the turbulent Trahern Channel. The channel wove in and out of Manticore's five islands. Its currents were known for their ferocity, but they were nothing he couldn't handle by way of boat and a steady hand.

Riding along the Plains of Cerebria, Aloysius quickly traveled over the Grimbold River bridge, and then he could see the Duer Mountains taunting the sky with their peaks in the distance. Snow caps atop great giants of earth and stone stood as monuments to the landscape. Aloysius recalled seeing their spiked forms at a young age. He wondered if even the strongest birds or dragons could fly up to their peaks. Aloysius had always desired to climb them; perhaps he would after delivering the message of war on the horizon. Again, he thought just how lucky Aedan, Nestor, and the people of Brèdon had been to have him there to take down the invaders. It was different, killing men, he thought to himself. Much different than spearing fish or other game to eat. The feeling empowered him. He could stop angry men now. If need be, he had the ability to exact justice on wrongdoers.

With a swollen head and an empty belly, Aloysius trotted farther. "I should have rationed better. Mother would disapprove of my lack of planning," Aloysius said aloud. His stomach spoke to him like a monster from the deep, but he was confident he could find something in the area to make into a meal. Despite his hunger pangs and his tongue itching for something flavorful, he did not lose sight of his mission. He had to stay focused; otherwise, yearnings could distract him. Distractions could prove dangerous. He began remembering his plan. Reach the small town of Cathair. Board the ferry to the main island. Trek to Archere. Find that delectable smell and consume it.

"Wait. What?" Aloysius asked himself in mid-thought. "What is that smell?" Aloysius' active young brain could not overpower his desire to eat. "Is that venison?" His heart began to race. He took deep breaths. Inhaling the aroma of salty charred meats, Aloysius became like a dog, finding his way home by scent. With his nose pointed in the air, he kicked his horse forward. The odor gripped him now. He could smell smoke. Hickory fumes blended with greasy meat. Then Aloysius' ears filled with soft laughter.

"Cathair! I must be nearby!" Aloysius shouted, looking down at his horse. "Go, boy! Run before I decide to eat you instead." With that threat the horse and famished young man sprinted down the plains toward meaty bliss. Man and steed weaved in and out of a cluster of trees as the laughter and talk grew louder. Aloysius could taste the meat on his tongue. Finally, he emerged from the small grove and came upon a sight much smaller than a town; a troop of people were settling in for the night.

The troop had erected several tents surrounding two large fires. One had over it a boiling pot of stew, churning its coalescing ingredients. The other warmed a freshly cooked deer, rotating on a rotisserie. Aloysius could hear the grease dripping into the fire. The sputter against the coals played like light drums in his head. Initially, Aloysius could see about twenty people. Men, women, and small children. Most of the troop were taller and larger than average—a dead giveaway that they were Cerebrians.

On the opposite side of the camp lay two cerberus. One, a female, was smaller than the other. Her fire-orange fur made her stand out, even in the darkening light. The male stood a head taller. His brindled coat allowed him to blend in with the surrounding environment. He could be very useful during night-time hunts if his owner chose. Aloysius' appearance in the camp stirred the group. The young children fled to their mothers, while the available adults walked forward to address the newcomer. Even though Ruxar had never seen war until recently, that did not mean conflict and danger did not still exist about the land.

"Hello there," said Aloysius. "I've been traveling a great while, and I require some of your food." The group looked at him, faces as frozen as statues. Then eyes squinted and heads shook. "Did you hear me?" Aloysius asked.

"Oh, we heard ya, boy," said a robust Cerebrian woman, stepping forward from the middle of the troop. "It sounded like you are demanding we feed you."

"Demanding? No, no, no. I was merely—"

"Merely thinking you were going to take food from us. This deer will feed us for tonight and into tomorrow, and we have a long way to walk." She closed her proximity to Aloysius with every word uttered. "You see, we don't have fancy horses like you, boy."

"Even if you did, you folk couldn't ride them, being so big and all," Aloysius blurted.

The woman smiled at Aloysius with her teeth, and the others shook their heads in irritation. "Why don't you just do yourself a favor and trounce back to whatever posh city you came from, huh, little boy?"

"Little boy!" cried Aloysius. "Could a little boy stop a whole army from destroying a city?" He looked around for reactions. Only confusion and snarky smirks could be found on his audience's faces. "Would a little boy be a part of a resistance?" Irritation began to transform into frustration. "The Soldiers of Fire, we are called! In fact, I am their leader!" exclaimed Aloysius. In that instance, the Cerebrian clan's frustration and annoyance erupted into great bouts of laughter.

"You, a leader?" said the woman.

"Who would follow you?" said another in the crowd.

"And into what exactly?"

"Soldiers of small twits is more like it!" said another Cerebrian, and with that, a second harangue of belly laughs echoed in the dusk.

Aloysius, feeling his cheeks glow red with anger and embarrassment, stood up on his horse. The people eyed him queer-like. He swung his bow from his back and drew an arrow from his quiver with a swirling maneuver. Cerebrians' hands landed on blades and axes to defend against a shot. Aloysius, seeing his grave error, quickly aimed upward and away from them.

"Pick something!" he blurted out. "Anything."

"What are you getting at?" asked the woman.

"If I can shoot three targets in a row, no misses, you let me eat with you," Aloysius stated, doing his best to regain the troop's confidence.

The woman eyed his stance, wrinkled her brow in thought, and looked to the other members. Curious looks shot at her and then back to Aloysius. "Three targets? In a row?"

"Yes, any three. You choose."

"And if you succeed, you eat with us?"

"Yes."

"And if you fail?"

"I'll ride off. Won't bother you again."

"All right," said the woman. Aloysius breathed a quick sigh. "But you'll be leaving that horse with us."

Aloysius' mouth contorted and strained. He knew they had him. "Agreed," he said hesitantly. "So, pick your three." At this point, nearly the entire Cerebrian troop looked about the area. Trees, rocks, patches of grass—the choices were endless.

"That tent post there." The Cerebrian woman pointed to the outermost tent just to the right of Aloysius.

"All right. Done."

"The rock patch behind the camp. There is a small spot of grass between the rocks. Hit the grass from your horse there."

"Great. Easy. Done. Next," Aloysius said eagerly.

The Cerebrian woman smiled. She could feel Aloysius' hubris vibrating off him. She wanted to make him work for his meal. "There's a cluster of small birds in the grove behind you. Brown heads with green breasts."

"Great. Simple enough."

"You didn't let me finish," she said, smiling with her teeth and eyes now. Her entire face was brimming with glee. "You need to kill two of them with one shot."

Damn! Aloysius thought. *I shouldn't have acted so arrogant.* "Yes, of course," he said, after clearing his throat. His confidence began to dissolve with the last request. But he needed to eat; that was all that mattered.

"Well? Begin. We are all waiting, oh mighty leader," said a man in the crowd.

With that taunt, and still standing atop the horse, Aloysius lowered his bow. Steadying himself, he honed in on the target to his right: the tent pole. With one exhale, he moved as fluidly as water down a river. The shot twanged, followed by a piercing knock. The arrow stuck in its target. Aloysius grinned widely. The Cerebrian woman nodded in mild amusement.

She then glanced and pointed at the second target—a cluster of stones with miniscule greenery between them. The crowd had grown nearly quiet. Mice-like whispers squeaked about the people. Aloysius focused once more, this time paying attention to the winds. Being accurate was much easier when there wasn't a captive audience or food and his horse on the line. No matter; knowing he needed to trust in his Manticorian capabilities, he let loose another shot. Another deep breath and sharp exhale released his projectile. The arrow's long body bowed and wobbled like a dancer. Everyone watched his shot lob high and then lose altitude with great force, landing out of sight.

A young boy sprinted to the target sight. Aloysius' brow sweated in anticipation. His stomach growled and impatiently choked his intestines. All the others eagerly awaited the results. "He did it!" cried the boy. "It's stuck between the rocks!" Aloysius seemed to have made a fan out of this showcase of his skills. He still had one shot remaining. Dusk's end was looming. Light and timing would be everything to nab these tiny brown and emerald birds.

Aloysius did not wait for another taunt to encourage his movements. This time, he sat in his saddle and turned his horse around. He looked at the wiry mess of branches and the dancing birds within them. The creatures scattered and pranced like bees in a hive. His eyes squinted in the pale orange glow of evening. He snatched the arrow and drew back the string. His heart thudded against his chest like a bass drum. His breathing was now deep and slow. All of his muscles clenched tightly so as not to let loose his grip and, with that, his aim.

Aloysius mustered all of his senses. He looked for the intersections of the jumping birds. He listened for cue calls and chirping. He felt the air and his chest rhythmically beat within him. His nose caught the odor of fruit being gathered by the woodland warblers, and his tongue watered from the taste of the satisfying meal he yearned to receive. A brief moment of quiet stilled the land and the crowd. Then, like the beginning of a tune, an airy whistle screeched. The arrow twirled toward its mark. Aloysius' bow dropped around his arm and onto his back.

Someone stepped forward to verify the shot. A man of great stature lumbered toward the tree where Aloysius had aimed. He scanned and searched for a good while. Nothing. Another man came to aid in the search. Nothing. The woman who had chosen the targets walked with conviction to the two men.

They stopped to look at her. "Nothing here," one man said.

"Oh, really?" she snapped back. The men followed her eyes to an adjacent tree. Attached to its great trunk was an arrow and two emerald-breasted warblers. One still clutched a twig in its grip. "Looks like the little bastard gets to eat with us after all." Aloysius instinctively smiled at the comment, and the notion of a full belly.

CHAPTER 16

HIDDEN FURY

Riding northeast toward his homeland, through Cerebria and into enemy territory, had been easier than Aedan had expected. He hadn't run into any travelers, the weather hadn't been too hot or cold, and his supplies would last him for another three days. Riding Niul, however, had proven to be the hardest part of his adventure yet. His legs felt weak from riding, and his back ached unmercifully after stopping every night. By Aedan's count, he had been traveling for more than two days, occasionally stopping to feed and water his horse.

Now, however, he needed to become more vigilant. He soon passed the Cerebrian city of Maccus, and hours later, he crossed the border into Hydraria. Aedan then decided to stop early before the sun was too low in the sky so he could set up for the night. Luckily, a small stream lay close to their temporary campsite, allowing Aedan and Niul both to take a long-deserved drink. Next, Aedan found a tall sturdy tree and tied Niul to its trunk; then he grabbed an apple and fed it to the mighty beast. Niul quickly ate it up in two bites, core and all. Aedan followed suit, grabbing a piece of dried meat from his supplies and devoured it. Then, his body heavy from the day's ride and his mind full of thoughts, Aedan rolled out a small blanket on the ground near his steed and tried to sleep with barely a piece of meat in his belly.

• • •

The next morning, Aedan awoke chilled and his eyes aching. Anxiety and restlessness had replaced sleep. Niul, however, was still slumbering. *Who knew horses sleep so much?* thought Aedan. Aedan rose from the ground, shook the blanket out, stretched, and began to collect his things from the previous evening. Once Aedan finished, he ate another piece of dried meat and gazed at the beauty of Hydraria's outskirts. The Bron Mountains jutted from the ground, miles and miles from him. Clouds were drifting in the sky, and tree clusters were staggered throughout the land. The trees were a lush green, surrounded by golden grass and lightly browned earth. It was quiet and beautiful—just what Aedan needed to see before his journey got any more exciting.

After Niul woke, Aedan saddled him, led him to some tall grass and water, and then after Niul's breakfast, began galloping northeast toward Dragonia once more. Since crossing into Hydrarian territory, he was constantly checking his weaponry. He had a pair of straight swords, a well-proportioned dagger, his bow, and a full quiver, thanks to Captain Igne and the Cerebrian royals. Hours went by without so much as a few birds screeching in the midday sun. At a distance, Aedan noticed something on the horizon coming closer. It was flying, gliding on updrafts like a leaf caught in a breeze. He pulled his bow from over his shoulder, drew an arrow from his quiver, and placed the two in a ready position on his lap, being careful not to lose sight of the creature. Niul walked steadily. Aedan could feel the great beast breathing steadily beneath him. They had become one with their breathing—a soothing sentiment.

A few more moments passed and Aedan still kept his eyes fixed on the winged creature getting ever closer to them. He was unsure what he would do if or when it got closer, but he wanted to be prepared all the same. Another span of moments floated away, and still Aedan was unclear about this creature. By this time, a myriad of guesses swam through his head. *Maybe it's a large eagle, a small dragon, or an enormous crow?* Either way, the creature continued to soar ever closer to Aedan and his black steed. At last! Aedan could make out the creature's body. It was rigid and hard. No feathers. Definitely not an eagle or a large crow. Its wings were cloth-like, kept taut by a strong skeleton. It possessed four legs, all of which had claws like a cat. Aedan also noticed smooth flesh on its skin; not a dragon. That realization alone made Aedan breathe easier, and he put away his bow. Dragons can be wonderful companions when trained from a young age, but a wild one, depending on the type, could spell a death sentence if one were unlucky enough to encounter it. Luckily for Aedan, this creature was much smaller than a dragon. Finally, he realized it was a gargoyle.

Strange, he thought. *Gargoyles never venture this far southeast. Something must be driving gargoyles from their hunting grounds. Have the Hydrarians reached Gargolia as well? And what of Nestor? He will surely find trouble if Gargolia has been tainted by villainy.*

With those frightful images in mind, Aedan put his heels into Niul and whipped the reins to get the horse up to galloping speed. The pace quickened and Aedan's thoughts continued to fester. *Has Cerebria been attacked again? Are the Hydrarians really that well-armed? How organized are they? What is truly at work here? What will it take to stop the madness?* As Aedan's thoughts raced through his mind, Niul and he raced along the easterly hills of Rolant toward the still unseen edge of Deirdue Forest. Tree roots jutted from the earth like large fingers. Aedan figured he could reach the tree line and follow the forest all the way into Dragonia. There he would be safe. The challenge was getting there unseen.

Without warning, Niul neighed loudly and tumbled hard onto the ground, throwing Aedan several feet. Gasping for breath, Aedan opened his eyes wide. His vision had become fuzzy, and his ears were ringing from the sudden stop. Once Aedan caught his breath, he slowly stood up and stumbled uneasily toward the magnificent creature. Aedan realized their great pace was now going to slow greatly. Niul's front leg was twisted awkwardly—broken. Aedan ran his hands through his hair in mild panic and began to pace rapidly. The once strong, majestic horse was nothing more now than a large ink spot on the ground. Aedan knew that a broken leg—a long-term injury—took months to heal. However, out in the middle of nowhere, a horse with a broken leg meant a different fate.

There was no way Aedan could drag Niul anywhere. Where would they go? Nor could he fix the leg. The only humane act was to put Niul down—to let him die quickly, rather than leave him out in the elements. Aedan took a moment to stand up and step away from the broken beast. He could hear Niul breathing heavily, and he could sense his pain. Aedan had only killed a horse once before when he was a boy. The stallion had been sick for weeks, and it wouldn't stand up. He knew then that if a horse didn't rise after a certain amount of time, it would never get up again. Instead of waiting for the poor old horse to die slowly, he did the merciful thing and pierced its heart. Aedan had never forgotten that day. Unfortunately for Aedan and Niul, a similar event would now take place. Aedan turned around slowly and knelt down to the beautiful black stallion. When Aedan looked at Niul's large dark eyes, he could see horror in them. Niul looked up at Aedan, never breaking eye contact.

"You'll be well soon. It will only hurt for a moment, and then you will fall asleep," Aedan said. "You are a great horse, and I hope I have done well by you. I will always remember your strength." With those words, Aedan unsheathed his dagger, and in one quick motion, he punctured Niul's velvet black coat and slowly watched his breathing slow, until nothing was left but the body of a once great and powerful steed.

With little time to mourn, Aedan completed the task of saying goodbye. Then he found sticks and branches to cover Niul the best he could. Hopefully, then Niul's body would be left alone by the creatures in the area. Aedan's mind now had to be set on the task of getting to the tree line to ensure a clear path to Dragonia. After bowing his head in regret, Aedan gathered up his supplies and began to walk toward the distant forest. By this time, the sun was leaning closer to the horizon, allowing the moon to take center stage in the sky.

Just as Aedan felt the loss of his companion sink in, a new threat emerged from the hills surrounding him. Three men, armed with bows, arrows, and scythes, stealthily succeeded in ensnaring Aedan. Aedan stopped suddenly.

"I don't want to fight," Aedan announced.

"That's good," said the tallest of the men. "We don't want to fight either. However, we do require your supplies—weapons, too."

Aedan gave the tall man a wry look. "I'll be keeping my belongings today. You three appear to have plenty."

"All right then. How about you come with us then? We have been told to look out for stragglers to be brought in for questioning."

"No. I have someplace I need to be. In fact, you're making me late," said Aedan, continuing to walk.

The three men stiffened and drew their bows, holding their position. "You are coming with us now, or you will be shot," said the tall man, seemingly salivating at the chance to kill. Aedan said nothing; he held his ground, glancing to both of his sides, catching a glimpse of the other two, each readying an arrow aimed at him. "I will give you till the count of five to get on the ground," said the tall man.

Aedan remained silent. He continued to stare deep into the tall man's eyes.

"One!" the man shouted. Aedan didn't move. "Two!" Still, Aedan stayed strong. "Three!" The man's voice was growing louder. "Four!"

Aedan took a deep breath and held his gaze. A bead of sweat trickled down Aedan's cheek. He could feel the wind hard on his right side. It cooled his rapidly heating body. His arms stung with eagerness, and his legs were charged, ready for a fight. Aedan had a plan in place; all he had to do was wait. Finally, he heard the final number.

"FIVE!"

The three archers let loose their arrows.

Aedan could see the long shafts and pointed metal flying toward him. He could see the look on the men's faces, and he could feel the screaming survival instinct within him. Aedan, feeling the wind push against his body, sensed the men's eagerness to deploy their lethal desires, yet he oddly found himself in a state of tranquility. Something powerful within him coursed through his veins and took over his movements. Aedan erupted like a fiery beast from the breadth of a mountaintop.

Aedan exited his trance and began moving with a deliberate and deadly purpose. The arrows on either of his flanks had been released barely a moment apart. He spun to his left, simultaneously pulling his bow from his shoulder. The movement, so quick and forceful, caused one arrow to kiss and whistle past his right ear, while another was abruptly blocked by the sweep of Aedan's bow. Without thought, Aedan finished his spin by reaching into the anticipated path of the tall man's arrow, catching it by its neck, within blinking distance of his head. Then he spun the arrow between his fingers, drew back, aimed, and released it. The arrow, originally intended for him, found its way to the tall man's throat, lodging deeply within his flesh. The reaction on the tall man's face spelled disbelief and horror. He grabbed at his neck, hoping to deny his blood's escape from his wound. His efforts in vain, he dropped to his knees, collapsing where he stood.

The other men, witnessing their leader's demise, drew another arrow and attempted another volley. Aedan would not let that happen. Quick to react, he drew an arrow from his quiver and fired at the man to his left; his arrow made impact with the Hydrarian's chest. The man quickly shuddered and fell to the dirt before releasing his bow. Aedan redirected to the last assailant. The Hydrarian fired at Aedan, missing his leg. Aedan drew his dagger and leaped upon him as a wolf, jumping high, knife point leading the way, driving the blade deep into the man's eye. The Hydrarian yelped for a split instant, and then, like the others, gave way to Aedan's hidden fury.

Aedan stood up slowly, hoping not to lose his balance. He felt tremendous relief. The rush brought on a weight of exhaustion that crashed into his body. He staggered to a small group of trees and buckled at their roots. Aedan positioned himself against a sturdy trunk and laid his head back. Breathing heavily, and confused and exhausted, Aedan found that his mind was unleashing more questions.

How did I kill those men? It was as if part of me could sense their actions before they happened. Did I really catch an arrow? How did I move with such speed and agility? Is this the passive skill Nestor mentioned? These thoughts and others made their way through Aedan's mind, but his desire for answers was surpassed by his need for water, food, and rest. His mind swimming with concerns, Aedan took several deep gulps of water from his pack, and then he rapidly found himself falling asleep beneath a tree in the middle of the Hydrarian countryside.

CHAPTER 17

THE CHARMER

Nearly a day had passed since unleashing Ulysses' great army from Jormungand. As the last man exited the capital, Ulysses ventured into the darkness of the storm that had been blowing since the night before. The turbulent conditions were as relentless as his passion for conquest. As Ulysses rode over the hills of Rolant, the rains fell like small blades against exposed skin. The winds blew with such ferocity that Ulysses could feel himself being pushed almost to the point of toppling off his stallion. As Ulysses continued into the Senta Valley's fields, the storm gales continued to bash and batter the king and his mount. Not until the foothills of the Pleon Mountains did Ulysses glimpse the beginning of the end to the harsh weather.

Over the next day, Ulysses combated more intolerant environments from within the mountain trails. Over cliff sides and sharp rocks, he made his way through the treacherous terrain for one purpose: to recruit. Foot after foot of every agonizing step that his horse trotted increased Ulysses' determination to reach his destination. His mind could not be clouded with miniscule thoughts of weather, comfort, or safety. For Ulysses thought of the consequences his family and fellow Hydrarians would face if he did not succeed.

At last, he arrived at the small, impoverished town of Broga. This small borough was the key to his victory.

As Ulysses reached the broken wooden gate of Broga, he immediately spotted an elderly man standing upon a watchtower, eerily eyeing him. The old lookout squinted sharply, bringing his aged eyes into focus. This did not intimidate, but annoy, the confident king. With a shudder and a swing, the gatekeeper opened the rickety gate.

"Oh, King Ulysses," the gatekeeper exclaimed, bowing, "how fortunate we are to be in your presence!"

"I am here to see him. The beast keeper."

"Ah, yes. Follow me. Right this way."

As Ulysses followed behind the scraggly elder, he noticed Broga's condition. The homes once made of fresh wood had rotted from the harsh weather. The streets were pooling festering marshes for insects and other pestilence. The townspeople showcased themselves as true objects of Broga's neglect. The villagers' small frames and greasy hair were compounded by clothes full of filth from working in extremely damp environments that could make a fish weep and squirm.

"Here we are," said the gatekeeper cheerfully. "Is there anything else I can do for you, my king?"

"You can leave me," Ulysses said. "Your smell offends me."

The lookout's face churned sour at the king's comment. Then he spun around to waddle back to his post. Ulysses rubbed his nose irritably and knocked on the dilapidated structure's rotting door. No answer. Several more deliberate knocks were eventually met abruptly by another elderly man.

"My king!" he said. "The great Ulysses. What brings you to Broga? You are a long way from your throne, my liege." The elderly man's appearance epitomized Broga's shabby outlying existence. His stomach-length beard was tangled into knots laced with dirt and it housed many petite twigs. The skin under his eyes hung low, and his frail body showed off bones similar to underfed livestock.

"I have come to recruit," said Ulysses. "Wait, how do you know who I am?"

The old man smiled. "I have my ways. My sight reaches far."

"I don't understand."

"You don't have to, my king. You only must rule and leave the world's intricacies to the odd and old ones. Now, you seek to recruit? Is that all?"

"Yes, recruit. And I require information."

"Recruit who? And what knowledge could I impart to the almighty King Ulysses?" asked the elderly man.

"The kind of people and knowledge involving the hydra, and their breeding grounds," said Ulysses.

"Why would you care about my beasts and their offspring?" asked the old man.

"I require allies—strength. I have recently come to believe that my kingdom and Broga will mutually benefit from my campaign."

"And you think I could be one of those allies?" asked the elder.

"I hope so," said Ulysses. "Although, I'm unsure if I can trust you."

"What makes you think I can't be trusted?"

"Instinct," said Ulysses.

"What gesture would be required to establish a bond between you and the people of Broga?" asked the man.

"Start with your name."

"Fareed. But my people call me 'the Charmer.'"

"The Charmer?"

"Yes. It references my uncanny, albeit useful gift of controlling even the most stubborn and powerful of hydra," said Fareed. "And now that you know me, what do you require of me and my people?"

"Most, if not all, of your fittest people. This will include boys and girls from age sixteen on to your elderly. Also, I require the packs of hydra that live in the fields of Kazimiera."

"Well," said the elderly man, taken aback, "that is all of our people. What do you require of us? We are a dying, cursed people, some would say."

"Before I answer," said Ulysses, "I need your word never to speak of our conversation."

"All right. I agree. I promise," said Fareed, drooling with anticipation.

Ulysses paused, hesitating before he spoke. "I have attacked another kingdom: Cerebria. As we stand here, my forces are marching into the country to begin the invasion." Ulysses paused again. The weight of his words hung on his tongue. "I am starting a war. This war will come swift, but the cost of lives on both sides will please our beloved Jormungand and raise us up."

The old man buried his head into his hands before he spoke. "You want our help fighting your war? You want to use hydra as weapons to destroy our neighbors, to bring anarchy, death, and destruction?" Then, just as Ulysses thought the old man did not want any part in his plan, the old man lifted his head, looked deep into Ulysses' brown eyes, and sprouted a jubilant smile. "Broga is with you. We will help you fight this war. I have been waiting my entire life for a ruler to rightfully return Broga to its revered position in our kingdom. My people will be pleased to hear we no longer have to live like rodents."

"Excellent," said Ulysses. "I will expect all of your people to be ready at any moment. Expect my communication soon. I want you to be the one who leads the hydras to Jormungand. Are we in accord?"

"Yes, my king," said Fareed.

"Soon a group of my warriors will be here to escort you, your people, and our beasts. From there, you will receive further instructions." Ulysses stepped away from the shack. "I am glad to have you as an ally, Fareed."

Fareed bowed his frail head. "I wish you a safe journey."

Ulysses returned the farewell to his new ally, Fareed the Charmer. Then he walked back to the crumbling gate, untied his steed, and continued his arduous journey to secure more weapons for his arsenal as he rebirthed Ruxar through conquest.

CHAPTER 18

THE ABYSS

The sun had just begun to peek out from the horizon. The wind was still and the air cold. Aedan woke to a sudden desperate chill. As he slowly rose, he could not remember why he was lying on the ground. His body ached grievously. His arms were weighty and his muscles tender.

Then, suddenly, it all flooded back to him, like a ship taking on water, quick and sobering. The ride into Hydraria, the fall, Niul, those men! What had he done? Was it a dream? His questions were answered the moment he turned around and saw the product of the evening prior. Aedan stood, staggering about like a newborn foal. His body's weakness was dancing with the shock of what he had done. It was a gory sight indeed: two men with arrows grotesquely protruding from their cold bodies, the other with a large hole where his eye used to be and a large puddle of blood surrounding his head.

Aedan, still shocked by the sight, began to question his reaction. He had not behaved this way during or after the gruesome battle at Brèdon. But during the battle, he had not been able to catch arrows or move as swiftly as a cat, nor jump as high as a creature with wings. It seemed as if he were beginning to discover himself, and he had a feeling this would not be the only discovery that would churn his stomach and fog his logic. He knew there would be plenty more to accomplish on his journey to stop Ruxar from crumbling.

After a few moments of gathering his thoughts and washing his head and face, Aedan bid his unfortunate victims farewell and continued toward the forest. He figured that even though he no longer had his great steed beneath him, the forest would still supply him with the appropriate food, water, and cover from any passersby. The day seemed to travel by more rapidly than his movements. The sun appeared to be skipping across the sky rather than its normal meandering. Before long, it was sunset again. The pale oranges and faded pinks caught Aedan's eye before he realized the sun was becoming heavily enveloped by the horizon. Snapping out of his stupor, he felt his body still aching from the fall and the fight. His legs seemed to disappear from under him, numbing angrily. Aedan had been walking all day, and if not for the constant checking, he might have believed he was now floating from the waist up. *A few more miles*, he thought. *Just another hundred more steps until I can rest.* Aedan's eyes were heavy and his stomach hollow. His arms felt like heavy tree limbs being weighed down by snow and ice in winter.

Before Aedan could consciously make the decision to stop for the night, his body made it for him. Collapsing suddenly to the dusty earth, he finally let his mind and body meet in a whirling mashup of the senses. He had been suppressing his pain and discomfort to reach the tree line before nightfall. Sadly, his efforts were in vain, and now he might have to rest for another full day before he could continue. Aedan cursed himself for being so stubborn, but his self-loathing was short-lived. As his body quickly relaxed, his mind began to slip deep into sleep. But before his eyes shut, he could feel a distinct vibration emanating from the ground. Normally, an anomaly like this would wake Aedan's whole self, but this time, it just assisted in his passage to slumber.

As Aedan's exhausted body slept, his mind dreamt. Deep in the chasms of his psyche, images and people floated past him. Some he knew, some were strange, some pleasant, but the clearest sights were ones of great terror and chaos. He saw a great city full of buildings that towered high above the clouds, brick work so masterfully done that the people who admired it wept with awe. Great rivers and lakes surrounded the city, shimmering like crystals and diamonds. Aedan could smell heavenly scents of freshly baked bread and meats being basted and cooked to perfection. He could even taste ales, wines, and other exciting beverages concocted to suit every palate. Songs, coupled with male and female singers and a variety of instruments, performed glamorous ballads for his ears. Finally, he could hear blazing laughter—the laughter of men, women, and children as they enjoyed the festivities, embraced life, and indulged in its pleasures. Then a cloud, once buoyant and fluffy as wool, began to fall upon the city. The cloud grew dark as red wine and shrouded the glamour and excitement with a ghoulish veil. To Aedan's dismay, he discovered the cloud's deep red hue was not of wine, but blood.

Shadows floated from alley to alley. Gracefully landing with ease, even the most complex acrobatic move seemed smooth as water. Great black ghosts were now descending onto the once wondrous city, and the people who had once thrived were now being cut into ghastly pieces. The road became laid more with limbs than brick. The once glimmering rivers and lakes were now deep with their occupants' blood, and the shadows' origins were now becoming clear. Shadows born of fire in the night—a great blaze had grabbed hold of the tallest buildings with orange and gold hands, ripped down massive sections of them, and perpetuated the havoc.

Men and women alike clamored for any sort of weapon they could use against the shadows and fire, but their efforts were useless. They were being swallowed up as swiftly as the bedlam began. All they could do was hold on to each other tightly. One last embrace from their loved ones, their children, before the fire and shadow drank them all, encapsulating all light, hope, and beauty into the abyss. To Aedan, this force seemed to have an unquenchable thirst—an appetite that could consume the entire world if it desired. As Aedan started to recoil from the sights, he felt paralyzed, his whole body unable to move, his eyes being the exception.

Aedan saw a figure, a giant creature with eyes black as obsidian. A small crooked grin peeled across the figure's face, showing teeth that had been grinded down to points. Its muscles protruded from its limbs in a grotesque display, and its body was emblazoned with scars from injuries no mortal man could survive. His skin was as white as milk and his war cry as shrill as those of tortured beasts. The dreadful being spoke. "I am Death! I am the ruler of all that is dark and cruel. No man or creature can overcome my might. All shall bow down to me. Pray for my mercy, for I will be your one and only god!"

With those words, the shadows faded. Still asleep, Aedan felt his eyes burning from the sweat trickling down his beaded brow. He could feel himself trying to wake. Subconscious questions fired through him like arrow volleys. *What was that figure? Its presence felt old and all-knowing. What did he mean to pray? And what in the name of kings is a god?*

CHAPTER 19

BLOODIED ASH

Muffled screams and a cold sweat finally jolted Aedan's conscious. He gathered his thoughts, realizing those screams were his own. The dark world he had dreamed about lingered in his mind like a sour taste. The blackness blurred figures in Aedan's environment. His last recollections were of the outdoors, but now everything felt artificial. The shadow's shapes were irregular and the air close.

"Oh, good, you're awake," said a female voice.

Startled, Aedan tried to stand, only to discover his legs wobbled awfully and a searing pain pulsated through his head. "Who are you? Where am I?"

She approached cautiously. "It's quite all right. I found you lying on the ground, moaning and whining terribly. I thought maybe you were having a fit, so I brought you here."

Aedan rubbed his eyes. "And where is here?"

"It has no name. It's not supposed to."

"What is that supposed to mean?"

"It means this place does not exist. Give places or people names and they matter, have a purpose. This place is not to have any such thing."

"So, then where are we really?" asked Aedan, his frustration mounting.

"In Hydraria, not far from where I found you."

Aedan breathed a shallow sigh. "Why help me? You don't even know me."

Her lips tightened into a grin. "Honestly, you remind me of my boy."

"Your son? You helped me because I look like your son?"

The woman sat back, her stare looking into a fond memory. "No. You move like him. When you sleep, that is. He would talk in his sleep. Nonsense mostly, but I could always tell how he was feeling by how he slept. It's a mother's gift."

"Well, where is he? Your son."

"He's gone. They took him. They took everyone who mattered to me."

Aedan sat up, his eyes adjusting to the night's light. He finally realized his rescuer had brought him into a simple tent. "What do you mean by that? The Hydrarians took their own people? How?"

"I'm sorry. I shouldn't be talking to you about this," she said, rising to her feet.

Before Aedan could say any more, the woman had left the tent. He could hear her sobbing just outside the curtain. Aedan took the opportunity to inspect the Hydrarian town with no name. He moved to the closed flap, parted the cloth, and peered through the small opening. On first sight, he noticed many tents, just like his crying rescuer's. Three small wooden buildings sat in the center. Pairs of men dressed in cloth and leather armor strode about, armed with simple swords and carrying torches as they performed patrols. Aedan heard distant shouting coming from what he could only assume was a place of ale and debauchery.

The woman reentered the tent, poised once more. The redness in her eyes was the only remnant of her breakdown. "I'm sorry. It has not been easy these last months."

"I can only imagine," Aedan whispered. "I'm still confused as to what is going on here."

"Let me start with my name. I am Gilda."

"Gilda," Aedan repeated. "I am Aedan of Dragonia."

"A Dragonian. I wondered from what country you came. You do not have the air of a Hydrarian."

"Is that supposed to insult me?"

"Not at all. Just an observation. Your spirit feels freer than ours. Wilder even."

Aedan eyed Gilda queerly. "Thank you, I think. So, tell me, what brought you out so far from this nameless place that doesn't exist?"

Gilda dropped her chin, stared at the floor, and began to speak. "I was leaving. Running away. Running to your country in all honesty."

"Away? From all this? You must have a good reason—perhaps because your king has started a war with the Cerebrians," Aedan said.

"There is more to it than that. They took my sons and my husband from me. Swept them away. Convinced them all to join."

"If they were convinced, that means they all had a choice. A choice to invade friendly lands and attack people who have done nothing ill to anyone."

"No!" shouted Gilda, covering her mouth from fear of being overheard by the watchmen. "No, it was not so. Powerful people came to our home. Dozens entered our house, uninvited, and ordered my family to obey the king and his new order's requirements. His royal decree. For to resist would mean to rebel against the country itself."

"No king can do that," said Aedan.

"Ulysses is no king then. He is a beast. A monster that rips apart families."

"Why didn't you resist? Why didn't you fight back?"

"I insisted they leave at once. But my husband did not want to tempt their anger. He said he could not imagine what they would do to me if we did not comply. I was powerless."

"This doesn't make any sense."

"At the time, it seemed the smart move to sit and listen. There were five armed guards with each recruiter. We might have been killed, but now I feel I would rather be dead together than alive separately, not knowing if any one of my boys has died."

Aedan's silence spoke to Gilda. He had no words for the grieving mother in the tent. Aedan knew that words often cannot heal a dying heart. The two sat together, quiet, listening to time slip by, waiting for one of them to break the silence.

"I'm sorry," Aedan finally said. "I'm sorry for what happened to you—to your family."

Gilda nodded, eyes watering. "Thank you."

"How old are your sons?"

"They are both teenagers. My oldest is nearly a man."

Aedan smiled at the thought of himself as a young man. "I bet he is a hard worker. Is he the one I remind you of?"

Gilda chuckled; it was nervous laughter. "No. You remind me of my youngest. But yes, my oldest is a good worker. Just like his father and me." She lost herself for a moment, entranced in the past. Finally, she blurted, "What are Soldiers of Fire?"

Aedan snapped out of his calm. Fear flooded him. "What? Where did you hear that?"

"You said it in your sleep. What does it mean?"

"Nothing. It's nonsense."

Gilda scooched closer to Aedan. "You understand that I am a woman who has mothered two boys, yes?"

"Yes."

"And in doing so, I have been gifted with the ability to know when men are lying," said Gilda, smugly. "You can trust me."

Aedan nodded, but was apprehensive. "If I tell you what it means, and you betray me to your people, I could be a dead man."

"You know my feelings about my people. If anything, I will betray them after what they have started."

Aedan wanted to trust her. It felt right. However, Aedan could not help but shake his instinct about keeping the resistance group a secret, especially behind Hydrarian borders. Then he was struck by a lost memory. The memory of another woman, a Hydrarian, Turia, at Brèdon. She, like Gilda, disagreed with her country's actions; perhaps Gilda could act on her principles just as her kin did. "All right. But I'll need to start from the beginning."

So Gilda sat and listened while Aedan retold how he had come to the nameless town in the middle of Hydraria, his stance on the war brewing, and his mission to reach his homeland so he could do his part in preventing more bloodshed and misery. *A truly amazing occurrence*, thought Aedan. *Those I thought were enemies are merely future friends, afraid to lose loved ones. So much so that most would stay seated at a time when we all must stand to stop the rising tyranny.*

"What you are saying is that a group of people is already fighting?" asked Gilda.

"Yes. Come with me to Dragonia. Together we can find your husband and sons. We can free your family."

"How many are you?"

"Not many, but that number is on the rise, it seems," said Aedan, smiling.

Gilda nodded slowly. "Then, as a new recruit, I feel the need to inform you of this place's true intent."

"Oh?"

"The army has been using this place as a checkpoint. Parties bring to here newly recruited warriors like my family, supplies, and even prisoners—those who won't comply. They don't last long. So many already have been murdered, just for saying no."

Aedan's blood burned at the thought of people being put to death for simply disagreeing with their king. "Tell me, why are you not fighting? Why did the army not take you?"

"They did. I am in a different division. I support the army for other needs."

"Other needs?" asked Aedan, concerned.

Gilda looked away, ashamed. Her eyes filled with tears. "How can I ever be whole again? They have taken so much from me."

Aedan reached out to Gilda, gently grasping her hand. "Where did you place my weapons? We need to go hunting."

• • •

The next several moments were fueled with rage and confidence, stealth and ferocity, steel and fire. Gilda and Aedan exited the small tent like shadows, skulking and sliding between the cracks in the dark. Gilda followed closely to Aedan, guiding him among the maze of canopies and small structures. Aedan's first victim met a swift demise among the cloth coverings of another young woman's shabby home. Gilda was quick to ease her troubled thoughts as the men who had once ravaged them fell, choking on their own blood.

Aedan and Gilda moved like bladed silhouettes. One guard at a time was struck down, thereby releasing two, three, or four girls at once. The girls freed themselves of their confines and fears, Gilda all the while being their guardian, their inspiration, their liberator. Gilda seemed to have found her purpose, and now she meant to enforce it. She watched as Aedan dispatched another guard, this time scooping up the downed man's torch. They used the red blossom to ignite the torch for their cause, one tent, one structure, and one monster at a time.

Havoc transformed into chaos in the night. Captives became the captors, and the lot of them fought brutally for salvation. Aedan and Gilda rallied the few fighters to escape as the flames grew. The drunken guards were useless in chasing the fleeing women, who were now well on their way to safety. Nor could most of the intoxicated men fight off the fate their past actions led them to.

"We must go! It is done!" shouted Aedan.

Gilda lit another tent. "No, we must make our mark first."

Aedan looked at her, confused. The fire's roar sounded like a constant booming voice in the night air. "What do you mean?"

Gilda jogged to a large stone and began smearing words on it. Her ashened hands left traces of letters to spell a message to their foes. The smile on her face grew large; finally she would make her mark on the world. But as quickly as she had rubbed her hands along the stone, her face blanched to the color of the ash with which she wrote. Aedan ran to her side, scooped her up, and ran behind the rock. An axe blade had sunk deep into Gilda's back, thrown out of the darkness and smoke.

"No, no, no! Gilda!"

Her eyes slipped back and forth between living and dying. Her breath was erratic, and her body fell limp. "I…I…I'm sorry."

"No, no. There is nothing to be sorry about. We need to go now. We need to find your boys. You did so well tonight. I need you, Gilda. Your sons and your husband need you."

Gilda shook her head slowly. "I love them. I love. I—."

Gilda's last utterance fell flat, and then her final breath left her throat. Aedan lay her down as gently as a newborn upon the earth. He looked up to see nothing but blackness and fire. He rose and turned to face her message—it was incomplete. Aedan finished her message with ash from his palms, and added his own. In the night, among the glow of orange and red, a stone in the middle of Hydraria outside a town with no name painted in bloodied ash read: "We are the Soldiers of Fire. For Brèdon. For Gilda."

CHAPTER 20

NONSENSE AND DISBELIEF

"So there we were, staring down the shafts of our arrows. There must have been tens of thousands of them!" said Aloysius, retelling the story of Brèdon. All of the children sat by firelight, listening, leaning into the newcomer and his epic tale. "As the Hydrarian army advanced, you could hear many of the fighters in the town blubbering like babes, begging for milk. Everyone was looking to me for answers. The clang of swords and armor running to the walls sounded as millions of anvils and smiths worked at once."

"What did you do?" asked a little boy, his eyes fixed on Aloysius.

"Something no one else thought about." Aloysius paused for a moment. "I left the line suddenly and ran to get the oil from a cellar. There had to be some there, I thought. So I grabbed as much as I could and told everyone to dip their arrowheads in oil."

"Wow. So then what happened, mister?" asked a little girl, her hazel irises glistening in the camp's lights.

"I told them all to fire on my command, of course!" Aloysius' face held a large smirk. "As I saw them light up the tips, I told them to take aim, and then ordered 'Loose!'" The children's eyes grew wider, and their faces filled with amazement. Their little minds could see hundreds of smoking red and orange projectiles falling to the ground as if the skies were collapsing.

"Wow," said one child.

"Ooo," said another.

"That's incredible. I don't believe it."

"I don't believe it either," said Vanna, the woman who had granted Aloysius clearance. "You tell a good story, but I think you, young man, are completely full of shit."

Aloysius scoffed and shrugged. "No. It happened." He looked back to his captive audience. "Then, as all the fire arrows fell to the ground like lost stars, the earth erupted in a huge wall of fire!" He emphasized his words by yelling and raising his arms above his head. "The screams of the invading army were enough to make your heart stop beating. But we couldn't think about their pain. We had to keep fighting. I ordered my warriors to fire at will." Aloysius began to roll on the ground, pretending to shoot arrow after arrow, making whooshing sounds as he reenacted the harrowing scene of fire and death.

"No way!" the kids said together.

"Yes! Indeed!" Aloysius got closer to them now. "Then, as we loosened our last shot and flames turned to embers, we heard something." He gave each child a curious look. "And do you know what we heard?" he asked.

"Nonsense. That's what I am hearing," said Vanna, still not convinced.

Aloysius gave her a snarky look, and then he looked back to his adoring onlookers. "Nothing. We heard nothing. The men who survived the fire ran away. All that remained were the charred dead. That fire must have burned for hours during the battle. Long enough to squash their hope of getting into the town." Aloysius stood up now with pride. "They applauded my astounding leadership and called me a hero." He raised his head high, closed his eyes, and grinned smugly. "But I told them we were all heroes today. In fact, I said we should all now be known as the Soldiers of Fire! A group of people who will not stand for such acts. A resistance! A fighting force that will repel the Hydrarian assault on our countries! Then together, we set off to warn your king, Rordan, of the dangers that threaten your lands." The kids were all smiling now with great exuberance. "Now I am on my way to Manticore to alert my kinsman of the same, in hopes that another attack will be prevented." Once finished, Aloysius bowed his head.

The children clapped. "Great story," said one.

"Do you have any others?" asked another.

"Oh, it's not a story. This was a telling of real events that happened only a week or so ago," Aloysius replied.

"We are not impressed. Don't fill their little heads with nonsense. They won't be able to sleep tonight," said one mother. "Come along, dear; we have to get to bed." She pulled her little girl by her wrist.

"But, mother, I want to hear another one," whined the girl.

"She's right, you know," said Vanna. "Telling tales of large battles and great armies is stupid to mention, even as epic tales. It could give people the wrong idea."

"Again, I'm not lying," said Aloysius. "I fought off a gigantic army of Hydrarians. They flew their flags and everything. People died—loads of them. It was ugly, but we prevailed all the same."

"Because of you, of course?" Vanna shot back.

"Well, you did hear the story."

"Yes, I did. And everyone here thinks you a liar, a damn good one, mind you, but a liar nonetheless."

Aloysius stood there, taken aback by her impression of him. "I am telling the truth. An army attacked a town. People died, and they were run off by a huge fire. So how am I lying?"

"Whether you know it or not, people tell stories to get others to like them," said Vanna.

"And it worked," said a teenage girl, listening from inside one of the tents.

"Zavia, don't believe this boy," said Vanna. "He doesn't have our best interests in mind."

"But he's so adamant that this attack occurred. Shouldn't we listen to him?" Her black hair reflected the firelight and appeared like a silhouetted sunrise to Aloysius. "What if he is telling the truth, and we are walking toward something we can't fight?"

"Zavia, you are too young to understand the intentions of men," said Vanna.

Aloysius looked at Zavia, smiled, and turned back to Vanna. "One moment I'm a boy, and the next, a man. Sounds to me like you don't understand what you're talking about, madame."

Vanna shook her head and walked slowly toward Aloysius. "You listen here. There will come a day when that tongue of yours will get you into a mess you can't talk or shoot your way out of." She stood over Aloysius now, like a mountain dwarfing treetops. "And I will kill you before you bring down any of my people with you."

"That won't happen. I save people. In fact, I do believe I saved Zavia here earlier from a droll evening." Aloysius again smirked boyishly at Zavia, who was already giggling at his words.

One swift jolt and Aloysius was tossed to the ground like a bird struck by a rock. His cheek and jaw ached from Vanna's sudden slap. "I'm warning you, boy, and you better listen. Tell all the stories you want, but don't sell them as truths." With that, she skirted away toward the deer meat now being served by the fire.

Aloysius sat up, rubbing his cheek. "Well, that was a surprise."

Zavia walked over to Aloysius. "Sorry about her. She's protective of us; that's all."

"Well, could she maybe wag her finger at me next time? That was a bit uncalled for, yeah?"

"Actually," said Zavia, "you got off easy. You impressed her earlier with your bow."

Aloysius beamed. "Well, I am—"

"But then you disrespected her," Zavia said, draining Aloysius' smile. "Even after she gave you food, shelter, warmth, and even, to my surprise, let you live. She has taken down a passerby once or twice for being half as rude or threatening as you were."

"I wasn't being threatening!"

"Aloysius, you strode into camp on a horse and demanded food with an armed bow," said Zavia with indignation. Her dimples were accentuated by her expression and the lighting. "Come now; I want you to meet some people."

The two stood up, and Zavia took Aloysius by the arm, leading him to the other side of the camp. There were four others. A young girl of fourteen perhaps, with the same black hair as Zavia, and three boys. All around the age of eighteen—the same age as Aloysius. The clique's members chatted among themselves, laughing and enjoying the last of their deer meat and stew.

"Everyone, this is Aloysius." Zavia tightened her hold and gestured to him. "Aloysius, this is Zara, my little sister." Zara stood only inches shorter than Zavia, but the long black hair and dimples confirmed their relation.

"This tall lad is Tacitus." Even without standing from his leaning position, Tacitus was several inches above Aloysius' head.

"Good to meet you," said Tacitus, chewing on a bone from his meal. "Glad Vanna only slapped you. You seem like a fun guy. Foolish, but fun."

"And this brute is Basilius," said Zavia. Basilius gestured back politely and returned to shoving an entire rib into his mouth.

"And lastly, this is Hagan."

Hagan hopped up quickly and shook Aloysius' hand. His grip felt like a tree hugging Aloysius' palm. Aloysius could feel bones in his hands popping. "Good to meet you. You're quite the archer. Where'd you learn to shoot like that?"

"My father taught me," said Aloysius. "Plus, I've had years of practice out fishing on the Trahern."

"So you're from Manticore, yeah?" asked Hagan.

"Yes. Born in Atwater, a small island."

"You see many actual Manticore beasts there?"

"Many, no. But we have one that lives with us on our boat. Its quills help us make spears. They are great for protection and loads of other things."

"Like your accuracy?" asked Hagan. That's how you shoot so well, right? The passive skills people get by being around animals like that." Hagan looked at Aloysius and smirked. Everyone else was quiet now.

"Yes, that has something to do with my abilities." Aloysius squinted his eyes curiously. "Why does that matter?"

"It doesn't," said Hagan, smiling. "We have those same advantages. I mean most of us anyway. I myself have a little more strength than most. Basilius here is probably the strongest among us." He pointed to the burly boy, who was still more interested in his food than the conversation. "Well, not including our two dogs." The group turned to look at the beasts. The cerberuses' three heads were competing for the bloody entrails of the group's kill. Aloysius noticed how their paws were like frying pans and their claws like thick-bladed tree branches.

"Yes, they are quite remarkable. I must say, much larger than the manticore beast," said Aloysius, realizing how lucky he was to be alive and standing among new friends rather than being food for their pets.

"Yes, smaller like you," piped up Tacitus, finally spitting out the bone. "But, somehow, you have the biggest mouth I've ever seen on a person. Are you all like that in Manticore?"

"Excuse me?" said Aloysius, feeling a twinge of anger.

Zavia stepped between the two. "Let's not ruin tonight by peeing all over ourselves, boys." Zavia turned to Aloysius. "You have a real knack for making people want to hit you; you know that?"

"I'm just sayin'," Tacitus finished, "you claim to be this big leader of a resistance in a war we know nothing about in a world that hasn't seen more than a small skirmish in its history. Seems a little suspect to me."

Basilius chuckled like a deep horn. "Haha, 'fishy' 'cause he's a fisherman. Good one Tac."

"Shut up, Bas," said Tacitus.

"It does seem off that you have this grand story and nothing to show for it," said Hagan. "No proof, no other witnesses, no injuries, no burnt clothing. Nothing to show you were there."

Aloysius looked back and forth at the three boys. He contorted his mouth to keep from saying the wrong thing. His bottom lip and tongue rubbing against his teeth hardly kept him in check.

"I believe you, Aloysius," said Zavia. "Zara, doesn't Aloysius seem trustworthy to you, too?"

The quiet teenage girl, who had been silent throughout the discussion of Aloysius' honesty, replied, "Yes, I think he is telling the truth. He is just a really good storyteller."

"Thank you, ladies," said Aloysius, feeling validated.

"I bet ya he doesn't even know where Brèdon is," said Tacitus.

"That's a lie," said Aloysius. "I could take you there right now and show you the scorch marks and where we buried the dead. You could even talk to those folks I led and saved."

"That sounds like a great idea, ol' boy," Hagan said, smiling.

"Yeah! Let's go see!" said Zara.

"You'll take us, won't you, Aloysius?" asked Zavia.

Aloysius stood. He stared at everyone. All of them ready for him to make his next move. He knew if he took them to Brèdon, he could be putting them into danger. He needed to complete his mission of telling King Remus of the Hydrarian threat. In his stomach, he knew he should just accept these people's disrespect and go about his business in the morning. But the nonsense and disbelief of these Cerebrians ate at him.

"Yes. I'll take you all to see Brèdon," said Aloysius. The group cheered, some genuinely and others sarcastically. "On one condition...."

CHAPTER 21

BRANDY SMILES

The next morning, Nestor awoke to swelling ocean waves crashing against the port house. The force of each break made the small home sway and creak like a ship out at sea. The sounds overtook Nestor's senses enough for him not to notice Samuel's elderly form eagerly packing for his final move to meet his daughters. The two men took the next several hours to gather the supplies needed for each journey. Samuel became acquainted with his new steed, and Nestor did his best to recall his younger days on the water, in hopes those memories would reinvigorate his rusted sailing skills.

Once the two old men exchanged knowledge of each other's travel means, Samuel and Nestor said their goodbyes and parted ways. Nestor had to accomplish one task before setting sail. He could not bring himself to tell Samuel of his intentions, so he waited many hours until he was sure the old port keeper was out far enough not to see the flames. The old Gargolian would set the port ablaze to thwart the Hydrarian advance. No longer could the small port be used to transport supplies secretly. Nestor spent the next several days manning the small craft, usually manned by three people, fighting to maintain a northerly trajectory. If he was not tightening lines, he was redirecting sails, or steering his best alongside the shore. Nestor's vessel sailed close enough to land for the old man to locate his destination, but not too nearby that passersby could identify it as anything ominous or interesting.

The real problem Nestor discovered was since he was one man doing the job of three, he could not sleep, at least not horizontally. Many times, Nestor found himself leaning against the helm, staying true to his path, only to be startled awake by strong winds lurching him farther out to sea. Nestor's tired state cost him several hours of redirecting the boat back and forth, snaking the coastline. Thankfully, the clear nights made it possible for him to see land and the stars for navigation.

Finally, on the third day, Nestor arrived at his destination: the port of Broinn. The noon sun sat high in the sky. Broinn was a small town, but its port continued to serve as a mecca for traders and travelers throughout the kingdom and benefited as a point of embarking for Ruxar's southern regions. Nestor's tired mind lurched onward to the marina at Broinn. He located a spot to moor and tied the small craft to the dock. Having adequately secured his seaborne steed, Nestor proceeded to the dockmaster. Moments later, Nestor encountered the man and learned of an inn nearby with vacant beds. With no money, and exhausted from three days at sea, Nestor was able to sell the small craft for a sizable sum—enough to obtain him lodging for the night, a meal or two, and perhaps a ride to his hometown of Darnis.

Nestor so wanted to see his wife, Phaedra. He longed to regale her with stories of the past weeks. He needed to gain her insight into these wretched times of uncertainty. He knew, however, that rest took priority. His age was showing. In his army days, it was not uncommon for him to go with as little as an hour of sleep at a time and to march for days on end. Reminiscing aside, Nestor located the vacant lodge and found his bed. As soon as his head hit the pillow, Nestor fell into a dreamless and, thankfully, visionless sleep.

• • •

The next morning, Nestor awoke refreshed but sore. His body still ached from the hard ride and his sea voyage. After several minutes of stretching his stiff muscles, he set his sights on a hot meal and a means to Darnis. With a sharp mind and his goal weighing heavily, Nestor traded the rest of his money for a strong, gray and white horse.

Setting off, Nestor knew the rest of the journey home would only take half a day at most. His mind wandered along the way. Thinking about his vision of Brèdon on fire and the young hero being struck down made Nestor's chest tight and his stomach flutter.

"Who was the hero? Was it Aedan? I need to hurry. King Xenos should be able to help us," Nestor thought aloud.

After what seemed like hours of open plains dotted with trees, the old general reached Darnis. Darnis' size had grown significantly in the last several years. With the erection of new homes and expanding farm land, Darnis was becoming more and more urban. Its town square continued to swell with new traders, selling goods and providing services to help its growth. Nestor loved seeing how the development had flourished since his retirement from the army years ago.

Nestor eagerly rode through Darnis. His heart raced with excitement. His mind's eye could see the front door to his home. He greatly desired to feel the comfort of his wife and small house. When he turned the final corner, there it stood—a quaint wooden structure with small fences surrounding a private garden, a small stable with two horses, soon to be three, and a gargoyle named Fajer roaming the property. Nestor smiled as his tired eyes laid sight on his land. The scene became brighter when a slender woman with silver hair stepped over the threshold. Phaedra smiled gently at the sight of her husband on horseback. Nestor clamored off the horse, twisted his back to stretch out the aches, and walked forthright to his wife.

"Hello, beautiful," Nestor said, reaching for her and leaning in for an embrace. The two wrapped each other in their arms. They kissed lightly. Nestor's mind cleared and his anxieties quieted.

"It's about time you came back," said Phaedra, smiling. "I was beginning to get worried. When you said you needed to investigate that vision of yours, I began to wonder if it got the better of you."

"Got the better of me?" Nestor replied. "When have I ever let anything happen to me?"

"I could tell a few dozen stories, my love," said Phaedra, as the two walked arm in arm toward the house. Nestor grinned at the comment, knowing she was the expert on the subject. The pair reached the house and were greeted by a fire roaring in the fireplace and the smell of stew brewing in the pot. Nestor's home calmed his nerves. However, in the forefront of his mind, he knew his stay would not be for long. He needed to regain focus and head back out on the road to Kunagnos, the Gargolian capital.

"My dear, I'm so glad you're home," said Phaedra, breaking the silence.

Nestor nodded. "I'm afraid I won't be able to stay for more than a day."

"But why? You have been gone for nearly a month, and I have missed you greatly," Phaedra said as she wrapped her arms around him again.

"I must go. There is trouble in the kingdom. War is coming," Nestor replied. His face turned from delight to dread. "I'm glad to report that the vision I had was prevented, but at a terrible price."

Phaedra's eyes filled with concern. "Exactly where did you go? All you told me was south."

"I traveled far. I found myself in Cerebria, in a town called Brèdon. I met a young man there. The one I saw in my vision. He, I, and the townspeople prevented the place from being destroyed by the Hydrarians."

"The Hydrarians? You're sure?"

"No doubt. I was there. I saw their flag waving. I fought them. I killed many of them." Nestor's eyes dropped. "I thought I was done fighting." Nestor shook his head and looked back up to his wife. "After we pushed them back, three of us traveled to Ansgar to meet with their king. We told him the tale and then went our separate ways. Each of us is pursuing a mission to accomplish the same goal."

"Father?" said a new voice, appearing from around the corner bedroom.

Nestor whipped around. "Orion! I didn't expect to see you here." The two came together, embraced, and separated. Orion stood slightly taller than his father, with thick brown hair, a sturdy frame, and deep brown eyes.

"When did you get in?" asked Nestor.

"Last night. I received mom's letter that you had been traveling. She sounded concerned, so I came down from my post at the capital to check up on her."

"Orion, it's so good to see you. We haven't seen you in over a year, and you look more and more like a leader than ever before," said Nestor, brimming with pride at the sight of his son.

"Thank you, Father. The title of lieutenant weighs heavily on me, though. Many men look to me for guidance. I learned how to manage myself by listening to your stories." The pair exchanged grateful looks. "But what did I hear about an attack? Hydrarians?"

Nestor nodded fervently. "This is most important, and you being here will make my presence more pertinent. I need you to travel with me to Kunagnos. I need an audience with the king."

"I don't have that authority. You served Xenos as general; are you unable to request a meeting since stepping down?" Orion asked.

"No, I am able. However, we did not part on good terms. My leaving the army was as much his idea as it was mine," said Nestor mysteriously.

"What happened?"

"It's not important at the moment," Nestor replied. "What matters is that you can vouch for me. You can be my ticket to talk with him, warn him of conflict."

Orion looked worried. "I don't want to abuse my new title."

"This is too important to let your worries stifle your nerves. We need to act. The lives of thousands could be at risk, if not the whole kingdom—Ruxar even."

Orion let out a sigh of submission. "All right. We will ride out tomorrow."

"Early, as soon as the sun hits the horizon," said Nestor.

"You don't think the Hydrarian movements will make their way up here, do you?" asked Phaedra.

"I don't know," said Nestor. "At best, what happened down in Cerebria only involved the two countries. But when we met with

Rordan, he gave no impression of motive for an attack from King Ulysses. Just keep a watchful eye for anything. Question newcomers; keep Fajer close. We don't know what to expect. Violence is a cruel master, and we are its playthings." Nestor turned to his favorite padded chair and took a seat.

"So," said Phaedra, "since I only have both of you home for another night, let's make the best of it." The two men smiled gently at her. They could all feel the uneasy energy of unknown future events. The fear of uncertainty lingered among the small family. They did their best to distract themselves with the comforts of home. Phaedra finished the stew, and the three delighted in the hot broth and sustenance. Nestor pulled out a hidden bottle of honey brandy to share. The liquor helped the family shed the stresses of modern times and regale each other with army stories and tales of a younger Orion throughout the evening.

As the night drew to a close, Orion wished his parents a goodnight and retreated to his bedroom, feeling his inebriation. Nestor and Phaedra, too, went into their room. The couple, high on bliss, came together as husband and wife until finally drifting off into slumber, absent any ill thoughts of the future.

CHAPTER 22

THE ENEMY'S DEATH STROKE

Magnus' mind swirled hazily, his head pounded, and his body was heavy. He had blacked out after his attempt to escape the prison. The last he remembered was the general lying on the floor, and he was wielding swords. He remembered contemplating the general's fate, but in the darkness, he also recalled seeing a vague figure of a woman, and then nothing.

"What happened?" Magnus asked himself. As his vision slowly returned, he noticed he was in yet another cell. Except this one contained no bars. He had no way of seeing who or what was coming. The door was a thick slab of steel accentuated with one fist-size window. "I want to go home," Magnus said softly. "I need to get out of here. I need to get back." Before long, the steel door opened, allowing the muggy air to escape and cool air to rush in. In the doorway stood a man. The man Magnus had almost killed.

"It seems you are not very trustworthy," said Anwar smoothly. "However, I can rely on you to behave erratically. Just like at Brèdon."

"Well, you did a poor job; it was easy to repel you, like a cat with a small bird. You Hydrarians have always been weak," Magnus replied.

Anwar drew his hand, back-fisting Magnus for his comment. "You are a fool for doing what you did," Anwar claimed.

"Yes, perhaps, but at least I didn't lose to a group of villagers," said Magnus.

Anwar's scarred face twisted into a wretched, toothy smile that made Magnus rethink his comment just before a barrage of fists pummeled Magnus' face, stomach, and chest.

"Is that it?" asked Magnus when Anwar had finished. "Are you truly an army general? It is known that infants from my country can hit harder than you." Magnus chuckled to conceal his pain.

"I may not be as strong as I was in my youth, but my knowledge and experience in dealings with wretches like you and your people would make even you weep, Magnus of Brèdon."

"Why do you harm him?" called a velvet voice. "You know it will get you nowhere. He is a Cerebrian; they are the most durable of any race in Ruxar." A woman entered into the light. She stood smaller than Anwar, her hair as black as a storm cloud with eyes to match. Her complexion was elegant but stern.

Anwar acknowledged her presence with a shallow bow. "I must thank you again, Princess, for saving me from this brute. It seems I underestimated his desire for freedom."

"It is my pleasure, General Anwar. A man of his stature, and particular stubbornness, cannot be broken physically. He must be broken down in other ways. Or at least, that is what you have taught me, teacher."

"Yes. How do you intend to do that?" asked Anwar.

"Well, that's simple," she replied. "I expect I will be successful at extracting his knowledge without even touching him. If I do it correctly, he will scream what he knows to me."

"Ah, yes," said Anwar.

Magnus' worry about his situation began to elevate. *What is she eluding to?* he wondered.

"Do you recall when I was a child, General?" the princess asked. "When I would receive treats without doing anything for them? All I had to do was close my eyes and the chefs would come out with a whole platter of sweets, just for me."

"Yes, I recall vividly," said Anwar. "I also remember what you did to the guard who scolded you. The one who accused you of stealing those sweets."

"Ah, yes. Poor fellow couldn't speak for days. Threw himself at a nesting hydra; crushed before anyone could save him. That is, if he even wanted to be saved," said the princess.

Magnus' glances at the pair became erratic. He was unsure what to think of this princess and her story. Perhaps it was all a scare tactic, but what if it wasn't?

Before the conversation could continue, a uniformed soldier appeared at the cell door. A messenger was with him, holding a letter in his outstretched hand.

"General Anwar," said the messenger, "a communication for you, sir."

Anwar gripped the letter, snatching it from the messenger's grasp. "Leave us."

On the courier's departure, Anwar stepped out, followed by the princess. The door slammed shut, echoing in the blackness. Magnus could still hear their voices quite clearly, using the thin window slide to eavesdrop.

"It's a communication from your father," said Anwar.

"What does he say?" asked the princess. "Does my father ask about me? Am I to travel?"

"No, Morrigan, he does not," Anwar replied. "Why does it matter? You know he wants you here to learn interrogation. Your skills are still needed here in Echidna."

"All right, then what are his orders?" Morrigan asked.

"He writes to inform me the army is being sent here. The soldiers arrive within the week," said Anwar as he read.

"Where are you to lead them?" asked Morrigan.

"Well, first..." began Anwar, now whispering, so that Magnus only caught fragments of his words. "Then we will turn our attention to...."

Magnus began to panic. Would his home be attacked again? He thought of his people being killed and their homes burnt to the ground. He thought of Aedan and Nestor. What if they were still there? They surely could not face another force. Worst of all, he was helpless to do anything. Chains, cells, and his enemies' will denied his getaway.

As Anwar and Morrigan finished their conversation, they slowly made their way back into the cell. Anwar was still holding the letter, skimming it intensely to not miss anything. Morrigan, however, had now become fixated on Magnus. She leisurely circled him like a wild animal stalking prey.

"You are probably wondering why I haven't sent you off to be killed," Anwar said to Magnus at last. "It's due to information. We desire to learn details of the Brèdon siege."

"I'm not telling you anything. I don't believe any of what you people say," Magnus replied.

"Who led your town to victory?" asked Anwar. "It wasn't you. Who conjured the walls of fire? Did you have word of our advance prior?" The general looked back to Morrigan. "Did you get all those questions, Princess?"

"Every single one, General. I'll see to it that he talks," she replied.

Magnus focused. All he could do was scowl at Anwar. He so desperately wanted to stop him. Nothing would make Magnus reveal Aedan or Nestor's identity. "I won't talk. You have proven to me that you are not worthy of breaking my spirit," he said, ready to burst from his shackles.

"Who said I would break you?" asked Anwar scornfully. As he spoke, Morrigan walked in front of Magnus, knelt, and peered deeply into Magnus' large brown eyes. "No, good Cerebrian, I will not break you. That job will be graciously overseen by the princess. She, as you may recall, has ways of dealing with strong stubbornness. Down in the dungeon, it was she who made you weak. It was she who dropped you just before you could end me. You will find her will incredibly formidable, even for a student." Anwar chuckled with a wide sneer.

Before Magnus could even think about moving, he was again paralyzed. Except this time, his breathing remained fully functional, and he continued to be conscious for the whole tribulation. He then saw Morrigan close her eyes, and he could feel her in his head. His thoughts and memories were open to her, like a book about to be read. He could not understand how she was doing this. He was frightened for his safety and feared for his life. He'd never been so afraid. Not even when he had seen Anwar's army outside of Brèdon. She was asking him questions he did not want to answer, but it did not matter; she still dipped her mind into his and pulled out faces and names of people in his past. Finally, Morrigan found the memory of the battle, like a star in the sky. Magnus tried to resist. He had to. But she saw in his mind Aedan and Nestor. A break in the princess' connection to his mind threw Magnus against the cell wall, his breathing labored. His body was no longer paralyzed, but nothing important had been relinquished.

"That is merely a taste of what I am capable of. I have many devices that will drive you mad, and I am in control," said Morrigan, swiping a finger down Magnus' cheek. She stood up, turning back toward the door, tossing a smile at the general. "I think I will have fun with this one. For one so strong, he has a weak constitution for mental torment."

Anwar returned the smile and gestured for them to leave the cell. "Come, Princess; we have much to discuss. Let us leave the Cerebrian to his mind's suffering. You will be back soon enough to continue the session."

"Yes, very soon. I'm eager to try more."

Magnus watched as the two strode out and closed the steel door. The clatter and clang of the metal rocked Magnus' ears, sending spikes of red lightning through his scalp. His eyes watered amid the throngs of invisible stabs. His entire existence of using his strength would be pointless in this prison. His mental fortitude was all that stood against his kin and the enemy's death stroke.

CHAPTER 23

THE WICKED

Morrigan entered the room, pacing among the sharpened implements. Somehow, she felt at ease surrounded by organized instruments of death. Echidna's armory was a mere arrow in the quiver that was Hydraria's weaponry. Her pride would not let its standing be cheapened by its lack of use, so she used the space as her muse. Morrigan's mind wandered within the room, searching for inspiration, ruminating upon her role—her destiny within the kingdom.

"There must be more," she thought out loud. "I want to transcend this base title of *princess*."

"You are a princess," said Anwar, entering the armory unannounced.

"Can't a girl have some privacy?" Morrigan asked, embarrassed.

"I see you are still talking to yourself. It was cute when you were a girl, but now it is starting to feel less so. You are a woman now, Morrigan."

"Tell that to my father."

"I have. In fact, he sent you here because he wants you involved in the movement. He trusts me to teach you to be more than heir to a useless crown."

Morrigan picked up and inspected a lengthy dagger. She eyed its gilded hilt and curved blade. "What then? Shall I become only what my father wishes me to be? Why can I not choose the route I take in the crusade?"

"If memory serves, you chose this outpost to start your training—away from your parents, away from the capital."

"Yes, but to what end?"

"Your mastery of weapons and mental manipulation, for a start. Already, you have shown immense strength in the deception of the senses. You have brought many traitors out into the light."

"Yes, but I want to do more."

"More what?" asked Anwar, perturbed.

"I want to fight, Anwar."

"And your combat training does not count, why?"

"I want to kill for our nation. I want to lead warriors into battle."

Anwar sharpened his gaze upon her face. "Battle is not for you, Morrigan. Save the dirty deeds of open combat for the wicked."

She sprung upon Anwar, whipping the lengthy blade upon his neck. "The wicked? Are you saying you are one?" asked Morrigan, eyeing Anwar coyly. The sparkle in her eye reflected off the sharp metal.

"More than you can know, my dear princess," said Anwar, emotionless, and motionless to her threatening advances.

"What is it that makes you so morally destitute, old man?"

Anwar batted the dagger away as one would a fly and turned to the armory door. He placed a heavy hand on the iron handle, then spoke. "Nothing that shall concern you. Not when there are other militant matters at hand that require your insight."

"Oh?"

Anwar released the handle and turned back to face the princess. An idea sparked in him. Her childish, yet skillful, self inspired Anwar somehow to take a chance. "I have reports of a resistance force rising. They seem to call themselves the Soldiers of Fire."

"A resistance force? How is that possible? My father has but only begun the campaign."

"I am afraid our foul defeat at Brèdon may have sparked more than a minor setback. It seems our Cerebrian friend knows more than he has let on."

"I'm not so sure. He has undergone much attention, and while he has broached much of the battle, he has divulged nothing of a group of resistance fighters."

"Morrigan," Anwar said, placing his hand on her shoulder, "I need you to push him harder. Break him. Do whatever you can to learn the identities of those he fought alongside."

"I have tried most of my tricks. He hasn't cracked."

"Everyone has a breaking point. You have three days, Princess," said Anwar, pulling the door open.

"Until what?" Morrigan asked.

"The army. It will arrive in three days' time."

"And?"

"An army cannot lead itself."

Morrigan stepped forward to Anwar. "What are you saying, General?"

"I'm saying I am putting you in charge of your father's army—of the first wave of the invasion."

Morrigan leaped toward Anwar. "Oh, thank you, General! But what of you? Where will you go?"

"I have other matters I must attend to. Matters that will elevate us higher than any dragon or gargoyle can fly to stop us." Anwar grasped Morrigan's shoulders and brought her back to her own space. "You must earn your ascension to the throne. And you must do this by fighting among your people. Lead them to victory. Now come along; we have much to discuss."

CHAPTER 24

IMPENETRABLE FEAR

The family of three rose to roosters making their wakeup calls. The clouds were wisps of white and the sky a blissful blue. Nestor and Phaedra lay together in the warm air of their home and held each other closely. Nestor was at a point in his life when savoring the good was just as important as stopping the bad. Once the two had risen, they went on to making breakfast and drinking tea. Orion, being a military man, was up with the sun.

"Good morning, Mother. Morning, Father," said Orion, smiling wryly.

"What's with you?" asked Nestor.

"Out by the time the sun hits the horizon, huh?" said Orion cheekily.

"Well, maybe the brandy hits me harder than it used to."

"It's quite all right. I honestly didn't even think you would be up by now, with all the traveling you've been doing," said Orion.

"Well, I'm up, and we should really be getting our things together for today's ride."

"That's quite all right, Father. The horses have been fed, watered, and packed. All they await is our asses to sit in the saddles," said Orion with a proud grin on his face.

Nestor scoffed with surprise. "Well, haven't you come a long way from whining about doing your chores in the garden. The army has done you well," Nestor said smiling. "I guess you will take good care of your mother and me when we get old." Orion smiled wide, and his deep, brown eyes lit up from their bantering.

The three shared their breakfast, said a long goodbye to Phaedra, and were on their way. Phaedra held both of her men for as long as they would allow. She kissed them both on the cheek and let them go reluctantly.

"I love you both. Be safe," said Phaedra. "Oh, take Fajer. I fear you will need him more than I." Nestor reluctantly agreed. She watched the pair mount their horses and gallop away toward the capital, with Fajer flying overhead.

Once father and son were far enough away, Nestor pulled back on his reins to bring his horse to a walk. Orion, seeing this, stopped his horse completely for his father to catch up.

"Something wrong, Father?" asked Orion, looking concerned.

"I need to tell you about Xenos and me."

"Father, you said it wasn't important."

"But it is. I didn't want to get into it yesterday. I wanted to enjoy our precious time together as a family. Plus, your mother gets upset when I tell it. So I do my best to avoid the subject."

"All right, if you think it is worth knowing. Please tell me; we have a long ride ahead of us," said Orion, with a twinge of annoyance in his voice. Nestor nodded and began his tale.

"Xenos, our king of this great nation, is a good man, but a cursed one. Xenos' family, like all other royal families, raises the beasts our kingdom is named for. In this case, his family chose a gargoyle bloodline that was cursed with nightmares. Dreadful, dark, twisted nightmares. So over time, as the two species grew up and died together, a trait was born among his kin. Those exposed to their gargoyles would endure horrific terrors as they slept. Regardless, Xenos taught himself and his family members how to endure them. It made his kin who accepted the curse impenetrable to fear. Those who failed to accept the curse ended their lives. Xenos lost many loved ones to this. I saw him rise through the death to become an excellent king—a man I worked alongside for my long career in the army. I am optimistic Xenos will provide the support necessary to aid the Cerebrians. However, my and Xenos' relationship was altered drastically the last few years of my leadership.

"Many years earlier, I witnessed King Xenos travel with the army across Gargolia to aid those in need. At the time, there were reports of feral rogue gargoyles swooping down from the sky and snatching livestock, attacking townsfolk, and even carrying villagers off to consume them. The odd behavior gained Xenos' attention when I reported our own village, Darnis, was being harassed by many of the winged creatures. These flying beasts, as you know, prefer the darkness of night to hunt. However, the wild ones were seen landing on rooftops, growling, and biting locals when the sun was at its highest.

"King Xenos announced that a full scale hunt was to be organized to capture and eliminate these threatening gargoyles. Among those involved in the hunt was Xenos' son, Darren. As prince of Gargolia, it was expected the young man would be thrust into battle with both men and beast. This conflict was to prove his worth, to show what kind of man he would be. I promised to keep Darren safe during the hunts.

"During the first months of tracking and hunting, all went well. No injuries. No casualties. It was even Darren who figured out the creatures were suffering from a new illness preventing them from sleeping—like a viral insomnia. This is especially bad with gargoyles. The gargoyle has a deep connection with the mind. The mind is powerful, but not invincible. Soon, these flying hunters of the dark became confused about fantasy and reality. Our gargoyle caretakers developed a remedy that allowed the paranoid creatures to sleep, in turn, effectively curing the illness. However, the longer a gargoyle remained awake, the stronger and more unpredictable it became.

"One morning, we were returning to the capital. The hunt had been a major success. Xenos even planned to ride out to meet us on the very road we are traveling now. Darren and his men had caught three gargoyles two nights prior. Our caretakers had run out of supplies, but they were going to aid the animals once we arrived at Kunagnos that night. Sadly, it did not go according to plan.

"The beasts are smart, as you know, son. You have seen Fajer, that sneaky bastard, open windows and pick locks with that tail of his. This was the day I learned never to trust a caged gargoyle, especially a sick one. Well, we had become dangerously comfortable with these crafty creatures. We thought we knew all their tricks and how to take them down. We were wrong. It started with a huff and a sharp click. That was the only warning. What followed led to the bloodiest fight involving a gargoyle I have ever witnessed.

"One gargoyle unlocked its cage with its shard-like tail. It slunk through the grass like a cat. Then it struck like lightning and thunder, screaming. I saw a man being snatched up by his head and dragged until he separated at the neck. I saw the gargoyle's sharp, swordlike tail cut men to pieces. Only seconds had gone by, but we had already lost three men. Soldiers grasped their bows, but before an arrow could be strung, the beast pounced, lacerated, and mauled the men into ground meat, only suitable for worms.

"Darren, seeing the events transpire, immediately began to dart around as the gargoyle did. Erratic movements to contradict erratic movements. His acrobatics were graceful. He unsheathed his sword and shield. Darren trailed the beast. Keeping up with the swift hunter was difficult, but he stayed within three paces of it the entire time. Every step was met with more blood and screaming comrades. Arrows finally began flying, whizzing past Darren's face and body. His nerve, as strong as rocks, helped him gain on the delusional animal.

"Once Darren was within striking distance, the deranged gargoyle snapped around like a cracking whip. Lunging at Darren, claws, teeth, and tail fought to land flesh, but Darren would not let it. He parried and blocked and countered and slashed, drawing blood, breaking the beast down. Until I screamed an order to the other men. That sound was enough for Darren to lose his concentration. The gargoyle sensed this and struck right through Darren. The mad animal had just enough fight left in it to rip him open. The two worthy warriors fell, side by side, dead.

"That scene was but an hour over when Xenos arrived. He dropped to his knees when he found his son eviscerated. I did my best to comfort him, but the blow was too great. No number of words or actions I had for Xenos would quell him. He had lost his son, and under my watch. My leadership had gotten Darren killed. Our relationship was never the same after that day.

"After Darren's death, Xenos began to let the curse win. His iron resolve deteriorated. He stopped sleeping. He questioned everything I did. He began to slip into madness, just like those sick gargoyles, just like the one that had killed Darren. After several more years of being challenged and blamed, I finally decided to take my leave. I found a successor, and then I did my best to live my life the best way I could."

Orion's mouth was slightly agape. "Oh, my. Father, I had no idea."

"This is why I need you today. I need you to use your position as both a lieutenant and my son to convince Xenos to see me." Nestor's eyes filled with tears from the memory. "I need him to hear me. This is too important."

"I'll do my best, Father. I want to help," said Orion, lending his hand to his father. Nestor looked up to him and nodded gently.

"Then let's get moving. We need to get there before dark. Gargoyles hunt after sunset, and I don't want to be mistaken for a meal," said Nestor. The two men kicked their horses and away they raced, northward to the capital.

CHAPTER 25

MADNESS

Day swept away and made way for night. The sunny day of riding with his son through the Gargolian countryside had made Nestor feel complete. Joy filled him even in the capital's presence. The two men were moments away from the great city of Kunagnos. From a distance, the city's skyline was tall and tapered. Its great halls and castle's spires caught the eyes of all travelers. Smoke plumes wafted about, circling upwards along the monoliths. In Kunagnos, birds did not dot the skies and rooftops; instead, gargoyles perched atop structures, leering and skulking about in hopes of catching an easy meal.

Nestor and Orion entered the city by way of a guarded bridge over a small river. Orion, being well-known among the guards, was spotted and allowed to enter without any fuss. The guards would not say anything concerning their lieutenant's guest either. Nestor's happiness and pride carried strong within him as he watched his son saluting and being saluted on their way deeper into the settlement. They trotted on toward the castle's barracks. Orion looked back to his father, grinned gently, and turned his head toward their destination.

"I must consult the king's advisor to request a meeting," said Orion. Nestor nodded. "I remember."

The two men tied up their horses, checked Fajer into a specially catered pen, and entered the barracks. The stone structure tunneled dozens of paces past small windows, allowing light for transit. Nestor followed his son. They crossed paths with several soldiers who were transitioning for guard duty or performing other tasks.

"Where is the general?" asked Nestor. "I remember coming down to the barracks often to oversee the living quarters and morale of the men."

"He is most likely in his chambers," said Orion. "The general does not wish to be disturbed unless it is important. He is not you, Father."

Nestor grinned at his son's comment. He had heard that General Bram did not work well with the men. He had also heard of the general doling out harsh punishment for small offenses or mistakes. The story of a young recruit losing a pinky finger and being flogged for falling asleep on duty came to mind. In Nestor's generalship days, it would have been a loud verbal correction, followed by a series of undesirable chores and duties. That usually did the trick. But he realized the stories he had heard were all third or fourth hand, and not by anyone in the army. Nestor had never heard Orion speak ill of his general, thankfully.

They reached the end of the lengthy barracks hall and passed by tables of soldiers at mealtime, still dressed in mail and coverings with the gargoyle sigil: a fierce, black gargoyle silhouette on a backdrop of yellow. The beast's form accentuated its teeth, dagger-like claws, sharp-angled wings, and almost catlike tail that came to a deadly point. Nestor gestured to the men, wanting to salute, but he felt that would have drawn too much attention. He and his son were on a mission, of course. Finally, once passed the sleeping quarters, they came to a room. Inside was a man, well dressed in the colored robes of their nation.

"Lord Advisor Segeric," said Orion, "I have urgent business. I must request an audience with his majesty."

Segeric looked up, eyes wide and mouth taut. "Lieutenant," he said, "you cannot barge in like this and demand a meeting. Can't you see I am working?"

"My apologies, Lord Advisor," said Orion. "This is an urgent matter."

"Yes, you've mentioned that. It still does not change anything," said the advisor, looking back down to his work. He picked up his quill and began to scribble a note onto parchment. "You must be careful, Lieutenant. You have only just earned rank. You wouldn't want to upset the general, would you? Or worse, the king. You know they don't take kindly to unnecessary distractions."

Orion glanced at his father. Nestor shot him a look of annoyance and frustration.

"Do you think an attack on our soil is urgent enough for them?" Orion asked the lord advisor.

Segeric looked up, puzzled. He stood up slowly to match Orion's gaze. "Attack? Nonsense."

Orion looked to his father and then back to Segeric. "Lord, I need you to arrange a meeting with the king. It is vital to our future in Gargolia. My father witnessed everything." Orion gestured to Nestor. "He is the one who needs to tell the tale."

"Your father? He is old. They will not believe him. Men his age are senile at best," the advisor replied.

"My name is Nestor of Gargolia, former general of this army," Nestor said. "I still retain my proper mental faculties, and it is imperative you do as my son says for the good of the kingdom. I will not let a small man with a large title dictate how we are to protect our kingdom."

"Now see here, you—" began Segeric.

"Tell Xenos that his old general is here and has troubling news," said Nestor, abruptly exiting the advisor's office.

"Father!" cried Orion. "Where do you think you are going?"

"I am going to find the king myself. I don't care what they do. He needs to know about Hydraria. About what they have done."

Orion stepped forward and grabbed his father's shoulder. "Not like this. You can't tell them what happened if you're dead. They will kill you on sight if you barge in like a madman."

Nestor's breathing was heavy, his face hot from frustration. He placed his hand on his son's hand and gently removed it. "All right, we will do it your way."

"Thank you, Father. Now, let's see if I can salvage this encounter."

The father and son reentered the advisor's office. Orion looked at Nestor and then back at Segeric. "I apologize for my father's outburst. He is a passionate man."

"I can see that," said Segeric, still standing. "I did not realize you were the son of the previous general, Lieutenant Orion."

"Not many do. I was taught young to make my own way rather than ride on the reputation of my family's success."

"Very well. I'll allow it—only because if the king hears about this, he may punish me for not allowing your father an audience," said Segeric.

"Thank you, Lord Advisor," Orion replied.

"Remember, Lieutenant, this is a favor. You owe me now," said Segeric.

"Just arrange the meeting," Orion replied, aggravated. "My father will be waiting in the barracks for your call." Orion turned and walked out, perturbed by the little man.

"Wait. Where are you going? Won't you stay?" asked Nestor.

"I must see to my duties, Father. I fear the general and king will see this arrangement as an abuse of my power," said Orion.

"I'm sorry if this causes you any ill treatment, my son, but this is too important not to address." Nestor now felt guilty for asking Orion to use his influence.

"It will be fine, Father. I will check in on you in a few hours. Perhaps you can join me for dinner tonight once your meeting is complete."

Nestor nodded lightly. Then his son strode off with a purposeful step. Nestor walked back to the barracks' food hall and took a seat at a table. His worry grew as he thought about how this meeting might affect his son's new position in the army. His thoughts weighed heavily on him. Memories of Brèdon and the battle were still fresh in his mind. He could still smell the fire burning even now. The heat of the blaze that had ultimately saved their lives was what pushed him now to fulfill his duty. He needed to ensure that his part would be completed, like any good soldier would do. Nestor only hoped the fire that drove his actions didn't get anyone hurt in the end.

Several hours passed, but no meeting happened. Nestor was beginning to think the advisor had disregarded Orion's request. What could he do now? Nothing. He knew he had to sit and wait for his time. If he made a scene, he might create a sour situation that could bleed over to hurt his son. He wouldn't do that, not yet at least. He was going to behave, as he had been told to do. Then, with the sound of iron hinges singing and locks clanging, Segeric, the advisor, stepped around the corner.

"You are being summoned, past general Nestor. The king is very eager to see you," said Segeric.

Nestor stood up, collected himself, and started following the now tight-lipped advisor. Segeric led Nestor through a large wooden door and into another hallway, lit by torches. Nestor recognized these halls well. He hadn't thought about them since he had stepped down as general. The odor of stale air and ash reigned in the hall. Silence between the two men continued until Segeric slowed his pace and turned to Nestor.

"You are about to be in the presence of his majesty himself, plus General Bram and others of his court and army. They expect you to speak only when spoken to, and I suggest you use all of your years of army training to remember how to speak politely." Nestor's tongue remained still while the man finished his condescending etiquette speech. "Do you understand everything I told you?" asked Segeric.

"Yes. All of it," Nestor replied. His stare did not break Segeric's.

Nestor followed closely as Segeric led him through yet another torch-lit hallway to an iron door. The door had the Gargolian sigil emblazoned upon it. The effigy's silhouette in the firelight seemed to make it move about on the iron canvas. This door seemed familiar to Nestor. He began digging through his memory to locate where he had seen it before. However, Segeric had led Nestor to a part of the castle he had since forgotten as a general. Nestor quickly dismissed the familiarity as an old man's memory parting with age.

"Ready?" asked Segeric. Nestor nodded.

The iron door was dutifully unlocked and pushed open by the advisor. It seemed to Nestor that sitting behind a desk reading a parchment might make a man knowledgeable, but in the process, it weakened the body. Nestor aided Segeric's pushing until the door was ajar enough to walk through. Nestor stepped out slowly. He recognized the room—the castle's main hall. It was clad in the drapery of the kingdom's colors. Floor to ceiling windows lined the walls, allowing the hall to fill with natural light. The floor was an ornate tile of shimmering mauve speckled with gold flecks in the floor.

Nestor crossed the threshold into the hall and laid his eyes on the king. Xenos sat upright on a wide, oaken chair. His position was the highest in the room. Next to him lay a dozing, ash-gray gargoyle. Its body would rise and fall with every inhale and exhale. Alongside the wall stood many men, including Nestor's successor, General Bram. The general was remarkably tall, almost a whole head above most citizens. His hairless head shined in the light of the dwindling day. He stood erect, in full suit and mail, with a sheathed sword on his hip.

"Please, come face me, old friend," said Xenos calmly.

Nestor proceeded forth, walking by the many soldiers along the wall. He eyed the general and gave him a tip of the chin. The general sat as a statue, leaving Nestor's nod unacknowledged. Nestor reached the steps of Xenos' seat and kneeled as instructed by the advisor. Nestor bowed his head, awaiting instructions.

"Arise," ordered Xenos.

Nestor stood up slowly. He was showing his age. With stiff knees and achy back, Nestor wrestled with himself to stand as gracefully as possible. Once standing, he could see the king's face now. Xenos' eyes presented a red tint. The irises of his youthful, hazel eyes had grayed immensely. His hair was thinning and near a stark silver. Nestor could see small patches missing on his scalp. The skin on his face was dotted with sores.

"It is good to see you, old friend," said Xenos, his voice wheezing.

"You as well, my king," replied Nestor.

"It has been many years since you departed," Xenos said. "And now you return, only to demand my counsel."

"A request, my liege. I have an urg—"

"Excuses!" shouted Xenos. "You come into my city and harass my advisor."

"No! Your majesty, please," said Nestor. His heart started to race faster now.

"Do not raise your voice to me!" yelled Xenos. "We do not take kindly to those who speak out of turn, no matter their past titles."

Nestor took a step back and glanced at those on the sidelines. Everyone stared at him. He looked back at the king, who had now stood up from his chair. Xenos' legs wobbled as he rose.

"Now, I will forgive your insolence, but only once," said Xenos. Nestor bowed his head in respect, noting that the king's voice was shaking. "Now, you informed my advisor that you had news. News of an attack on our soil. Please enlighten us with your tale."

Nestor waited a moment to begin. Then, summarizing both tragedy and hope, Nestor told the tale of his quest. To Nestor's credit, he felt his retelling was improving. He admitted to being a visionary, with the ability to see into the future when sleeping. He told of the battle, and he spoke of the Hydrarians' act of war.

"So, you see, your majesty, and the rest of the court, this is a situation worth addressing immediately," Nestor ended, feeling he had delivered the news with enough emphasis.

"I see. I see. This is grave news indeed," said Xenos, now walking down the steps to Nestor. "However, something you mentioned didn't make sense. Why did you bring me news of another nation? Earlier, you claimed the attack to be on Gargolian soil." Xenos' eyes widened, his gaze shooting through Nestor.

"In fact, my king I did not say that. I simply said there was an attack that could affect our kingdom."

"Are you calling me a liar?" shouted the king. "First, you force your son to order a meeting with me. Then you threaten my advisor, and now you lie to me and my entire court!"

"My king, that is simply not true."

"Quiet! Damn you!" Xenos yelled as he stepped out to Nestor and slapped him across the cheek. The echo of the strike rang out for several moments in the great hall.

Nestor recovered his composure from the strike, and then he decided enough was enough.

"No! King Xenos, you and your court must listen to me!" he shouted. He stepped back to avoid another slap. "Our allies in the south need our help. They can't do this alone. The Hydrarians will assuredly invade our lands next, burn our villages, pillage our homes, and kill our citizens if we don't eliminate the threat now!"

Xenos looked at Nestor and smiled. "Why would I attack the Hydrarians?" His eyes glazed over. Nestor sensed Xenos' long festering grief, which had caused him to slip into madness.

"We need to help fight," Nestor replied. "Send emissaries on missions of peace, something! If the King of Hydraria declares war on one country, we need to help stop this war. It could destroy us all."

Xenos ordered men from his court to open another door across the hall—the main entrance. Once the doors had been pulled back, a series of soldiers in formation marched into the hall. At first, Nestor believed them to be Gargolian, but to his shock and dismay, they wore Hydrarian colors.

"What is this!" yelled Nestor.

"Meet our new allies, General," said Xenos. His wicked smile displayed all of his teeth now—at least those that were left. Many had fallen out, leaving gaps for his tongue to caress. The same illness that had infected the gargoyles many years before had indeed infected the mind of Nestor's king.

"How? Why?" asked Nestor, completely bewildered.

The Hydrarian force continued marching toward Nestor. They stopped in a straight formation, and an order rang out to surround Nestor. A man of stature and poise appeared as a snake from its den. Anwar slithered himself into view, sounding off another order to his troops.

"Ulysses, their king, approached me several months ago, via General Anwar. He discussed the shortcomings of the other three kingdoms. He offered to help me in exchange for my assistance in his crusade."

"Help you with what? To what end?" demanded Nestor. The old Gargolian now realized his drastic misunderstanding of the situation.

Anwar stepped forward, approaching Nestor. "Victory, of course." The king's scar shimmered in the room's glow.

"Ulysses knows I suffer from the gargoyles' accursed nightmares. Whereas in my youth I was strengthened, in my elder years, the darkness has crippled me. I can't sleep for but an hour or two a week. Ulysses has people who can remedy this. As for his crusade, I don't care about the outcome. He made valid points about Ruxar—how it was an unworthy land with those other people and creatures among us. It is time to eradicate the weak and keep the strong, Nestor." Xenos ended his speech with a gesture to the Gargolian guards.

"That's it? Cure your affliction, and you help mad men destroy innocents?"

"No," said Anwar. "In agreeing to become allies in this purge of undesirables, my king has promised your kingdom a large sum of land—the entire country of Cerebria to be exact."

Nestor's chest tightened. "Despicable! Both of you. All of you!"

"As despicable as starting a war with my country?" asked Anwar.

Nestor's brow furrowed. "What are you talking about?"

"Now that your involvement in the death of so many Hydrarian troops at Brèdon has been confirmed," said Anwar, "I could potentially sway my king to attack Gargolia as well."

"That will not be necessary," said Xenos, looking worried. "Nestor does not represent my kingdom. I do!"

Nestor was helpless. He stood still, awaiting their grasps. His mind swirled. His king had betrayed him—betrayed his people.

"Is this all because of Darren? Is that why you are siding with men like Ulysses and this general here?" asked Nestor, searching for any shred of the old Xenos.

The king thrust himself onto Nestor, grabbing his throat. Nestor grabbed at the king's wrists, but to no avail. Xenos' grip was incredibly strong for one who appeared so frail. Nestor could feel his body begin to fight for air. He thrashed about, attempting to remove Xenos' hands from his neck. The world around him was fading into gray and evolving darkness. Then, as if by miracle, light began to show once more. The grip on his neck loosened, and Nestor fell as a pile to the ornate floor.

Bram stepped forward. "My king, perhaps we can use him. He was there at Brèdon, which means he helped fight off the first wave. We can use him to find out how and who survived, or save him as a gift for Ulysses when he arrives," said General Bram, holding the king's hands, allowing Xenos to lean on his sturdy frame.

Breathing heavily, hands shaking, Xenos replied, "To the dungeons with him."

In a matter of moments, Nestor felt himself being scooped up by soldiers of much greater strength than his own. Hearing dabblings of chatter among the men who were forcibly imprisoning him, he finally recalled what the iron door signified. The iron door was a passageway to imprisonment, torture, and execution. Nestor was now a captive in a war he had never wanted to fight, imprisoned by a mad king he never wanted to see again.

CHAPTER 26

THREE PAIRS OF EYES

Gasping for air, Aedan reached the Deirdue Forest's tree line. He took a moment to judge the distance to his homeland of Dragonia. Behind him, he could see where he had come from. The unnamed town still plumed smoke. The rolling Hills of Rolant budded across the landscape. The great wall of rock, known as the Pleon Mountains, was visible on his way to the trees.

That must mean I'm somewhere in the middle of the Senta Valley's edge. Once I make it to the Grindan River, I only have a short distance to the Dragonian border, he thought.

It sounded so simple. Aedan's plans always sounded so simple in his head, just like rescuing Gilda. Before it got dark, he decided to hold up for the night next to a large maple. His body still ached from his encounters with the Hydrarians, and his fall, his time in the settlement, and his long journey across the valley. Lying a few feet within the forest would hide him from enemies and shield him from any rain. Gray clouds were now tumbling over each other in the distance, and Aedan could smell the oncoming storm looming ahead. The evergreen trees and the moss invited Aedan's throbbing body by providing padded ground to sleep on.

Before he could amble into slumber, however, Aedan unpacked what was left of his food rations: a large strip of meat and a long, stiff loaf of stale bread. After eating, he followed the meal with a hearty gulp of rainwater, now culminating in leaves just feet from where he lay his head. With his stomach full for once, his thirst quenched, and his body on soft ground, Aedan was at last able to sleep a dreamless sleep—the kind all heroes need to recover from long endeavors.

The morning broke, birds chirped, branches cracked, and rainwater thumped like untrained children on drums in the dense forest around him. Aedan woke to a dabble of large raindrops splashing him rudely on the cheek. Aroused by a wet wakeup call, he sat up, alert but calm. His sleep had been undisturbed, which had been greatly needed to regain his strength. He stood up, legs unsteady but strong, and his head clear. The only element he could not diagnose was a low thundering feeling that drummed his entire body.

At first, Aedan believed it to be the chill he felt as he woke up. But this feeling was different. This felt mammoth. What could it be? What could be so gargantuan that it could shake the earth like a quake? The answer was obvious; he had just not wanted to believe it. It was a hydra. He'd seen the hydra beast emblazoned upon hundreds of flags, breastplates, banners, and posters since Brèdon. Not once, though, had he seen one in its truest form.

When Aedan turned around, the gray-skinned mountain beast rose higher than any peak he had ever seen. Even being led by men, its four legs seemed to travel miles with each step. The girth of just one leg Aedan deemed worthy of crushing a castle in each great stomp. The beast's tail swayed like a feline maintaining its balance. The gargantuan creature's body was rippled with muscle and fat that could be seen with every heavy step. Aedan looked up now to see its head. It appeared a serpent more than any other, or possibly something resembling a dragon. Its immense jowls hung open like cave mouths. Inside its jaws were enormous long teeth, and down the back of its never-ending neck was a thick, scaly mane that armored it from anything sharp. The second hydra was a close twin to the first. However, the third hydra, in the rear of the group, the oldest, had multiple heads. Three heads to be precise. As hydras grew they sprouted more heads. No one had seen a hydra grow a head from combat in hundreds of years. The three heads, with three different pairs of eyes, and three different minds, looked around aimlessly as the beast's sluggish sauntering continued.

Aedan began to recall childhood stories of their neighbors to the south. The tamers of these hulking beasts were old and wise. Their sagacity gave them many strategies to handle such animals, but for whatever reason, the huge beasts could not be trusted around the achievements of man. Hydras had been known, generations ago, to wander into towns, villages, and cities, demolishing them with a single stroke of their monstrous feet.

Aedan snapped out of his recollections. He could hear chatter, low muffled voices, and high-pitched shrieks accompanied by the heavy walk of the colossal hydras. Men in hoods led the mountainous beasts with ease. Ropes attached to each were as loose as drapery.

Who are they? Aedan thought.

Viciously, his eyes were ripped toward a cruel sight—one of chains, children, battered parents, and chiming chides from soldiers of the Hydrarian nation. The Hydrarian men were plastered with new shining armor. Their odious actions brought joy to their faces. Smiling, laughter, and excitement ran through them as soldiers mocked the prisoners, who were entrapped in garbed steel and tripped over themselves.

Aedan, crouching, began to move as a beast on the hunt under cover of the forest canopy. His feet were swift and quiet. His senses heightened and his reaction to sound intensified. He continued to pursue the group of beasts, soldiers, and prisoners from the tree line, until they finally halted.

"What say you, Ky?" asked one Hydrarian soldier of his brother. His dark blonde hair slid out of his helm as he spoke. "How long do you bet this little twig of a man could last?"

"That depends, I think," said Ky, a stocky man with dark brown hair, "on whether we have him fight against a tree trunk or this prissy little woman here?" The men began to laugh as they pointed to one of the prisoners. She was slight in build, with amber hair. Her face was stern, but even from a distance, Aedan could see her eyes were puffy from tears, and her cheeks gave off the sun's rays in small twinkles of dread.

Another soldier began. "Which pair do you think the commander will pit first? Maybe the soldiers from Cerebria, or the angry brothers? If we're lucky, we'll see some ladies fighting. That would be a sight indeed!"

"There you go again, thinking with that small thing between your legs," said the dark-haired Hydrarian with a bellowing laugh. "Don't be so eager. You don't want to inflate your expectations. These are the very first fights the king is sanctioning. We don't want to be disappointed." The eager soldier withdrew from more comments and took a sip from a cup; Aedan wished it had contained poison.

Fights? Aedan thought. *The Hydrarians are making their war prisoners fight?* His mind began to swim, flooding with strategies, a plan perhaps to rescue the ten or so captives held hostage by their sadistic enemies. Without more thought, Aedan rushed into action. Unfortunately, being patient was proving difficult. His breathing was quick. He could feel his heartbeat in his neck at the thought of dispatching those foes once and for all.

Aedan grasped his fortitude and quelled his nerves long enough for the party to continue on their path. Aedan, unrelenting, followed as he had before the halt. As agilely as he could, he gingerly grasped his bow and an arrow from his quiver. He laid the arrow in place and then stopped movement. He focused all he could on one of the fifteen or so enemies. His breathing steadied. His mind calibrated the wind and the footsteps of the heavy hydra planting their feet, making the earth shutter with every stomp. Aedan brought the zealous arrow to his eye, released it from his bow, and let it soar. It soared and wisped through the air, rotating its perfect design, cutting through the wind as scissors over leather. Aedan's eyes followed it as it dipped its head directly into the neck of one of the malicious men. He went down fast and quiet.

Thankfully, the troop had no sense it was under attack by a stealthy assailant. Aedan snatched a second arrow, armed his bow, and sent the deadly device away. It traveled just like the first, hitting its mark in an unshelled soldier's skull. This time, however, it did not go unnoticed. The men began to rally. All armor and weapons were donned; swords, axes, daggers, bows, and sickles were all unsheathed. This response did not deter Aedan; it merely gave him the strength to continue.

Without thought, Aedan had sent another two arrows into flight. The first ricocheted off one man's chest plate. The second managed to bury itself deep in a soldier's throat, killing him instantly. Aedan walked and reloaded another arrow. Feeling back in his quiver, he realized he had two left, and he needed to make them both count. His first spun and arched, hitting a soldier squarely in the upper leg, invoking an incisive scream, causing the man to bleed to death in moments. The blood turned his once shiny armor into a swirl of red and dark, earthy brown. Aedan's final shot planted itself into one of the wicked warrior's eyes. The man's body slumped in on itself. The soldiers who remained clamored for shields against the deadly hits.

Aedan dropped his bow and quiver, unsheathed a sword and dagger, and engaged two of the swordsmen immediately. Just as men in mines would hear the clang of work, Aedan heard the clang of battle once more. The swords bounced off each other, and recoiled, sending intense, vibrating shock waves through Aedan's arms and hands. He did his best to ignore the feeling. Another swipe of his sword and another soldier said goodbye, hollering. More soldiers fell upon Aedan. All he could do now was retreat and parry. Swipes of his sword no longer made any purchase.

The prisoners, previously terrified, screamed and clamored together, doing their best to protect their little children. Aedan, seeing this heartfelt self-sacrificing attempt to shield their loved ones, was distracted long enough to be walloped from behind on the top of his skull, sending him in a spiraling path to the ground. Aedan closed his eyes and hoped his enemies would end his life quickly.

CHAPTER 27

EMBERS OF RESISTANCE

"Wretched ingrates," cursed Ulysses, with muffled breath as he perused messages. "What gives them the authority to disturb our advancement? These Soldiers of Fire don't answer to any one flag."

"Are you saying they are of a different nation, sire?" asked Amos, Ulysses' messenger.

"No, idiot. I'm saying this resistance group, if you can call it one, is composed of rogues and arsonists."

"Are you worried?"

"Of course not!" declared Ulysses, continuing his search for new information.

"I can't imagine this band of wretches, as you say, could truly make an impact on your vision, eh?"

"No. No," said Ulysses, his voice trailing off into thought. "Look here. A message from my army heading to the dog lands tells of a Cerebrian rider charging into the ranks of my supply wagons."

"Yes, sir. I was the one who intercepted the communication."

"What else did they say?"

"The men who encountered the rider added that his beast was brutal; it tore through our warriors as easily as a piece of bacon. No mercy."

Ulysses sighed. "Well, then, we must advise our archers to carry crushed ostium flowers. That should slow the vile beasts down."

"I will make a note of it," said Amos, feverishly writing on a piece of parchment. "What other information shall I return to our forces, my liege?"

"Tell all you encounter to be on the lookout for small groups or lone riders. It seems their reach is far and wide within Cerebria."

"How so?" asked Amos.

"One instance here tells of a small port on the most western coast, at our southern border. It was being used to transport goods and soldiers. Now it is in ruin. Smoked and burnt. No sign of any dead, either. They must have been watching us a long while to know about that asset."

"Was there not an old keeper there?"

"Right you are, Amos. Put out the word for his whereabouts. Perhaps he can tell us why his home went up in flames."

"Of course, sire," Amos said, adding to his notes. "Where else have the brigands struck?"

Ulysses fiddled with the last of the letters, opening it aggressively. "It seems their reach continues to grow. This time in our own country. Damn them!"

"What will you do, my king?" asked Amos.

Ulysses' face glowed with anger as he continued to read. His focus sharpened with every passing detail he digested. "This son of a whore."

"What is it, sire?"

"We lost a checkpoint."

"Sire?"

"It, too, like the port, is in ashes. This, however, is much worse." Ulysses closed his eyes and pointed his nose to the sky. He took a deep breath and returned to the letter. "Not only is the checkpoint destroyed, but several of my men were killed and others wounded. I lost workers in this fire, and it seems one of our own people aided in this havoc."

"How can that be, my lord? All have sworn fealty to you and our cause."

"It does not matter now. The treasonous bitch is dead."

"And what of the man?"

"He escaped out into the plains."

"Our men will capture and end him, in the name of our savior, King Ulysses."

"No! Capture only. We need people like this man if we are to fulfill our true purpose."

"What makes these people so special, sire?"

Ulysses looked up to Amos. "Once the smoke cleared, and the bodies were counted, the writer of this letter says he saw two messages written in ash and blood on the stones just outside the settlement. One said, 'We are the Soldiers of Fire.'"

"And the other?"

"'For Brèdon,'" Ulysses replied.

"You're saying?"

"That those who defeated us at Brèdon and these rogues are the same people. I want them alive. I want them to feel agony before they see the end. Their every breath insults me and our nation. Send word to our man in the east of my coming. I want to see progress."

"Yes, my liege. I will write this up right away and ride out at first light," said Amos.

"No. As soon as the ink dries. We must move as fast as the wind if we are to smother the embers of resistance."

CHAPTER 28

CHAINS AND STONES

Nestor sat in the dark dungeon, negotiating with curious rodents to leave him be. Being in chains was a new experience for him, and he did not particularly enjoy his new jewelry. The cold metal choked his wrists, and small beads of steel remorselessly chafed his skin. His legs were held down by cuffs and disappointment. He was seething mad at himself for believing King Xenos would help him after the events of Darren's death. The king was never the same after that.

Nestor couldn't sit in self-pity. He needed to get to Orion. Nestor had no reason to stay in his homeland. He had a duty to protect his family. They all needed to travel east to Dragonia. From there, they could get a proper foothold on the spiraling conflict. He hoped Aedan was already there, moving pieces into play that could stop the Hydrarian advance. Nestor was unsure how long he had been down in the dark caverns of the Gargolian dungeon. He had been less than cooperative on his commute. The guards had slammed an object against his neck to make him more malleable to the transition.

The question Nestor now had was, *How long do I have until they decide to kill me?* Nestor wondered about Orion. Would he be taken too? All Nestor could do was try to sleep in the cold, dark cell, where he was unable to move more than a few inches. Perhaps he could access his visions to help aid his escape. Perhaps all wasn't lost yet. Only time would tell.

• • •

Hours slipped by. Nestor's sleep was sporadic at best. His eyes fluttered with images, but nothing solid. He could not focus while so uncomfortable. The cold crept into his bones like maggots in a corpse. His muscles spasmed and ached. Sitting on the hard stone made him dearly miss Phaedra and their bed. He closed his eyes once more and saw Phaedra. Her hair was moving with the wind, her smile on her face. She was ushering him to her. He effortlessly strode to his beloved. Her embrace felt warm. Nestor could feel his breathing slow and his heart beating a calm rhythm.

A sharp, natural jerk of his cramping muscles tugged him out of the memory. Disappointment and anger flooded his head. He hated the king for this. He hated the Hydrarians. He hated his visions for showing the future, and most of all, he hated himself for being so foolish. Nestor couldn't fathom that he could change the future. It didn't matter. Brèdon was attacked, the people were saved, but now it appeared through his mind's eye that Brèdon had or would be assaulted again. The same people who had perished in his first vision would inevitably die the same way. Perhaps Aedan was already a dead man. Aloysius, too? Nestor's self-flagellation reached a peak. He held his face in his hands and began to sob. No more thinking, just feeling.

As Nestor's sobs echoed in the stony tunnels, his body and mind meshed. His body fell into slumber and his mind's eye whisked him to the familiar sight of Brèdon. This time, Nestor was not experiencing a scene for the very first time. He had witnessed it before on his journey home. Once again, he saw the town he had helped save on fire. The flames licked the skies, smoke smothered the senses, and the Hydrarian soldiers hacked away at defenseless souls.

In the distance, Nestor could see the sad scene once more. The silhouette of a man fearlessly fighting for innocent lives. The man was overrun by wicked men. That tall, ominous shadow striking him down, meeting the same fate as the others he was attempting to save. As the hero's body landed with a thud, Nestor's mind awoke. The vision had reassured him. If he got out, he need not go back to the doomed town, but east to prevent a further cataclysm.

CHAPTER 29

DARK, LUCKY MOMENTS

The day continued on for Orion. Once he had left his father in Segeric's capable, yet rude hands, he returned to his duties. It felt good to be back in charge, but he had enjoyed the brief moments with family. His army life had become his only life for many years; however, the sounds of his parents' laughter hung around in his mind as he made visits to soldiers training, those on watch, and to his constituents to discuss happenings within the kingdom. He looked forward to meeting with his father at day's end.

As the sun began to set and Orion's duties were completed for the day, he made his way back to the barracks, back to Segeric, and, he hoped, to a pleased father. His steps inside the barracks were quick and light. He felt excitement. He desired to know what the king and his father had discussed. Perhaps the army would be riding out soon to deal with the Hydrarian threat. Orion made sure not to inform anyone of the matter until the highest ranking among them knew.

As Orion reached the end of the long hallway, only feet from the turn to the advisors' office, he overheard a conversation coming from inside the office.

"Are you serious?" asked a man.

"Deadly serious. Lieutenant Orion's father is in custody," said Segeric. Orion stopped suddenly. His ears opened to every sound at that moment.

"Does he know?"

"No," Segeric said. "And we aren't going to tell him. As far as the lieutenant is concerned, his father is back at home with his mother." Orion's heart began to beat into his ears.

"Won't he find out? I mean, he could just ride home and see for himself."

"Not with the work that is coming. The general made it clear we are to keep Orion busy with preparations to aid the Hydrarians. Then dispose of him," said Segeric. "Besides, the old man wouldn't keep his only son in the dark. Orion knows what his father was here to discuss." Orion stepped lightly back the way he had come. He knew at any moment Segeric or his assistant could come out and see him. Orion was thankful for the time of day. The sunset had nearly erased all light in the hall, and the acolyte had not fulfilled his duty yet. With that luck, Orion was able to slink out of the trap left by the snake Segeric.

Orion began walking. Nowhere in particular. Just kept walking. He needed to figure out what to do. In a matter of moments—dark, lucky moments—Orion had discovered deceitful acts and realized the Hydrarian threat's true depth. His father had not only been right about the danger the Hydrarians imposed, but he had been duped by their cunning. Now Orion only needed to figure out where his father was being held and how to get his father out. Unfortunately, in his entire time within the army, no one had been taken into custody on his watch. Few conflicts couldn't be settled by separating folks and letting them sleep off their stupor.

This was much worse, however. His father was now being held as a prisoner of war. To get him out through diplomacy would not work. As he had heard from Segeric, they were only going to use him until preparations were complete. What preparations? What were the two kingdoms' plans? Orion tossed the thought aside until he could figure out his current predicament. Thankfully, Orion had already checked in with his superiors. They wouldn't be expecting to hear from him until the next day. He had time to make something happen—as long as he didn't cross paths with Segeric or the general.

Aimless walking led Orion near the city's northwest wall. It appeared that mild panic and contemplation had taken him farther than he had anticipated. This part of the city was for officers, such as himself. He was close to his living quarters. Being an officer in the Gargolian army brought with it many pleasurable amenities, including his own home. He gingerly strode down the street, looking for anyone who might be out of place. When he was satisfied that no one was around, he made his way as gracefully as a newborn foal to the inside of his home. As he swung the door closed, he realized he was an easy target to follow. Being loud and clumsy was a terrible trait to have when attempting to be unassuming.

Orion took a few moments. He breathed deeply, realizing nobody would come looking for him tonight. No one knew he and his father had made plans to meet later today. No one knew for sure about his involvement, or even his understanding. Perhaps the king would release his father in the morning. All would be forgiven, and he could go about his business.

"I heard wrong," Orion said aloud to himself. "That must have been it. I was eavesdropping and didn't hear the full conversation." Orion played out that theory in his mind several times. He had to do something. He couldn't go asking for his father's release, and he would surely die if he tried anything too daring on his own. He needed help, and fast. Orion was about to expose a terrible truth to his people, and he was not going to do it lightly.

Orion gathered his composure and exited his home in a dignified manner. His mission now was to find the troop he had risen through the ranks with. All were scattered about the city since different ranks and jobs had separated them over time, but they were still bonded by shared experiences of servitude and brotherhood. Orion was optimistic they would help. Although, asking them to betray their kingdom for brotherhood could prove damning. Leery of the future, Orion trudged on to find his brothers.

CHAPTER 30

A KINGDOM OF BROTHERS

Tius, Euric, and Hathus were men of passion, ingenuity, and at times, utter stupidity. But they were Orion's brothers of dutiful servitude, and he trusted them above all others. In fact, he trusted them to be finished for the day, just like he was. Orion trusted the three men would be sitting around a table at the pub moments from his house. If not all three, one would surely be present with a beer in one hand and another likely at the table for company.

As Orion stepped into the pub, his nose flooded with the aromas of cooked meat, mead, and sweaty patrons. The roaring fire in the establishment's center could thaw the coldest brow and replace frost with beads of sweat. The cool autumn night's touch fell away as Orion walked back to their usual table. One of his brothers, Euric, a tall man with a broad stature and bronze skin, turned just as Orion passed the old wood hearth.

"Ah, good to see you, brother," said Euric, standing up to welcome Orion. "Everything all right? They said you'd gone on a personal matter almost two days ago."

"Euric, I need your help," said Orion, bringing his friend in close. The two men dropped to sit at the table.

"What is it? Another soldier out of line again?" asked Euric, jumping to conclusions.

"No, no. Nothing so routine. It concerns my father."

"What about your father? Did he not return?"

"No. Stop for a moment, Euric. Let me speak," said Orion, emphatically. Euric had been their group leader since the day Orion had met him. He was always thinking of what could come next, devising plans, and anticipating others' actions. However, sometimes he spoke too quickly for his mind to keep up.

Euric shot an irritated look at Orion. He sat back in his chair and said, "Okay, Orion; what has happened that has you so distraught?"

Orion looked around at the other pub-goers, then back to Euric. "My father, he is in custody."

Euric stared at Orion. Worry was spread across Orion's face.

"Is that all?" Euric chuckled and scoffed at Orion's problem. "So you found him, brought him here, and he got locked up for drinking and fighting?" Euric rolled his eyes. "You said it yourself—the great ol' General Nestor can drink to excess at times."

Orion, frustrated, slammed his hand on the table. "No," he whispered. The whisper did nothing to negate the attention he was now receiving from those around him. Orion took a deep breath and waited a moment until the patrons returned to their own conversations. "Listen, damn it. I went home to see my mother. She sent me a letter weeks ago saying she was worried about my father, who had seen something in his sleep and left."

"Where'd he go?" asked Euric, now being more patient.

"Apparently to Cerebria—to a little town called Brèdon. It's nearly in the center of the country." Orion stopped again to look around. He continued, once satisfied. "A few hours after I arrived home, my father arrived by horseback."

"That's great," said Euric. "He's safe and sound at home. So why is he locked up then?"

"Because he went to discuss the war that is starting. I haven't seen it yet, but it is at our doorstep, brother. My father encountered and fought back a Hydrarian army while in Cerebria."

Euric's mouth opened in awe. "I don't understand."

"Euric, my father came with me to talk with King Xenos. On my return to meet with him, I overheard Segeric and his assistant mention he was imprisoned and how I was to be killed once the time comes." Orion finished and sat back in his chair. The relief of a shared burden did not last long.

"You're telling me that our king—the king we swore to protect—has allied himself, allied our country Gargolia, with Hydraria, which has started a war?"

Orion nodded lightly. His eyes began to get hot from the room's heat and their conversation. "Come; we need to find the others and meet somewhere more private. I don't know how much time I, or my father, have." The two men stood up and made their way to the exit. As they reached the door, voices called out to them from the road.

"Hey! You two bastards just going to leave us without having a drink first?" cried Hathus.

"Yeah, that's not appropriate officer behavior," said Tius, jogging to meet up with Orion and Euric.

"Boys, we've got a serious situation," Euric whispered. "Don't say anything until we get to Orion's."

The four men walked briskly toward the small home. Euric's jaw lay stern on his face. His brown eyes scanned for suspicious movements. Orion began to worry about his brothers and how this knowledge would affect them. Euric had already begun to plan something; he could see it in how he walked. The other two had no idea what Orion was about to ask of them.

Once the four men strode into the house, Euric and Orion explained their odd behavior. Tius and Hathus grew quiet in the presence of accusations against their king.

"So what are you asking us to do, Orion?" asked Tius angrily. "Are you trying to die? How do we know you weren't fed a lie by your senile father?"

"My father is in his right mind, Tius!" shouted Orion. A tightness began to fill his chest.

"This is our brother Orion," said Euric. "He wouldn't lie to us."

"Orion isn't one to risk something like this because of a feeling," said Hathus. "I believe him."

"I just hate that our king could be swayed to launch our kingdom into war. And for what?"

Orion shook his head. "I have no idea."

"Look, why don't we all take a breath, and find Segeric or the general to straighten this all out," said Tius. His thin face grew red from frustration.

"I can't believe Xenos and the general would do something like this," said Hathus.

"Well, if they did, then there has to be a good reason," Tius replied.

Orion marched over to his friend, locking eyes. "And what reason is that, Tius? Are you truly this blind? What makes you not believe me? After all that we have done together—after all we have done for each other, you won't believe something like this could happen?" Orion's fury began to overpower his senses.

"Brothers! Brothers!" trumpeted Euric like a dignitary within a court of philosophers. "I have a plan to get the old general out and, hopefully, allow us all to live."

Orion turned to Euric. Hathus eyed him curiously. Tius looked at the three men he called brothers and said, "I won't be a part of this. You have all lost it." Tius looked over to Orion. "Ever since you earned the rank of lieutenant, you've been eyeing for an opportunity to send us further below you."

Orion jumped to Tius like a frog from a lily pad. "This has nothing to do with rank, soldier. I came to you as a brother in need, and you treat me as an enemy." The two men leered at one another for a long moment.

"Do what you need to, brothers," Tius spat. "I won't betray my kingdom, not even for my brothers." He paused a moment. "You have two hours, and then I'm going to Segeric with this. Hopefully, by then, you are gone or dead. At this moment, the two are the same to me."

Tius left with a thud and a slam of the door. A long silence overtook the room. The three remaining men sat in the quiet and reflected on Tius' words. Orion finally raised his eyes, peering at his two brothers. "All right, you heard the man. We have two hours. Let's hear this plan, Euric."

CHAPTER 31

BOOTS, BRUISERS, AND BRUNETTES

Aedan's vision blurred. His head felt wet from sweat and blood. His ears rang from the clash of metal to skull. Dust invaded his eyes, making it difficult to see his encroaching enemies. Aedan felt a sudden pull on the back of his neck. A large, scar-ridden man snatched him up, turned him on his back, and threw him to the unforgiving ground with a wallop. Aedan could feel the air forced from his lungs, and another great twinge of agony came from his head wound.

"How dare you!" yelled the scarred man, kicking Aedan's ribs with his equally stiff boots. Another bolt of pain resonated in Aedan's side as he lay helpless on the earth. "You just killed my men, you sleazy puss bag!" said the scarred man, continuing to thrash Aedan's body with his massive boots. At last, the beating stopped, but it escalated to him being dragged by his hair, lifted to his knees, and a sickle placed against his throat. Aedan's arms could hardly stay in their sockets. His muscles pulsated with such vigor that he could hardly continue kneeling. If not for the man holding him up by his hair, Aedan would have been a mess on the ground.

"You've killed your last Hydrarian, little man," said the scarred one, now ever-so-slightly inching the sickle across Aedan's throat.

"Stop!" said another. "Stop now, soldier. Put your weapon down. Shackle this man! We are taking him with us."

The scarred soldier hesitated, digging the blade deeper into Aedan's flesh. He could feel his warm blood travel down his chest. His heart began to beat as aggressively as drums. His vision cleared, and now his eyes were traveling between the assumed troop leader and the man holding Aedan's fate in his hefty hands. "You have to be joking, sir! He killed many of us! We can't just—"

"We can!" said the leader, standing up straight. "You will listen to me, or you will be the first in those trials when we get to Galicia!" With the threat lingering, the scarred man removed the sickle from Aedan's throat and once more kicked him with his massive boot, throttling Aedan's battered body to the dusty, blood-stained earth.

With a rush, Aedan was launched once more into the air, and brought to his feet by two more unfriendly soldiers. They forcefully escorted Aedan to the back of the chain line of prisoners, who were still reeling from the display of violence. The men shackled Aedan's hands and feet, attaching another chain to the prisoner in front of him. Aedan was now a hostage. His plan to meet his king in Dragonia had taken a grave deviation. He had failed. His head and shoulders slumped low. The prisoner train began to move again, aided by whips, leaving several dead as a feast for the fowl and beast to reclaim. Aedan could only hope to avoid their fate in the near future.

With the troop's movement underway, Aedan regained some sense. His pride was as blackened, bruised, and broken as his body. His will would have to prevail if he wanted to save himself. He was hopeful his friends possessed better luck than he did. With thoughts of others weighing heavily on his mind, Aedan began to survey the prisoners. He first noticed a tall, skinny man whose black hair resembled tar. Behind him was, Aedan assumed, the man's wife and son because the three huddled closer together than most. The wife was a sturdy woman. She had a strong confidence about her. Her light brown hair whipped in the wind as she glanced back at her little boy, the reflection of his father, but possessed of his mother's sturdy build.

Suddenly, Aedan's attention focused on the woman in front of him. In the sunlight, her dark brown hair bled varying hues of red. Her face curved softly and her eyes were a poised hazel. Aedan's eyes drifted down to her waist. Her hips seemed to sway as she walked. He could not help thinking he knew her. Her clothes were tattered and torn in places, no doubt by some of the wilder soldiers. Something about her seemed distantly familiar.

"What's your name? We know each other, right?" asked Aedan. She turned her head slightly. Their eyes met for a moment before she snapped her gaze back to its original position. *She is afraid of me? No, it must be the soldiers*, Aedan thought.

"Turia," she said, trying to appear quiet.

"Wait, from Brèdon? How did you get here?" He was eager for information both on her and the Hydrarian forces.

"Now is not the time," said Turia. "The men will beat you again." Aedan gave a nod of understanding.

The band of bruisers and prisoners alike continued solemnly to their destination—to a place called Galicia, a place unknown to Aedan.

• • •

Several hours later, Aedan's belly began to gurgle and fuss. His mouth was as dry as the desert ground. Traveling through the hot arid plains, Aedan noticed walls in the distance. Stone walls of a town, with large wooden structures inside them. As the caravan drew closer to the settlement, Aedan saw farms being tended to, and a small road being dug up for wagons to traverse. Aedan and the troop entered the township, where the prisoners were met by the rough and heavy hands of a welcoming team of guards. They icily stared at the captives in disgust, like they were nothing but rotting meat in the sun. The guards, assisted by the group of soldiers, escorted everyone to the base of a tall wood building. The structure was draped in the flags of those captured, and banners that said, "Praise Jormungand!" and "All hail, Ulysses, our savior!" Aedan could see a doorway leading to what he could only guess was his future dwelling.

Aside from the great wooden structure, Galicia held a few vendors who sold trinkets, food, and poorly scented wines. All the vendors eyed the captives. Then, as if out of nowhere, a great tent appeared. This unassuming shelter housed weapons, armor, and other combat paraphernalia. Nothing else, other than a well, could be seen from Aedan's vantage point just outside the gate.

No doubt, this is a checkpoint and rest area for Hydrarians, Aedan thought, and he turned his attention to the robed man striding toward the prisoners.

"Good evening. I'm in charge here. My name is Marcus." Marcus stood tall, with a broad jaw line and sharp facial features that accentuated his authority. "You have all been brought here to establish a new process. A process that will revolutionize our lives. That is, the lives of our people." A mocking smile formed as his last thought reached their ears. "You see, there is a war brewing. Our great king has decided that all of you, from every other nation on this great continent, are too equal to us." He stood firm and postured even more, inching taller. "We, the Hydrarians, are the noblest of people in Ruxar. We deserve to live like it." Marcus ended his last word sharply, smiled, and raised his eyebrows. Marcus clearly loved what he did. His smug smile transformed to a stern smirk as he began to speak once more. "Soldiers," he said, using the title as if he were addressing a dear friend, "who among this disheveled lot should be given the privilege—dare I say, the honor—to face one of our warriors from the west?"

The troop leader stepped forward, shot a sharp glance at Aedan, and turned his eyes back to Marcus. "I have one in mind, sir."

"Well, point him out. Don't keep me waiting," said Marcus.

Before Marcus could drop his last syllable, the troop leader fired another glance to two men, one of whom was the scarred soldier. The two jaunted over to Aedan, one on either side, and hoisted Aedan forward. "This one," said the leader. "This man ambushed us on the road. He killed several of my men, and cost me and my troop precious time."

Marcus, seeming confused and stunned by the accusation, replied, "This man? He is so puny. How could a man like this take on great Hydrarian soldiers like you?"

"It does not matter how it happened. What matters is he deserves to meet a fate as vicious as the one he delivered to my men!" hollered the troop leader, his face glowing with anger and his fists clenched, ready to strike.

Marcus, surprised by the leader's reaction, looked at Aedan. He strode toward the unassuming Dragonian, studying him as a scholar would a book. Then, as if possessed, Marcus belted a shrieking laugh that reverberated jaggedly in Aedan's ears and echoed throughout the town. The troop leader, unimpressed, grit his teeth in disgust at Marcus.

"If he is as vicious as you say he is, I cannot wait to see how he performs against a true opponent," said Marcus. Descending now from his laughing fit, he made sharp eye contact with the troop leader. "I just hope his performance is better than yours has been lately. Because if he does not put on a grand show for our guest, I assure you your master will take out his frustration on your head."

In that instant, the authoritative troop leader seemed to be replaced by a small boy scolded by his father. His eyes widened, mouth agape. The pigment of his skin faded as white as clouds. "He is coming? He is coming here?"

"He will be here in a few hours. He wants to be here when the first drop of blood hits the sand," said Marcus, whose eyes grew wide and his smile fuller still. "Our savior wishes to lead us into the start of this stage, just as he will guide us to the razing at Brèdon."

Brèdon! Aedan thought. *Who from the Hydrarian army was coming here?* Aedan's mind began whirling with thoughts. *Wait, he said the razing? The town is in danger again. That means....* Aedan's eyes began to water. His heart fell, knees weakened. *Oh, no, their army will destroy what is left. And the people.* He quietly mourned.

"Take them away; shackle them together in the cells." Marcus looked at Aedan. "And take the new athlete to the warrior holding cell. We don't want anything to happen to him that could jeopardize the ceremony tomorrow." Finally, once all the orders had been given out, the soldiers rallied and roughly escorted the prisoners to their new homes. Aedan knew his survival appeared bleak. He had all night to figure out a plan. Sadly, his mind was racing with thoughts of his friends, the other prisoners, and coming face to face with the person they called the savior.

CHAPTER 32

PRISON KNIGHT

Being led like a dog on a chain, Aedan helplessly felt sharp pulling at his wrists. The guards yanked hard if he fell even a pace out of step. They led him into the prison. Its rock walls and steel bars screamed hopelessness. Aedan could hear the coughs and bleating moans of the imprisoned as the blackness enveloped him. Squinting, he could make out small shadowy forms of young children being held by their mothers. Men, cradled by chains, hung against the walls struggling to stand by their own power.

At last, the guards stopped. One grabbed for keys and, in a swift motion, opened a cell. Aedan felt a jarring kick in his backside. He went lurching forward and crashed into the unforgiving stone wall. His body heat was escaping now, with every passing second since the sun's retreat and his incarceration. The door's hinges screeched as it shut, and the cell latch clapped in unison with the chuckling guards. Aedan's heartbeat quickened. His face was flush with anger. He whipped around and lunged at the locked cell. His cat-like pose amused the guards further.

"Save your energy for tomorrow; you don't wanna die too tired," said one guard, smiling.

Aedan closed his eyes and slunk to the prison floor, defeated. "How could I have been so stupid?" he said aloud.

"What did you think was going to happen?" asked a prisoner in the adjacent cell. "Did you think you would best them?"

"I didn't think I would end up in a place like this," Aedan replied. "I have somewhere I need to be. It's important I get out of here."

"Yeah. Likewise. No one here planned this either," the prisoner said with an exasperated sigh. Aedan slunk farther to the floor. His head now rested on stone.

"Oh, don't give up that easy," said the prisoner. "There is so much more suffering you get to endure before you rest." Aedan snapped a foul look at him. The prisoner smiled openly and said, "I'm Arthur of Hydraria, believe it or not."

Aedan looked at him. "Sadly, I do believe. I've seen it already. And I'm Aedan of Dragonia."

"Dragonian, aye? Not many of you folks around here. Mostly Cerebrian, and some disagreeing people of my kin like me."

"What is happening here?" Aedan asked. "How long have you been here?"

"Short of a week, and this illustrious palace you are currently being held in is a recruitment camp of sorts. On one side, they have procured people of other nations by fighting them, and the winners get to join their armies."

"What is the other side?" Aedan asked.

"Well, our hosts have decided to hold the families of those people hostage. Use them as collateral. Unfortunately, the young ones don't last long. Families are usually brought here with only one parent left to fight for their cause—whatever that is." Arthur finished speaking and spit, as if the words left a sour taste in his mouth.

"They're not just taking prisoners," Aedan said slowly. "They've already attacked a town. They'll burn it to the ground, finishing it off with everyone inside it."

Arthur looked up. His eyes were full of concern. He grasped the steel bars gently. "Where? Which one?"

Aedan looked up, his eyes meeting Arthur's. "Brèdon."

"What of the people? I know folks there from my travels."

Aedan couldn't bring himself to say anything. He just shook his head. Aedan could feel his eyes beginning to water. Slam! Slam! Arthur struck the bars of his cell. The echo harangued within the enclosed jail.

"No! Damn. What is my kingdom doing?" Arthur asked. "Those are good people. How do you know this? Where did you hear this from?"

Aedan exhaled a shallow sharp breath and said, "I was there. I was there when the Hydrarians attacked the first time."

Arthur and Aedan didn't speak for a long moment. Aedan could hear soft whimpering coming from his neighbor. Stuttering with grief, Arthur began to speak again. "You said the first time you drove them back. How many times?"

Aedan stood up. "We only drove them back once. That's all we could afford to do." Aedan told Arthur more about the events that transpired, and about Nestor, Aloysius, Magnus, and the towns-people. He went on to explain the path he had taken that led him to being imprisoned, and how he had discovered the fate of the lives he had helped to protect.

"This doesn't seem true. Why would my people do this? How do I know you are telling the truth?" asked Arthur, bargaining with himself over the truth.

"Why would I lie? Look at where you are—imprisoned by your own people."

"I don't know. Maybe you're a spy for them."

Aedan guffawed. "I doubt they would want me on their side. I mean, I sentenced dozens of them to a fiery death during the siege," said Aedan.

Arthur looked at this newcomer with further disbelief. "How exactly? Did you have one of those dragons from your country with you?" asked Arthur.

"Oh, no, we don't travel with dragons—too wild," Aedan jested. "No, Nestor, the Gargolian elder I met, taught me how to use fire as a way to deter a large force. In the end, it was me and another who caused the last blaze that nearly engulfed Brèdon. It did the trick. The Hydrarians ran off." Arthur stood, entranced. Aedan chuckled again. "The survivors named us the Soldiers of Fire. We swore we would resist the forces of tyranny at any cost." Aedan smiled softly at the memory.

"All right, Fire Soldier. What are you going to do about this predicament?" Arthur asked.

"I don't know. I heard them say I would be fighting tomorrow. Maybe I can make a move then," said Aedan.

"I doubt it. Too many eyes will be watching you. Plus, the guards and archers around the arena. Not to mention the small army camped outside that brought you here."

Aedan searched for inspiration. He thought of the prisoners' need to escape. If he was going to follow through with warning the other kingdoms, he needed to use what he had—his story. "I need to talk to the other prisoners," Aedan finally said.

"What good will that do?" Arthur sneered. "We're all caged, or did you forget the steel bars?"

"Did you see which way they took the group I came in with?" asked Aedan.

Arthur paused a moment to reflect. "Your group is with the other collateral types on the other side of the prison," he said.

"What does that mean for them?" asked Aedan.

"Anything really. I've seen people from over there get sold to tradesmen, and then some get used in other ways."

"What ways?" asked Aedan.

"I can only imagine. Many times, I've heard screaming for hours at a time, then just silence." Arthur's head dropped. "The soldiers and guards here take what they want. Your friends aren't safe."

Aedan sighed heavily. "Wait, you said that this side is warriors. Are you fighting tomorrow?"

"Yes," said Arthur, "and I'm not good with weapons. Tools, sure. Not weapons."

Aedan looked at him softly. "It will all be okay. I'll see what I can do."

Arthur's eyes began to glisten with tears of worry. "Not if you face their favorite fighter tomorrow. He is a large man. Strong. Gifted with the strength of the Cerberus."

Aedan looked at him. "Then I guess I am going to have to work fast."

• • •

Hours passed, and Aedan sat watching. He looked for patterns. Guard movements. The number of prisoners, how many could be fighters, and which ones needed protection. It appeared the majority of the captives were in need. Aedan searched for a weak spot in his cell. He grabbed pointlessly at the bars, trying to bend them.

Nothing. He scoured the ground, looking for anything metal with which to pick the lock. Nothing. He had begun to lose steam. He was grasping at dried-up ideas. Then a scream. The shriek echoed, bouncing off the walls and reverberating chaotically throughout the prison. All of the prisoners stirred. Many stood up to get a better vantage point.

Arthur looked back to Aedan. "This again—these people don't know when to stop." Arthur covered his ears. Aedan's chest tightened. His eyes and ears seemed to open more. Every sound and shape seemed sharper. His heart pounded like a drum in his ears. "Ay!" Aedan shouted. "Ay, give it up! You want a real fight? Come on this side!"

Aedan's voice coalesced with the screams. The other inmates turned to Aedan with fear.

"They are looking at you like you're dead already," Arthur told them. "We're all dead if we don't do something."

Then Aedan shouted to their keepers, "You bastards want to hear real shrieks, come and make me scream!" He kicked the side of the cell door. His hands grabbed the bars like a wild animal and he shook them violently, yelling and screaming with everything he had. No movement stirred for a long while. Moments passed, but he kept up the childish banging. His throat began to swell and dry from excitement. But he proceeded. The screams were still coming at them in waves of terror and shrill shrieks. "You Hydrarian motherless dogs. Come over here and show off to me!" Aedan screamed into the dank, stone prison.

The echoes faded. The screams ceased. Stillness overtook the halls and cells. Then tapping, low and steady tapping, like a drum beginning a percussive crescendo. Seconds sprinted by and tapping became thumping. The light drumming was now ambushing

Aedan's senses; his ears filled with sound like wind to a rising storm. Dark figures, clad in mail and brandishing knives, marched forth. Aedan's breathing increased. He moved backwards in his cell. A guard stopped at his door.

"What? Only brave when girls are screaming?" barked the guard.

"What? Are you only strong enough to beat on the defenseless?" asked Aedan, venom and flame in his words.

The guard smiled cruelly. "Bring her!" Two other guards galloped forward and dropped the young woman down on the ground—Turia. Her body smashed into the iron bars.

"Let her go! She didn't do anything to you," said Aedan.

"You want to take her place? You think you can handle us?" asked the guard.

Aedan held his stare at the man. "I've handled bastards like you before and won. What are you waiting for—permission?" asked Aedan, fueling himself now, preparing his muscles for the onslaught of fists and knives.

"Well, let me ask you, Arthur," said the guard, "is he dangerous? Should I open the door and find out?" Aedan eyed Arthur with one eye so as to not lose sight of the danger in front of him. Arthur's demeanor transformed. His worrisome eyes disappeared. Posture now erect, he leaned on the bars of his cell.

"Oh, yes, he is dangerous," Arthur said, with a smooth controlled push as he opened the unlocked door of his cell. "In fact, he was planning on an escape attempt." Arthur's mouth curled. "However, that isn't the best part. Aedan of Dragonia here is the founder of the Soldiers of Fire—the group that prevented the initial success of Brèdon's siege." As Arthur ended his utterance, Aedan's body began to shiver, a cold sweat overtaking him. He was exposed, more now than if he were fighting against hundreds of attackers.

The guard looked to Aedan and then back at Arthur. "Good work. Now get yourself cleaned up. You're beginning to smell like these worthless animals." Arthur smiled. His wicked grin stoked Aedan's rage.

"You're with them?" Aedan shouted. "You snake!" Aedan began slamming his arms against the cell. The two guards let Arthur pass, and the leader of the armed Hydrarians unlocked Aedan's cell. Like lightning, the men scrambled to Aedan. He snatched the top bars of his cell, then swung his legs up and into the chest of one man. Then Aedan hit another, stunning the two of them. The third guard drew a knife. The blade sang a sharp song as it was unsheathed. Aedan dodged left, then right, then jumped and struck the man in the shoulder of his knife hand.

The strike stunned the man. Aedan took control of the blade by way of the guard's wrist. Then a crash of pain swelled over him. The two other men regained action. One drove his boot into the back of Aedan's leg, forcing him to kneel. The other landed a punch to Aedan's left eye. Aedan was done. He thrashed like a wolf, still in control of the blade with one hand, while attempting to land blows on anything to make the pummeling stop. At last, the men ceased. "Time to die, you cretin!" said the armed man. The knife's deadly edge was against Aedan's throat. "No!" demanded the leader. "He has a special day tomorrow. Our leader will want to hear about this one." The knife-wielding man held Aedan tighter for a moment, then released him.

Aedan fell to the floor. The guards stood, surrounding him. "This is the man who defeated us?" one guard asked.

"It doesn't matter anymore. Our master will decide what to do with him. This piece of shit will either die in the ring or by some other means in here." The two guards nodded in agreement.

"In the meantime, take him to the arena holding cell. He can't get in the way of anything in there," said the leader.

"What about her?" asked one guard.

The leader knelt down and grabbed Turia's face. Her cheeks folded in his grip. He told her, "You should thank him for saving your life tonight."

Turia's eyes opened wide and she nodded. She looked at Aedan's bruised and bloodied form. "Th-Th-Thank you," she said, her voice cracking with fear.

The leader stood up. "Tell your prison knight in shining blood goodbye. After tomorrow, he is a dead man." The leader looked to Aedan with disgust, turned curtly, and walked away. The two remaining guards closed and locked Aedan's cell. Then they hauled Turia off as parents would an uncooperative child. Aedan and Turia locked eyes. He could see tears like diamonds falling from her face before she was dragged into darkness. Aedan lay down on the stone floor and fell into a listless state, his eyes examining his pains. Blood pooled by his arm. The cut he hadn't noticed began to burn. His muscles and organs ached from the guards' fury. Aedan's last sight was the feet of the guards coming to take him to a new cell for the soon-to-be condemned. Tomorrow, he would have to fight for his life yet again.

CHAPTER 33

MOONLESS SKY

Seemingly unaffected by their brother's desertion, Orion, Euric, and Hathus marched out into the night to tackle a new enemy—one they had themselves been raised in. The Gargolian army was corrupt, and soon it would be fulfilling the objective of its new allies, the Hydrarians. With that in mind, their intent was still to find Nestor and break him out with no alarm being raised. Perhaps if Euric's plan went well, no one would have to die.

Orion, dressed in dark clothing, lay in wait near a small building across from the barracks. The blackness of twilight hid his presence. Euric, clad in his usual officer attire, walked casually inside the long hallway. His footsteps were slow, precise. This night, in particular, benefitted the three men. A moonless sky greeted their rescue attempt. Even if they were somehow discovered, their identities could still be concealed.

Orion sat in the blackness, his fingers twitching in anticipation. His chest tightened, filling with the unknown and potential consequences of both failure and success. Not until a sound came upon the capital city was Orion shaken free of his anxiety. A snarling growl echoed in the night. The noise was reminiscent of two felines fighting—two very large felines. Orion moved to see the event transpiring. He cocked his head around the small structure to see Hathus chasing down two of the army's trained gargoyles in a fierce bout for dominance.

The two beasts slashed and scratched at each other. Their cries and screeches reverberated off the surrounding stone walls, so much so that they began to gain the attention of the barrack guards and others still on patrol.

Hathus followed closely behind the two dueling creatures, screaming, "Help! Help! Gargoyles escaped! Two rogue flyers in mutual combat!" As his thunderous voice landed on their ears, those around the barracks were too distracted to notice a dark figure move as a shadow in the night's ink. As Orion landed in the torch-lit passageway, he could see Euric at the other end, ushering him forward. Orion looked around and back outside, then made a dash toward his friend. Before Orion could reach him, Euric moved again toward the ever-deepening passageways. Orion could see now that Euric was clutching a ring of keys.

"Where did you get those?" Orion asked.

"Segeric's chambers. He won't know. Besides, you need to worry about getting out of the city." As he spoke, Euric continued down the stone hallway.

The two men ran down the hall, stopping at each corner. With every stop, they looked back at the way they had come, hoping to hear nothing but their own heartbeats in their ears. After what seemed like miles of navigating these strange, stony walkways, the pair finally made it to an old door. Three bars in the door acted as a window, perhaps for the guards to pester the prisoners. Euric began fiddling with the many keys on the ring. He tried one; no luck. Another, the same. Another; again no luck.

There must have been over a dozen keys to try. Orion's nerves were beginning to get the best of him. His eyes were stinging from the sweat falling from his brow, and his stomach could have collapsed into itself. He grew increasingly nervous by their lack of activity.

"How long does it take to unlock a door, damn it!" whispered Orion.

"Shut it. There are too many damn keys here," Euric fired back.

"Something isn't right. We haven't run into anyone down here."

"Yes, I see that. Tonight, it seems luck is on our side," said Euric, smiling, as he at last located the correct key for the dungeon lock. "Here we go, old friend."

The door creaked open from years of neglect and moisture within its hinges. Euric pushed it open and entered the prison. Urine's foul odor invaded his nostrils. Body odor stench began to make the men's eyes water. Orion gave an intolerant frown, doing his best not to let the smells and nerves overwhelm his awareness. Inside the small room were three cells. The first held no one—just chains and remnants of its former captive. The second cell also held no prisoner. Then, in the third cell, an elderly man with white hair and pale skin, and held up only by flesh and chain, dangled on the wall like a fish at a market.

"Father!" Orion said, stunned by his father's grotesque appearance. Euric again fiddled with the keys, this time matching cell lock to key on his second try.

"Hold him up, Orion. Take his weight off the shackles." Orion did as instructed, holding his father's motionless body in his arms. Orion's jaw began to quiver with sadness and anger at what the king had done to his father. His eyes swelled and he let a tear escape their grasp.

"Done. Let's get out of here before anyone finds us," said Euric.

"It's too late for that, officers," said the voice of General Bram. Orion's heart began to thump like bass drums. "Lieutenant, put down the prisoner."

Orion had already lifted Nestor and slung him over his shoulder. Orion wanted to speak, but he could not articulate. It was taking every ounce of energy not to obey his commander. Euric looked hard at Orion, glancing into his eyes and down to his side where his dagger sat.

"Lieutenant, put down the prisoner! Or we will take you all." As General Bram spoke, three more men stepped into Orion and Euric's view. "And you can die together tomorrow morning in the square," finished the general.

Orion stepped out of the cell, his father still on his shoulder. "So, that's it then? We comply and you'll just let us live?" asked Orion.

General Bram stepped forward. "Well, we won't kill you and Officer Euric here. Officer Hathus either. The three of you will be put on trial and banished for your treason. That is, unless—"

"Unless we join the new regime?" spat Euric.

"How could you allow Xenos to let the Hydrarians into our home?" asked Orion. "To use us and our people? Did you not hear what my father had to say?"

"Oh, I was there when the old man gave his testimony," said General Bram. "However, I agreed with Xenos on the alliance shift ages ago. We had only been waiting for the Hydrarians to strike. We will no longer be a lesser country."

"Is that how you see Gargolia?" asked Orion. "Lesser?"

"No. I believe we are strong. Although if we are to expand our lands, we will need help from other interested parties. One cannot defeat four," said Bram, now smiling. "Now, I order you to put the prisoner down!"

A long silence filled the room. Euric looked again at Orion and back at the general. "Fine," said Orion. With a smooth motion, Orion launched his unconscious father into the air at the general and his followers. The unsheathing of swords and daggers sung like metallic songbirds in the corridors. Euric lunged at the general's left and struck one man down instantaneously. Orion leaped forth, driving his shaking knife hand into the belly of the soldier to the general's right.

Nestor's dead weight crumpled atop the general. Euric swiped the hilt of his sword into the third man's head, rendering him null. Orion, seeing this, did the same to the general.

"Come on!" yelled Euric. He helped Orion acquire his father and they were off. Taking the only way out they knew, and keeping to the same strategy, they made their way down again, weaving around corners, hoping there would be no more unwelcome guests in front or behind them. As Orion and Euric came to another corner, Nestor began to cough. Orion placed Nestor down gently. He began to open his eyes at the same time.

"Ack. Ack. What happened? What's going on?" Nestor asked deliriously.

"We're getting you out of here," said Orion.

"Why does it feel like I've been hit by a runaway cart?" asked Nestor, moaning from his aches.

"I may have thrown you across a room," Nestor shot a bewildered look at Orion, "at General Bram," said Orion, with a guilty grin.

"Ph—is that all?" said Nestor. "I never liked that man anyway."

"We have to keep moving," said Euric. "I don't think we have much time. I hear soldiers coming."

"Father, we may have to fight our way out of here."

"Did we pass the door with our kingdom emblem on it yet?" asked Nestor.

"Yes. It was one hallway back," said Euric.

"Okay, take us back there. I can get us out of here, from there."

Orion scooped his father up again, and the three men set off to the door Nestor had passed through to discuss matters with the mad king. Once the trio reached the doorway, Nestor asked to be put down. He took a moment, then began standing and walking under his own power. In the meantime, Euric found the proper key.

"Now, once we open this door, follow me and stay quiet," said Nestor. "We are about to enter the king's throne room. A doorway is close that will take us out into the city streets."

Orion and Euric nodded, looking to their elder to turn the key and push open the door. The beautifully decorated hall, normally lit with the light of day, was empty of any combatants. The three men slunk out like small woodland creatures, keeping an eye out for predators. They scanned one side, then the other. Nothing suspicious.

Nestor led them. "Here we go, lads," he said. The old man opened the door slowly so the movement would not be seen and they would not be discovered. "It's clear. We have to move carefully. Speed will not be our friend; only darkness and stealth will give us our freedom."

Nestor moved aside for Orion to peer into the darkness. Sounds of soldiers wrangling gargoyles continued to clang in the night. Torchlights darting past in the distance made Orion hesitate. Euric nudged close and signaled to the next building. The two men nodded in agreement and, as lumbering shadows, pressed onward. Euric, now leading and in uniform, helped to conceal Orion and Nestor.

Euric started to stride with authority within the sparse streets, pretending he was concerned about the noises, while ushering on the father and son. The three men made it between a cluster of several market tents when the growling and wailing ceased.

"You two must continue on," said Euric. "Orion, you know the way."

"What of Fajer? He is still being kept in the gargoyle pen," said Nestor.

Orion shook his head. "No! You must come with us."

"Damn it!" said Euric, stopping to sigh heavily and contemplate his next moves. "We were seen by the general, and he mentioned Hathus. You and your father must get out of here. Acquire a horse if you are able, but not if it means revealing yourselves."

"But what about you, brother? You can't stay here either," said Orion, who began to fear for all of his brothers he had involved.

"I will retrieve Fajer and Hathus, then follow you," Euric said. "Do not stop for us. You can't wait. Your father must tell his story, and you, yours." Euric paused and produced a quivering smile. "Get ahead of this conflict, brother, before it consumes us all." Euric glanced at Nestor, then back to Orion, and then he was gone, swallowed by the moonless night once more.

Orion grappled with Nestor to help him stand and walk with some normalcy. The two men snaked through alleyways, behind buildings, avoiding late night movements of civilians and soldiers. They dodged lamplight and avoided curious eyes the best they could. In the silhouetted distance, Orion could see the wall, and with that, the gate he needed to pass through to make their escape. With squinted eyes, Orion could only see the standard two guards.

Orion knew if he were in his military colors, the guards would, without question, open the gates for him. However, that would mean eventual discovery much sooner than Orion desired. On the other hand, walking as a civilian with an old man would be suspicious given the time of night. No one left the city at night without discussing their purpose with the sentries.

"Trying to make your escape there, Lieutenant?" said a voice in the darkness.

Orion searched for the voice's origin to no avail. His breathing became heavier. Nestor, too, was looking for the source.

"I can't believe you did this," the voice said.

"Show yourself," Nestor replied.

"To betray our king and our Gargolian land is punishable by a lifetime of imprisonment. You're a traitor now, you know?" the voice said.

"I'm no traitor," said Orion. "The king and anyone who bows to the will of another country is a traitor."

Tius came into focus now, his full form appearing from the shadows. "You're wrong, Orion. The general told me such, and I believe him."

"You are blinded by faith, Tius. Blinded by your own passions. You think if you follow the general without thoughts of your own, you will be rewarded?" asked Orion, feeling hatred for a man he had once considered family. "Times such as these truly show loyalty and love, don't they?" Orion's eyes began to swell with emotions of fear, hate, loss, and worry.

"The general knows I tried to stop you. I went right to him after leaving your house," said Tius.

"I know the general plans to execute all of us," said Orion. "He told us himself in the dungeons."

Nestor's face was as contorted as a dog about to bite. "You piece of shit! You worthless boy! You call yourself a Gargolian? I bet once you feel Hydrarian steel swipe across your throat, you'll wish you had listened to my son."

Tius' demeanor and eyes transformed. Orion could see the rising shame in his eyes. "No, no, no. General Bram said you would all be sequestered and made to pay for your treachery."

"He lied to you, Tius." Orion's chest began to tighten. He could see the night sky transitioning now. "He and King Xenos have lied to all of us."

"Nothing good," said Nestor, "will come from the unification of Gargolia and Hydraria. If only you could have seen what I saw in Cerebria. Nearly slaughtered we were—hundreds of soldiers besieged a small town of unarmed farmers and tradesmen."

Tius' face morphed into a gray plume of confusion. His mind searched for answers. Conflicting information and jealousy had poisoned him, but Orion and Nestor's words seemed to drain some of the venom from his heart. "You need to get out of here," Tius finally said. "Come on."

Nestor and Orion breathed out exasperated relief. The two men hesitantly followed and waited for him to change his mind again. Waiting for another betrayal, they pursued Tius between more streets and alleys until they came within a mere block of the gate and freedom.

"Stay here. I will be back in a moment," Tius said. He began jogging down a street opposite the gate. Orion and Nestor looked at each other woefully.

"Can we trust him?" asked Nestor.

"What other options do we have?" asked Orion. "Euric and Hathus are busy with their own worries, and we can't leave without a blessing or an escort."

"Yes," said Nestor, "but he gave us up to that damn General Bram, who may be awake by now looking to decorate the city with our skulls!"

"Shh!" Orion insisted. "We have to trust Tius now. I want to trust him. We will deal with him later, if it is even up to us anymore."

After those words, the father and son sat waiting for long moments in silence, hoping not to see soldiers coming to collect them for ornaments in the throne room. The moonless night was almost the moonless dawn when Tius strode up, two saddled horses in hand.

"These are the only two I could wrangle," said Tius.

Orion took the reins. "Thank you, brother. I only wish you had believed me sooner."

"It would not have mattered, Lieutenant," boomed General Bram's voice. "Come out of the shadows and face your superior, and bring that dear old father of yours, too."

Orion's mood shifted. His hope of escape morphed into a pit of mourning in his stomach. Death's sour kiss would surely be delivered by the most brutal method. Bram was not known for mercy. Orion and Nestor picked themselves up from the alley and inched toward the pre-dawn light illuminating the open streets. In plain view stood General Bram and more than twenty followers.

"It's over, Orion. You and your father are now Gargolia's enemies!" shouted Bram. "Drag that traitor Tius with you as well."

The three men tentatively stepped out to face their fate. "How could you yield to them? How could you let our king yield to them?" Orion retorted, standing tall in the face of certain doom.

"Oh, dear boy," belted another voice, "I and my king can be quite persuasive." The vile General Anwar now slunk into view, joined by five of his guards.

"What happens now?" asked Nestor. "Attack more innocent people? Spread fear? For what? Land? Conquest?"

Anwar stepped forward. "The great General Nestor, one of the Soldiers of Fire. I have heard so much about you and your defense against King Ulysses' army with wretches and fire."

"If that is what you call an army, I am gravely disappointed in your standards, not to mention your leadership," Nestor replied.

Anwar smirked. "That's it; insult me all you wish. You won't be alive much longer to do anything else. Seize them!"

"Go. Take them. Throw them in the stockade," ordered General Bram. "For in the morning, we will execute them and relish their demise."

Orion and Nestor looked back to Tius. Tius' guilt hung heavily on his shoulders. "No running this time, brother. We see this through to the bitter end," said Orion, drawing his sword.

Tius nodded. "I'm sorry, Orion. I've killed us."

"Don't be sorry, boy. Be angry. Be fierce. Or we will be dead," said Nestor, unsheathing a dagger from Orion's belt.

The three men's enemies closed in on them, slowly ensnaring them in a desperate fight of fury, flesh, and futility. Orion looked to his father, smirked, and let fall a single tear. "If I am to die tonight, I will go happily in your presence, Father."

Nestor turned to his son with a quick embrace. "I am proud of you, son. Now let's show these vile scoundrels how real Gargolians fight."

Tius, Orion, and Nestor unleashed a roar, startling their encircling enemies. Their war cry sparked a charge and the three braced themselves for impact. Tius and Orion stepped in front of Nestor, prepared to shield the nearly defenseless man. Crackling, shouting, flames, and snarls overtook the sounds of approaching soldiers.

Several men looked up to search for the noises' origins. Tius and Orion took advantage of their distraction and started to slash and push at the soldiers within swinging range. The cries of men from the front and now the back grew louder among the clustering fighters. Orion did not question the clamor; he only thanked it for its birth. The three men staved off harsh sword slash after slash, slowly retreating into the alley. As the alley's shadows melted around the three men, the distracting roar erupted into pandemonium. Men screeched and shrieked, shouting curses and calling to their companions for aid.

"What is that racket?" shouted Orion, deflecting more strikes.

"I don't care," said Nestor. "Whatever it is, they appear to be on our side."

"Look!" cried Tius. "It's Euric and Hathus!"

The two rescuers fell upon the soldiers. Euric's shield and sword swung furiously among the knots of warriors, while Hathus stood behind him, reloading and firing bolt after bolt from his crossbow. A third rescuer emerged. Fajer dashed erratically from flank to flank. His sharpened tail and talons made purchase in the chests of terrified soldiers, ripping some in twain. Berated by their comrades' last screams, the soldiers engaged with Orion. Meanwhile, Nestor and Tius slipped back into the street and away from the action, routing to safety.

"We have them on the run!" shouted Tius.

"It's not over. Look at Bram and Anwar!" warned Nestor.

Bram and Anwar called upon more men—archers to take down the rampaging Fajer. The gargoyle's gnashing teeth dripped with men's blood. His yellow eyes now fixated on the generals.

"Archers! Loose!" ordered Bram.

A thin volley of arrows flew at the beast. Fajer tucked in his wings and spun, lunging into the line of archers and catching one man's arm in his jowls. As Fajer ripped the arm off, the rest of the archers scurried off to face simpler foes. Orion and Nestor smiled proudly at the beast. Fajer had always been a great companion. Now to see him in action encouraged the two to continue the fight.

The twinkling light of day began to blossom, almost overshadowing the fire behind the ranks of Anwar and Bram. Its flame increased with every passing moment. The blaze's heat could be felt by all now. Its sparks traveled, catching one roof on fire, then another, until only a wall of flame stood between the generals and the resistance of a few men.

"This must seem surreal, General—being caught between me and fire. Is it familiar to you?" asked Nestor.

"This ends now!" shouted Anwar. "I will not be defeated again by the likes of you. You are undeserving of my mercy."

"I have had enough of your mercy. You have twisted the mind of your last man!"

"Then end me here, oh great Nestor!"

"I can't," said Nestor. "But they can."

All alone now, no soldiers at his command, Anwar stood watching the light of orange flame be eclipsed by Orion and his brotherhood. Fajer joined Nestor, wrapping a protective wing and tail around his master. Tius, Euric, and Hathus encroached the general, pushing his back against the towering inferno, no escape in sight.

"Where is your king now?" asked Orion. "Where are your allies? Even General Bram has deserted you."

"It is time your filth be eliminated," Anwar replied. "It has been wonderful to see my enemies picking each other apart for me. Yes, I have lost, but if I lose, your people will have been defeated as well. Our fate is tied together now, young lieutenant."

The four men held their stances within several strides of the pinned Anwar. Sweat dripped from the general's brow. The heat and smoke choked his sight. His squinted eyes watered, leaving streaks of tears along his scar. Amid doom, Anwar grinned. One last quick breath of scorched air and Anwar erupted like a volcano, his fierce, exploding wrath unleashed. The old general leaped and dodged, slashed and stabbed with the grace of a mighty raptor. Orion's assumption of the man's abilities were shattered. He parried and swung in anger at Anwar. His three comrades did the same. Not a step was earned on either side.

Crashing pillars of burnt wood creaked and spat embers as upward winds swirled sparks around the dueling men. Soon, the street was snowing stars—balls of red hot light that danced among the clang and clamor of the battle. Euric and Hathus leaped as one creature while Orion and Tius converged at Anwar's feet. The swarmed general could do no more to stave off his attackers. Feet and blades made contact with Anwar; kicks and slashes drove him back to the firestorm's constant inhales and exhales, nearly breathing him in, beckoning him to fuel its raw power.

Nestor appeared as if to give his enemy a last farewell. A sharp nod to Fajer and the beast let fly a swift swoop of his tail, tossing the once great general into the flame. A smattering of painful cries sounded as Anwar burned. Then the small group of Gargolians stepped back from the heat to breathe a cool sigh of victory.

"I am sorry for what I did," said Tius, panting. "I should have trusted my brothers."

Orion nodded. "No time for apologies, Tius. We must flee before more men come."

"It is not safe here for anyone," said Nestor. "We must join the other kingdoms. That is how we survive. That is how we save Gargolia. Now let's move!"

"I'll be right behind—" started Tius.

Orion turned to witness his brother's face contort with pain. An arrow was stuck in his back. "No!" Orion cried. Tius fell forward, landing hard on the ground.

Hathus loosed another bolt from his crossbow, missing his target. "Damn it! Those cowards! Pick him up. We carry him."

Euric and Orion swept Tius' body up, dragging his lifeless corpse to the safety of the shadows. An enraged Bram emerged alongside the archers. "Fire at will! Kill them all!"

The fire, still burning, inched closer, sparks igniting everything they touched. Arrows zoomed overhead, alongside walls. "We must leave him!" shouted Nestor. "He is gone, son."

Orion's eyes filled with tears as he lowered Tius to the ground. Euric, too stunned to speak, did as the old man commanded. Hathus continued to shoot at the oncoming force. Fajer bellowed a deep growl. The four remaining men looked to the beast. Fajer eyed the firewall. The light seemed to entrance the gargoyle, hypnotizing him into a state of sedation.

"What is he looking at?" asked Hathus. "We need to run now!"

"Just wait!" cried Nestor.

Everyone turned their attention to the growing fire. Black smoke belched from flames. A scream shook them like hurricane winds. The gusts howled, forming a tornado of embers from the fire that had consumed Anwar. A charred figure, glowing in the red flame, limped out of the heat. Naked, General Anwar hobbled out of the blaze. His skin was mutating into that of a smooth, youthful man.

The fire that burned behind him was nothing but torchlight for the firestorm that smoldered in the general's stare.

All in his presence dispersed, running from the monster of the flame, running from a creature of fire, running from the man who had survived an inferno and was now reborn. General Anwar's nude, sculpted form locked eyes with Nestor. The old man's vision of great fear and turmoil had come to light, but what now lay in front of them even a seer of his caliber could not foretell. Nestor, being furiously ushered by his son, ran to escape from Kunagnos, their mad king, and a new and greater threat.

CHAPTER 34

APPLES AND COURIERS

Aloysius' one condition was to take a quick detour to the dock at Cathair. Even with some pushback, Aloysius was successful in using his wit and storytelling to convince the young clique of young Cerebrians to help complete his mission first. However, he did not want to take them to Manticore. They would be difficult to manage. He needed a different method. He needed a way to finish what he had started and still show these unappreciative people what he had done for their country.

The group of six waited until the men and women had retired to their tents. One at a time moved to the back of camp. No one would hear them over the cerberuses' scratching and snoring. The moonless night masked their presence as they moved like mice in the forest, light and silent. The six slipped away like stars at dawn. Once enough distance had been reached, their footsteps and breathing became heavier. A triumphant choir of nervous laughter was released among the young travelers.

"I can't believe how easy that was," said Zavia. Her smile seemed to illuminate the forest's darkness like a beacon.

"Told you it would be," Tacitus replied, smiling at his brilliance.

"Now what, Aloysius?" asked Zara, more apprehensive than her sister.

"We head on through the night until we reach Cathair. Once we arrive, we go to the docks," said Aloysius.

"Why the docks?" asked Tacitus. "I'm not going anywhere except to that damaged town with you."

"I'm sure he will explain everything in time," Zavia reassured.

"No," blurted Hagan. He stood taller and puffed his chest, "We need to know what we are getting into. If what you say is true, we could be heading into a bloodbath."

"We won't be," said Aloysius. "Cathair hasn't been touched. The old man I was with, Nestor, said the attack on Brèdon was their first assault."

"Oh, that's right," said Tacitus. "An elderly Gargolian with the gift of foresight. That doesn't sound at all made up."

"Like I told you all earlier," said Aloysius, "some Gargolian people possess strange gifts as passive skills, too. Not like Manticorian and Cerebrian folk. Their gifts can't be seen. Please, just trust me."

"So, what will we do at the docks then?" asked Hagan, crossing his arms.

Aloysius hadn't expected such heated questioning until their arrival. Still unsure what they would do, he said, "Well, uh, I was planning...." He looked at Zavia, who had moved closer to him. The look she gave him lit his inspiration like a match to dried kindling. "Couriers!" he announced.

"Couriers?" asked Hagan.

"Is that a type of food?" asked Basilius.

"It's someone who delivers messages," Zara explained.

Aloysius smiled at Zara. "Yes. Exactly." Aloysius stepped forward. "Instead of taking you to the Manticorian capital, we'll find many couriers to deliver a series of letters I will write. Those communications will be spread much faster than I could ever carry the story." Aloysius decided in the moment to keep Rordan's letter to himself.

"Brilliant idea!" said Zavia.

Aloysius grinned widely. "Then, immediately after, we travel to Brèdon, where you'll see proof of my story." Aloysius shot a look at Tacitus and Hagan. "Then everyone will believe me." The two boys sneered at Aloysius. They gave disapproving looks, but ignoring them, Aloysius began leading the way southeast to Cathair.

The rest of the night was quiet. Only crunching branches spoke as they traveled onward. The winds were calm in the nighttime, and movements slow. The same elements that had helped Aloysius and his new gang sneak away was also the very thing causing delay. Aloysius couldn't help but think the darkness would only continue for him. Running into these people may have brought him a small respite, but he wondered if meeting him had been the best thing for them.

Inner debates collided for hours as the youthful cohort traversed through groves of trees, across small plains and fields to at last reach their destination. By morning light, Aloysius could see the sun shimmer and illuminate the surrounding sky. The backdrop of the town twinkled and danced in the sunrise. The Trahern Channel could be seen from their vantage point on top of a small hill, leading them to the road into town.

Unlike other settlements, Cathair was defenseless. No walls. No catwalks. Nowhere to hide amid a full attack. Aloysius' mindset had changed since being involved in a siege inside a town. He was beginning to look at camps, towns, and even people as liabilities or assets, including his little band of followers. But at the moment, he was not worried about Cathair throwing any problems his way. Nothing they would face there couldn't be solved by a little diplomacy or a quick retreat.

By the time the sun was hitting the hilltop, the gang was descending into Cathair and onward toward the docks. "We are almost there," said Aloysius.

"It's about time. We've been walking all night," Hagan replied.

"If I had known we weren't gonna stop at all, I would have stayed back at camp," said Tacitus.

"I'm hungry," said Basilius.

"Oh, do please shut up!" Aloysius replied. He spun around toward the three so-called men. "All I have heard from you three is whining. Zara and Zavia here have had no complaints the whole way. How about you three strap on a sack and be more like the ladies!"

Chuckles from passersby made the three scolded boys blush scarlet. The girls smiled hysterically at Aloysius. "I have always wanted to yell at them like that," Zavia said. "They tend to be childish at times."

Aloysius smiled back. "You don't say? And here I thought I was being too harsh on them."

Zara ran besides her sister and Aloysius. "Thanks, Aloysius. Maybe they'll stop being so rude to you now."

"I doubt it," Aloysius whispered to her. "If anything, they will be more ruthless. But they won't be with you two around. I guess I'll just have to keep you close." Zavia smirked shyly and grabbed his hand. Aloysius did not anticipate the affection, but he did not shy from it. His and her fingers interlocked as he, she, Zara, and the three offended buffoons drew closer to the town's dock.

At the dock, they were welcomed by the smells of fish being processed in a hut at the head of the pier. The constant shuffling and bustling of fishermen, their customers, and passersby congested the thriving metropolis. A market just before the dock added to the overpopulation. Aloysius led everyone to the edge of the bulkhead. There they could all see the strong currents in action. The Trahern was known for its savage riptide and merciless waters. However, it was an excellent location to cast off from. The water could push a vessel out to the fishing grounds in under two hours. Along the way, workers skimmed their nets, catching the stragglers as the fish rode the tides.

Aloysius could smell the bait and the cooked fish in the wind. Often, his father and crew would prepare some of their catch on the way back to the dock. The entire trip took about a week to complete. Unfortunately, Aloysius and his crew would only fish close to his home island of Atwater. They seldom traveled to Cathair's dock to sell or buy items not accessible on the islands.

"Wow," said Zara, wonderstruck.

"It's beautiful," whispered Zavia.

"It really is," said Aloysius.

"I've never seen the channel before," said Hagan, eyes wide, taking in the sights. "How does one even navigate this?"

"Well, honestly," said Aloysius, "you don't. You let the water do the work, and eventually, you—"

"Wreck and drown," said Tacitus, squinting angrily at Aloysius.

"Uh, no," said Aloysius, trying to recover the moment. "The currents dissipate many miles out to sea. Or you can use the rudder to steer into the other outlying canals."

"You catch lots of fish?" asked Basilius randomly.

"We catch our fair share," replied Aloysius. "Well, anyhow, we must find a place to get breakfast. I know we are all hungry."

"What about your letter and the couriers?" asked Zavia.

"I'll write the letters while we eat," Aloysius replied, "and then we'll locate a few to carry them."

Aloysius, having been to Cathair's market before, walked to a small hut selling cooked fish and other goods. There, Zara and Zavia purchased some jam and bread to share. Hagan had enough money to buy several fish, which he handed out for everyone to eat their fill. Aloysius bartered with a man to give them fresh water and small containers for the road. And even Basilius, daft as he was, scrounged up nuts and other lightweight edibles from other vendors. Tacitus, however, took what was shared and pouted all the while.

Despite the uncomfortable meal, with Tacitus' incessant staring, and the crowded tables the six found to eat at, Aloysius was able to complete his letters to several important people throughout Manticore, including King Remus, the Manticore general, his friend Ledger, and his mother and father, of course. Once he had written the letters of warning, Aloysius employed the five for help in finding couriers.

Messengers who waited at the dock would carry messages throughout all the lands. Which courier would complete the task depended on the distance required for the task. Aloysius wanted one messenger per letter. That way, a larger chance existed of them reaching someone who could spread the word.

Aloysius gathered his little band of Cerebrians together and began his quick lecture. "The best method to spot a courier among the crowds is to look for a person wearing two packs. One for the communications, and the other for money, weapons, and food. No one else in their right mind would carry two bags because that makes each bag easier to pilfer. So watch out for pickpockets; they're as common as rats in a gutter out here." Aloysius stopped to see if everyone understood. When they all nodded that they did, he said,

"All right, get to searching. Meet back at the head of the pier once you have found your courier." With that, Aloysius randomly split up the letters. One to Basilius and Tacitus. One to Hagan. And Aloysius took the other two with Zara and Zavia.

"Zavia, you sure you don't want to come with us?" asked Tacitus.

"No, thanks. I want to go with Aloysius," she said. "Be careful you two. See you in a little while."

As the three parties went in separate directions, Aloysius could feel the heat of Tacitus' stare on the back of his head. He did his best to ignore it and focus on the task at hand, not to mention Zavia. He was thrilled to get some one-on-one time with her, even if that meant being chaperoned by her younger sister. Zara was nice to have around; she reminded Aloysius of his little sister at home. He welcomed the feeling of being wanted and looked up to.

After a short while, Aloysius and his two beautiful companions found and hired two local couriers who would be leaving the mainland in a few hours. Being gifted time, by finishing the task so quickly, Aloysius brought the girls farther down the pier, closer to the boats. Aloysius wanted to share more time with Zavia before the boys returned.

"What do you think of the boats?" asked Aloysius.

"Oh, the boats are lovely. I would love to sail on one someday," Zavia replied.

Aloysius anxiously looked about. "Would you ever want to come with me on my boat?"

Zavia turned and shot a cute look at him. "I would love that." She stopped and looked down at her feet. "But what about my people? They are all probably furious at us for leaving without their consent."

"I can talk to Vanna. It wouldn't be an issue," said Aloysius arrogantly.

Zavia grabbed his hands and looked into his eyes. "You show up, cause her problems, and then in the same night that she spares you, you whisk away five of her people like a common thief."

"All right, that does sound bad," Aloysius said, beginning to internally scold himself. "Maybe when we finish at Brèdon, we can meet up with your troop and I can explain—"

Zavia leaned in and pressed her lips to his. Aloysius felt her warmth. He pulled her in gently, and she grasped his arms to lock them together. As they parted from their moist kiss, Aloysius looked into her eyes and smiled a toothy grin. She returned the smile with a heavy embrace, wrapping her arms around his back.

"What are you two hugging for?" Zara asked, coming around a corner from admiring a ship. The two didn't answer; they just turned to her and smiled gleefully. "You two better cut it out. Tacitus already doesn't like you, Aloysius." Zara looked to her sister. "You know Tacitus fancies you, Zavia."

Aloysius made the connection now. Tacitus saw him as a threat. An issue he could handle, he thought.

"I'm well aware." She released Aloysius. They began sauntering back to the head of the pier, where Hagan was waiting for the group.

"You three just finish up?" asked Hagan.

"Yeah, just now," said Zavia, shooting a flirty look at Aloysius.

"Well, we must be off then, yes?" said Aloysius.

"Not yet. The other two aren't back yet," Zara replied.

Hagan looked about the surrounding crowd and spotted the tall Tacitus many buildings away. "They're almost here."

Tacitus and Basilius strolled slowly toward the group. A sinful smirk crawled above Tacitus' chin. He looked at his burly friend and nudged him hard in the arm.

"Ow. What are you doing?" asked Basilius.

"Remember what we talked about," said Tacitus.

"What did we talk about, Tac?" asked Basilius, more interested in the bag of apples in his hands.

Tacitus hit him on the head as if he were a child. "Remember, about the letter?" he whispered. "The one we threw in the water. You know we used the money Aloysius gave us to buy those apples instead of pay for a courier?"

"Oh, right," said Basilius. "The letter to the king. Haha. Yeah, that was good. Way better to spend the money on food for the trip to Brèdon."

"You idiot! He isn't taking us anywhere," said Tacitus. "He's lying to us with his stories and his charm just so he can get Zavia to like him. That was his plan the moment he saw her at the campsite."

"Are you sure, Tac? He doesn't seem like he's lying." Basilius took a bite out of an apple. "And why are you still on Zavia? You know she doesn't like you the same way you like her. You would have better luck getting one of the dogs to marry you."

"Damn you, Bas! I hope you choke on those stupid apples," said Tacitus. "All right, we need to shut up about what we did. Play along with me, okay?"

"Yeah. I understand, Tac."

The two boys rejoined the group of four. Basilius handed out the red apples to everyone, and Aloysius, with Zavia by his side, led the way out of town. The six would need to travel several days to reach Brèdon. There Aloysius could prove his story true, then possibly meet up with Vanna's group again and discuss spending more time with Zavia. Along the way, perhaps he could also figure out why Tacitus was sporting an uncharacteristic smile. He decided to put the worry aside and simply enjoy walking next to a beautiful girl while eating a delicious red apple.

CHAPTER 35

BLOOD LUST

A pale darkness surrounded Aedan as he sat awaiting his fate. Thin slivers of sunlight peeked into his cramped holding cell. The cheers and roar of a crowd of spectators kept him on edge. He couldn't see much of anything, and he grew ever more curious about what lay on the other side of the wall. *What will they have me do?* he thought. Suddenly, his cell's heavy wooden door flew open. Two armed men rushed in and grabbed him under his arms. They lugged him out into a much larger room. While being dragged across the floor, Aedan noticed small weapons scattered about—straight swords, rounded shields, helmets, and even armor. The two brutish men pulled Aedan to his feet, looked him in the eyes, and shoved a straight-edged sword and a rounded shield into his hands. He looked back at them, puzzled.

"You are about to be the first of your kind," said one guard with a devious smile.

"Don't die too quickly, you inbred dog!" spat a second, who also sported a wretched smile.

Still confused about what they expected from him, Aedan kept his tongue thoroughly still. He had learned early on that a wild and sharp tongue meant severe punishment for a man in his position.

The next moment came too quickly. The two brutish men led Aedan to a wooden door, pushed him forward, and pulled down on a thick piece of rope. The door raised fast, like a bird ascending to the sky. Sharp sunlight appeared and pierced Aedan's eyes like a spear. He advanced ever cautiously toward the blinding sunbeams until startled by a cacophony of cheers and excited howling.

Aedan, his eyes still burning from the dazzling sunlight, slowly regained his vision. He could see tall wooden walls all around him. Bleachers and seats towered over him like mighty trees in a great forest. People yelled and foamed at the mouth like rabid beasts, anticipating the action. He stepped forward. Still overwhelmed by all the sights and sounds, he noticed another door, the same size as the one in front of him moments ago. It also began to rise. From the looks of it, the only thing coming out of it would be from nightmares.

Just like a marble statue is revealed, the shroud of shadow concealing his opponent was removed, slipping off him like a wraith-like veil. The man entered the openness of the arena. Aedan's opponent looked to be eight-feet tall, with arms the size of wooden posts and legs as wide around as a small hut. Aedan's heart fell deep into his chest.

"How am I supposed to survive this?" Aedan thought aloud.

Horns sounded. A man sitting in a fashionable viewing section of the stadium stood up to address the audience. The crowd grew quiet, doing their best to be respectful.

"Welcome! Welcome to our new arena, here in the heart of the kingdom!" the man shouted passionately. "This day will be the first of many impressive spectacles." The entire crowd erupted with cheers, laughter, and hollers. The man in charge quickly quieted them and continued to speak. "Without further delay, I present to you two men. Two warriors armed and ready to fight to the death. No mercy shall be shown. Only one will survive this deadly and awesome showing of blood and savagery." The crowd grew more anxious. The anticipation rose like the heat of a great fire. "Now, let's usher in a great era for our kingdom! The match will begin *now*!"

As the dignitary's command fell, so did his fist, and the match was on. Aedan had but a moment to size up his opponent. Besides his adversary's sheer size and obvious brute strength, Aedan took note of the weapons he wielded—two heavy, straight swords. That meant his opponent was Cerebrian, so he would be slow, yet twice as deadly. By the time Aedan finished this thought, his foe was a sword's length away. A swift upward slice nearly split Aedan up the middle. Thanks to fast reflexes, he dodged it, barely. The giant man didn't stop there. A half-second later, he whipped the great sword at Aedan's neck. Instinctively, Aedan raised his shield, stopping the mighty sword, which ricocheted off his iron aegis and continued onward; the momentum of such a swing caused his opponent to spin to regain footing. Those few precious seconds allowed Aedan to crouch and roll forward, with his eye trained on the Cerebrian's leg. As Aedan began to unwrap himself from his roll, his sword made contact with the behemoth's right calf. A deafening howl erupted from the giant man, and the crowd exploded with exhilaration. They had just witnessed their first sight of blood, and they loved it. The crowd was filled with bloodlust, a hunger that would never be satisfied.

The giant man regained his strength as quickly as he had been cut, lunging at Aedan like a mad predator. Aedan reacted with a panicked flailing of his arms, which resulted in his being tackled to the ground by his massive adversary. The giant man dropped his swords, and proceeded to wail on Aedan with his stone-size fists. Aedan, being much smaller, curled his arms into himself to fend off as many blows as possible. At last, Aedan saw his opening, and struck quickly with all his strength. A swift, open-palmed strike to the large man's nose caused him to recoil.

Instantly, the giant man's nose gushed red. His hands flew to his face and he tightly shut his eyes. Aedan took this opportunity to push away from the Cerebrian, liberating himself, and locating his shield to his left. Then, without the slightest hesitation, he cocked his whole body back and brought down the iron shield against his opponent's right cheek. A wave of elation exploded from the blood-thirsty onlookers. Aedan's opponent had fallen face first into the sand. Quickly, Aedan grabbed one of his adversary's swords and threw it to the side of the arena, then snatched up his own. He had temporarily incapacitated his enemy and been able to remove one sword from the fight.

After Aedan had regained his sword and stature, the giant man had risen from the sand, bleeding, wearing a mask of red. The giant man rushed forward, unarmed. Aedan managed to avoid him by a swift side step. The enraged man lunged again. This time, Aedan bowed backwards, narrowly missing being tackled again by the behemoth. As Aedan turned to face his opponent, he saw that in the large man's attempt to tackle him, he had rediscovered his lost swords.

"Damn," Aedan muttered.

The warrior advanced again, this time strategically, and sliced at Aedan's head. Aedan brought his shield up and blocked the deadly slash. The large blade swooped down with such force that the sturdy iron shield dented and collided with Aedan's forehead, instantly splitting it open.

Aedan crumpled to the ground, and in an instant, the man was on top of him again, but this time, the large straight sword was at his throat. The Cerebrian towered over Aedan, smiling, his teeth covered in his own blood. Aedan surrendered; he knew he was finished. The crowd was ablaze with curses and murderous screams.

"Kill him!" he heard. "Take his head off!"

Aedan could only wait to be executed by this bullish man. He looked around at the sand and stared at the fine pool of blood he was making with his fresh wound. In his frazzled state, Aedan couldn't even begin to fathom where he was leaking red. Then the deafening uproar of the crowd was silenced.

"These two fought well—a great show of skill and violence," said the stout dignitary in the stands. "However, as the rules state, only one warrior may walk away victorious, while the other must be dragged out of the arena, never to fight again." A devious smile grew on the giant man's face, and the faces of those in the crowd matched it. Everyone looked to be possessed, their eyes wide and mouths agape with anticipation. This was what they had all come to see—murder in its most dishonorable form. Aedan just wanted it to be over; then maybe he could finally rest. Breaking the silence, the command rang out: "End this puny man's miserable life!"

CHAPTER 36

Blades and Maidens

Steadily traveling to Brèdon most of the day, Aloysius felt empowered. He felt energized by having sent letters of warning without venturing to the main islands. *Much quicker*, he thought. Plus, getting to kiss Zavia was a new highlight for him. Those few moments of embrace had nearly erased his memory of the terror he had felt battling Hydrarians. Aloysius' pace wore on the other five, however. He realized everyone had been awake for nearly two days now. It was time to stop and rest.

The sun was still high in the sky when Aloysius called for camp. Several hours of light remained. The time did not matter, however; everyone felt weary and lumbered to claim their spot of earth for the night. Tacitus and Basilius stumbled to a spot near a set of trees and collapsed, soon asleep. No fuss or sour looks. Hagan helped Aloysius with firewood, while Zavia and Zara located a small creek for gathering water and other edibles growing nearby. Once the four had what was needed for the morning, Hagan decided on a tree trunk to lay against; it overlooked the grove of trees where Tac and Bas slept. Zara waited for Zavia to land on a patch of dirt and then cuddled next to her.

Aloysius kissed Zavia gently on the forehead and remained awake to take watch. He would wake Hagan in a few hours to take over. Aloysius did not want to deal with the other two. He did not trust Tacitus. Basilius, on the other hand, was just daft and a little lackadaisical, but his proximity to Tacitus made it undesirable to chat with him. Once Aloysius scanned the surrounding area and found no threats, he aptly climbed a small tree overlooking the landscape. He could see everyone sleeping, and he had a clear line of sight in case anything strange should happen upon them.

One needed to be alert for such things as the occasional thief, or worse, an angry or rogue beast. Sometimes, even a tamed one would get territorial and take out its frustrations on people minding their own business. Aloysius recalled a time when a manticore had gone rogue and killed its handler. Later, however, he learned the handler had been mistreating it. Chaining and not feeding a beast as large and deadly as a manticore was a sure way to get yourself killed. After all, they could shoot quills from their tails a long distance.

Aloysius continued to reminisce on his little perch for several more hours. The afternoon had become dusk, and his eyes grew heavy as anvils. It was time for a shift change. He gingerly descended the firm oak and shook off the ache in his muscles. *Too much time sitting*, he thought. When he reached Hagan, he gently woke him. Hagan's firm jaw clenched as he rose, perhaps being aroused from a dream.

"What—what is it, Aloysius?" asked Hagan, trying to open his eyes.

"Hey, sorry, but I'm waking you for watch. It's nearly dusk. You've been asleep for about four hours," said Aloysius. "Next to watch is Tacitus, then Basilius."

"All right, all right. I'll stand watch. Sure thing. Just help me up, would ya?" said Hagan, perturbed.

"Thanks. I just don't want anyone or anything sneaking up on us," said Aloysius, eager to catch some sleep before they moved on in the morning.

"You truly worried about that?" asked Hagan, yawning.

"Yes. After what happened at Brèdon, and other times dealing with angered creatures. Definitely," Aloysius replied.

"Okay, okay. Stories for another time then. Off to bed you go," said Hagan.

Aloysius took that as permission and darted up to where Zavia and Zara slept. He found a spot near the girls and lay against a sturdy oak. Before he could take in the beauty of the sunset for another minute, his eyes closed as quickly as a hammer stroke, and Aloysius fell swiftly into slumber. Angelic sights floated across his eyes like clouds during a windstorm—scenes of Zavia and her black hair dancing while walking toward him on that dock in Cathair. Their kiss and closeness was his last thought before he was whisked away into a deep sleep.

• • •

Dusk had turned to dawn when Aloysius awoke, rejuvenated. The brisk morning air filled his lungs and jostled his muscles. As he stretched, the strain of yesterday's journey made itself known in a handful of remaining light aches. After a few moments of movement, his thoughts of Zavia roused him enough to inspect the group's alertness. The girls were awake but lounging in the waking sun. Hagan had resumed position at his tree after watch. Tacitus was still sleeping soundly, and Basilius was aimlessly walking about, swinging a thin stick and enjoying the audible whoosh of his makeshift instrument.

Aloysius peered around the oak. "Morning, ladies," he said.

"Morning, Aloysius," said Zara, sleepily.

Zavia smiled coyly. "Hi." Then she stretched widely. "How did you sleep?"

"Well enough considering I used a tree as a pillow," said Aloysius, returning her gaze.

Their flirty glances caught a now stirring Tacitus. Even in his sleepy state, he looked ready to insult or question Aloysius. Aloysius thought it strange that someone who had questioned him so much hadn't left their troop on his own accord. *Tacitus' interest in Zavia must be strong for him to follow me into the unknown*, thought Aloysius. Only another day or so and he would be rid of Tacitus and his ugly stares. After Brèdon, he would leave for home, for real this time, and ride out the conflict like he did every storm, with his family on a boat. Perhaps with Zavia. He still needed to convince Vanna. That was not going to be simple. He figured if he wasn't immediately impaled or mauled on sight, he would have decent odds.

Aloysius mustered the group and they ate what little remnants of food they had left—apples, wild edibles, and some small amounts of dried meat. After their meal, everyone assembled into formation and followed Aloysius on to Brèdon. He announced that with a swift stride, they could reach the town in another day or two. A collective groan spread through the group.

"You all decided to join me," Aloysius joked.

"Yes, but we thought we would have been back to our group by now," said Hagan.

"I'll get you back," Aloysius replied. "Where were you all headed anyhow?"

"To Maccus. We are meeting with other groups to purchase more goods and another mate for our male cerberus."

"Yes, our female is not bearing any young. So she will be used for protection on hunts," said Zara, happily displaying her knowledge of her people's business.

"Interesting," said Aloysius. "My people don't breed them. When our manticore dies, we will go find another in the wild to tame."

"That sounds dangerous," said Zavia.

"Oh, it is," Aloysius replied. "You have to be quick, both in terms of thinking and on your feet." Aloysius lobbed an arrogant grin at Tacitus' back.

Zara skipped ahead of her sister to walk in stride with Aloysius. "How do you tame a manticore? Won't their spines hit you before you are able to get close?"

Aloysius went on about how he and his family would manage snaring, wrangling, and finally calming the beast down enough to approach it. He had Zara entranced with his tale of danger. Zavia and the rest attempted to listen in amid the sounds of their footsteps and branches breaking. All but the sour Tacitus did their best to keep up with Aloysius' pace to hear the tale of life on a Manticorian island. Once the young Manticorian had finished his story, the questions began.

"Has anyone in your family been killed by one?" asked Basilius.

"Couldn't you use an herb to calm it down to prevent the beast from attacking?" asked Hagan.

"How big do they get? Can you ride one? I've heard they have wings; can they really fly?" asked Zara, thirsting to know more.

Zavia did not have any questions. Instead, she walked to the other side of Aloysius and latched onto his arm. The two kept in step with each other as they walked. The stares from Tacitus did not bother Aloysius too much. Everyone seemed to be on his side and ignoring the whining coming from the back of the line. Graciously,

Aloysius and the others ignored his snide comments and unthought-ful questions.

The sun slipped from the sky to the horizon and brought with it pale, purple-pink clouds that raced across the landscape. Aloysius called time to break for sleep. The group divided to complete tasks. Hagan and Basilius gathered wood for a night's worth of burning. Zavia and Zara located another water source and picked berries for supper. Surprisingly, Tacitus volunteered to venture out with Aloysius for a quick hunt.

"You know you didn't have to come along," said Aloysius, once he and Tacitus were away from the camp. "You could have helped the ladies with the water."

"What? And let you impress everyone with another story? No thanks," said Tacitus. "Plus, you will need my help if something big decides to cross our path."

"Trust me, I can handle one of your three-headed hounds," said Aloysius.

"Oh, sure. Because you fought off a made-up army by yourself? It's amazing that Zavia and the others trust you."

"I was not by myself, you twit. Did I not say I was with your kinsmen? Fighting with them, I saw good people die that day. Your people!" Aloysius turned to the towering Tacitus, who did his best to show how dangerous he could be. "I may tell it like it was glamor-ous, but it was anything but."

Tacitus eyed him curiously. "I...still...don't...believe you. You haven't been honest from the start. You convinced us to come bear witness to an attack that didn't happen to impress a girl you just met."

"That's what this is about?" cried Aloysius. "You are ridiculous!"

"It's true, isn't it? You aren't denying that you planned this elaborate scheme to steal her away."

"Steal her? I was unaware Zavia was something to be stolen. Perhaps we should inform her that she has no will of her own. She is to be stolen like a simple object." Aloysius turned to walk back to camp.

"You are twisting my words!" hollered Tacitus, following Aloysius with great speed. "Stop!"

"No! I think Zavia and everyone else needs to hear this!"

"I will kill you, Aloysius! Come back here!"

"Kill me?" exclaimed Aloysius. He spun like a top and leaped for the tall man, landing at his shoes, bow and arrow in hand. The head of the arrow was aimed a breath away from Tacitus' groin. Tacitus' confident momentum slammed into an invisible wall of fear. "You need to stop thinking with that, Tac, or I'll make you regret it." Aloysius held his position for a moment longer, then stood, turned, and shot upward at the tree canopy. "Now, let's get back before they begin to worry." Tacitus' face was still as stone. He was too worried about his member to react to anything Aloysius did. In the distance, a muffled thud was heard just beyond the tree where Aloysius had loosed his arrow. He ran over and found a squirrel lying on the ground, pierced by his arrow. Dinner was served.

• • •

The next morning, everyone woke as the sun's rays peeked through the canopy. Beams of light kissed them awake. Aloysius, still angry at Tacitus, slept with one eye open and one hand on his dagger. He did not speak to the group about Tac and their near-lethal argument. Aloysius was upset at himself for threatening Tac with the bow. Tacitus wasn't armed, and Aloysius was certain he could take him down in a fight if need be.

Aloysius first saw Zavia that morning walking back from a stream with their bottle of water. She glided over to him and sat down happily. "Sorry we didn't talk much last night," Aloysius told her. "I fell asleep as soon as I lay down my head."

"It's quite all right," Zavia replied. "All of this travel and little rest makes my head heavy by dusk. I would not have been any sort of a conversationalist anyhow."

"Well, today we can chat more," said Aloysius. "We should reach Brèdon by late morning. Then it will be off to Maccus to meet up with your troop. And, hopefully, I don't become target practice for an angry Vanna."

"I think you will be fine," said Zavia. "Just walk behind me when we first see her. And she won't be mad if you formally give her that horse you left."

Aloysius grinned. "I had completely forgotten about that horse. I guess I lost sight of it when I saw you."

Zavia's smile grew wider and her eyes glistened in the morning sunlight. "Well, aren't you a charmer," she said, and she pulled Aloysius' neck toward her. Their kiss was in full sight of the camp, but Aloysius did not care. He only cared about him and Zavia at that moment. Nothing else mattered…until a cry of hatred and pain rained out amid the bliss.

"You grimy bastard!" screamed Tacitus. Everyone stood up slowly, like one who had come across a wild animal and knew only slow movements would prevent attack. "I told you I would kill you! You damn liar!"

Tacitus' long legs and anger allowed him to reach Aloysius as quickly as a tree falling. His hands clenched into fists and his face was as hot as a skillet. Aloysius jumped to the right to lead the charging Tacitus away from Zavia. Tacitus reached him and swept his long arms toward Aloysius. His height made it so Aloysius had to dodge and move three times just to reach his body. Tacitus flung flurries of flying fists and feet in all directions, nearly missing each time. Aloysius' small stature and nimble frame kept him safe for the moment.

Aloysius' dodging maneuvers only increased Tacitus' fury. The tall Cerebrian saw the dagger on the ground, picked it up, and lunged again at Aloysius. At that moment, Zavia was screaming for Tacitus to stop. Zara added to the choir of pleas. Basilius and Hagan ran to Aloysius' aid like parents protecting their young from a ravenous creature. The two Cerebrian boys grappled Tacitus, controlling his dagger hand. With the assailant restrained for a moment, Aloysius took his chance and sprinted toward his attacker. He leaped, practically walking up Tacitus' body. As he reached the peak, he landed a swift but stiff kick to Tacitus' head, rendering him instantly unconscious.

Tacitus' head flopped to his chest as if he had no neck, and the blade fell out of his grip to the ground where he had found it. Hagan and Bas laid their friend down on his back. Everyone shot looks of confusion and anger at Aloysius. They looked at him as if he were the one who had just wielded the blade to kill their friend.

"What was that about?" asked Hagan, furiously.

"Are you okay?" shrieked a worried Zavia, wrapping her arms around Aloysius.

"He threatened me in the woods last night," Aloysius said, tightly squeezing Zavia. "He thinks I have been lying to all of you about Brèdon just to get Zavia's attention." He looked down into her eyes intently. "To steal you away."

"That's simply not true!" cried Zavia.

"Yes, I believe you, Aloysius," said Zara. "Tacitus was jealous of Aloysius, and you all have seen his temper. He has been known to shout at anyone with a different opinion."

"Whatever the reason, he still attacked you, Aloysius. We should bind him until we can talk with him," said Hagan, looking down, "when he wakes up."

• • •

Hagan and Basilius bound the unconscious Tacitus with leather straps from one of the bags. Aloysius convinced Basilius to carry his friend along the trail until he woke. The group quickly fashioned a stretcher to pull him along. He figured if Tacitus were to see how Brèdon had been scorched by blood and fire, and he talked to the townspeople, his anger would be redirected toward the Hydrarians.

For several hours, the five walked on. Aloysius felt a twinge in his senses. His instincts were smoldering. He could not pinpoint the problem. Perhaps a creature on the hunt, or perhaps something darker, lay in wait. Regardless, he checked for his dagger, drew his bow, and readied an arrow just to be safe. The others remained quiet as all the group walked deeper into the Turi Forest. Its dense undergrowth made moving slow. Aloysius explained that even though there was a way around the woods, he wanted to inspect Brèdon from a distance. Who knew what could be there?

"I know you said we needed to go through the forest, but I don't like this at all," said Hagan.

"I know it's not easy, but it is the safest option," Aloysius reassured.

"If we just left Tacitus behind, we could be moving faster," said Zavia.

"You know we can't do that," Zara replied. "He made a mistake, Zavia."

"I'm the one hauling him over all of this," said Basilius. "I'm with Zavia on this. Plus, I could use a rest. Do we have any food?"

Aloysius stopped for a moment to inspect the area. The thick forest floor was beginning to clear up into spread-out trees in the upcoming brush. "Yes. Let's stop for a break."

"It's about time," groaned Basilius, dropping the stretcher to the hard ground. "He is carrying me when he wakes up."

The five sat together and split the last remaining bits of food and water, even saving some for their devious comrade, who was now beginning to stir. "What...What...Where am I?" Tacitus asked. "Wait! Why am I tied up? Aloysius, you bastard! Untie me!"

Hagan and Basilius jumped over to him. "He didn't tie you up. We did," said Hagan.

"Yeah, you lost it," said Basilius.

"Bas? Why would you side with him?" asked Tacitus. "He's lying to you. To all of you! Especially to you, Zavia."

"Damn it, Tac!" screamed Zavia. She flew over to his side. "How about you worry about yourself and stop worrying about me! I don't like you! I have never enjoyed your company. You are a selfish, stupid ass."

Tacitus' eyes grew as large as saucers and quickly filled with hurt. "I had no idea you felt that way," he whispered. He stood up, towering over Zavia, but somehow appeared mousy by comparison. His mouth contorted and quivered awkwardly as he did his best to hold back further emotion. "Zavia..." he tried.

A piercing holler and screams of horror echoed through the air, wildly bouncing off the trees. The acrid smell of smoke in the distance filled their nostrils and burned their eyes. The six lowered themselves, crouching and striding toward the sounds and smells, moving ever so quietly to find the source. Aloysius took the lead again and bounded, ducked, and sprinted to reach the forest's outskirts.

What he saw was something out of his nightmares. It was as if he were watching it again, but from a different angle—Brèdon. Again. On fire. Smoke billowed out from the center, the walls turned to tinder and shattered sticks, and surrounding the tortured town was another Hydrarian army. This time, the townspeople were not so fortunate as to have Aloysius' bow, Nestor's knowledge, or Aedan's strong sword arm.

Aloysius felt his head spin. His eyes fogged from smoke on the wind and the stress of the scene. Helplessly, he watched as armored soldiers easily thrashed any resistance. A man defending his home was simply slain by a sword with the ease of batting a fly away. At last, Aloysius' five companions arrived to drink in the horror of their kinsmen's demise. One by one, the Cerebrians were attacking and dying among the flood of blades and armor and blood.

"Oh, no," said Zavia.

"Why?" whispered Zara, eyes welling up.

"What did they ever do to deserve this?" asked Hagan.

"You were telling the truth all along," said Tacitus.

"I don't believe this," said Basilius.

Aloysius turned to all of them. "It's worse than I anticipated. They came back to finish them all off."

"What do we do?" asked Hagan.

"We have to do something," cried Zavia.

"We have to go," replied Aloysius. "Start warning everyone in Cerebria. We need to go back to Ansgar. I went there with the other resistance fighters and told the king. I'm not sure how seriously he took our message."

"No way. We have to do something now!" said Tacitus, trying to keep his voice low.

"What are you going to do—fight off an entire army?" Aloysius asked.

"Yeah, Tac—Aloysius knocked you out with one kick, and he's half your size," said Basilius, giving his friend a look that said more than words could.

"They will slaughter us before we even manage to take one down, and then what?" asked Hagan.

Tacitus' breathing became heavier. His eyes swelled and tears started to fall like pebbles down his face. "You're right. You're all right." He stood up and started walking back into the forest. A sigh of relief swept over the rest of them. Then, in a whoosh of air hitting them, Tacitus leaped over the five and ran headfirst into the field, carrying a sharpened stick in one hand and a rock in the other.

Aloysius reacted instinctively now. Movement became unconscious. Thought, foresight, and questions of doubt evaporated. He climbed his way out of the woods, pursuing his once-attacker, who had thrust himself into a fight he would surely lose.

At first, the Hydrarian army did not notice the two running at them. Aloysius, with bow and arrow in hand, waited to see how they would react. Not a moment later, a wall of men realized the oncoming specks of men racing toward them.

Aloysius could see joints in their armor now—weak spots. He released his first arrow. It arched like a shallow rainbow toward the mass of warriors. A clang and a scream rang out. *Another arrow now,* he thought. He let loose another; this time it landed in a soldier's nape. Spouts of blood and life rapidly escaped him. Alert now to the incoming threat, a dozen men launched their own assault.

Tacitus reached them before they could set up formation. His legs stretched out and jostled the cluster. He threw the rock, and it made its mark against a man's nose. His stick jabbed and struck countless times, but it did little against his armored foes. Realizing his fate, Aloysius loaded and fired another projectile, which landed in another soldier's thigh. Tacitus took advantage and smashed his stick across the wounded man's face. Slashes of swords whizzed by Tacitus' form. Ducking, dodging, and diving, he blocked what he could with his stick.

Aloysius' slowed pace allowed Hagan and Basilius to overtake his placement. The two Cerebrians sprinted and collided with more armored soldiers. Hagan had managed to snag a sword from one of the fallen, and Basilius used his enormity and strength to boulder through a group of three Hydrarians. Aloysius continued to keep the enemy at bay by releasing arrow after arrow, striking each time. Shrieking and clanging was music to Aloysius in that moment.

Rocks began striking others, flying with enough force to inflict pain on many. Aloysius turned to see Zavia and Zara throwing large stones at the army. It appeared as though both of the girls possessed strength and abilities bestowed upon them from their three-headed beasts. However, the army kept drawing closer, so Aloysius' attention now turned to retreat.

"We need to go!" shouted Aloysius. "They will be all over us in minutes!"

Hagan hacked and slashed. Basilius pushed and threw men like dolls, and even tall, reckless Tacitus was evading strikes and landing deadly blows with his pointed stick. Then, without warning, as if the soldiers had fallen from the skies, the army had encircled the six. The girls had run out of rocks to throw as horns sounded. Trumpeting caused retreat and silence from the Hydrarian force.

The six backed into a circle inside the larger surrounding force. All six stood, preparing to strike. Aloysius felt his dagger being pulled out of his pocket. Zavia had commandeered his blade, arming herself with it. Hagan handed over another sword to Basilius to wield, and a small knife for Zara to hold. At this point, the encircling soldiers began to close in. The circle grew smaller with every step. Aloysius drew another arrow and held it steady, affixed at his enemy. Then a large pound rumbled the earth beneath them. A small path opened up among the soldiers' ranks, allowing an armor-clad maiden to stride inside the circle. Her black hair was tied up so as not to interfere with wielding a weapon. She had striking emerald eyes and a sharp nose pointed at the attackers.

"My, my, what a display of courage," the woman said, smiling. "You surely impressed me." Her steps were light and small as she inched closer to the cornered group. "Unfortunately for you all, I have suffered at your hands." She gestured outwardly. "What are we going to do about this, I wonder. I mean, you are all so young." She glanced at everyone in the party, eyeing them like meat to a starving jackal. "And talented. So much skill and strength among you all." Her hands fell to her waist and slid behind her back. "But you must be punished for your crimes." As she spoke, her arms folded to her front, revealing blades as long as her forearms. She stared at the metal like it was a mirror in a vanity. Her emerald irises glinted brightly in the metal's gloss.

"Please. We didn't mean any harm," said Hagan.

"Any harm!" roared the maiden. "You attacked, unprovoked, and killed a number of my soldiers."

"You provoked us, you bitch!" said Tacitus. "You burnt a Cerebrian town and slaughtered our kinsmen. That is provocation enough, in my eyes."

"He doesn't mean it, madame!" said Aloysius. "He was distraught when we came across the scene."

"Oh, distraught, was he?" She sneered. "And who are you to speak for him so confidently?"

"I am—"

"Nobody!" started Tacitus. "He's nobody. He is my soldier."

The maiden stepped over to Tacitus now. Only a few strides away. "A soldier? What for? Why does a young man like you need soldiers?"

"To fight you. To fight Hydrarians," Tacitus said fiercely.

"Oh?"

"We are the Soldiers of Fire, and I am their leader, Tacitus of Cerebria. I was here the day Brèdon was first besieged. I set the fire that swayed the battle in our favor."

The maiden grinned wickedly. "Oh, you? My father has been looking for you. Our general too. You made quite an impression on him." She gestured to her soldiers. The army moved away and made space for dozens of archers. "Drop your weapons," she told the six captives, "and get on your knees."

"No!" cried Aloysius.

"Shut up, damn it!" demanded Tacitus.

"All of you, drop your weapons and get on your knees, or we will see who can hold the most arrows, without using their hands," ordered the maiden.

"Princess Morrigan! Princess Morrigan!" shouted a man from behind the circle entrapment.

The maiden, now revealed to be a princess to Aloysius and his companions, grumbled, "Let him through."

The soldiers made another path, and in came a rotund man with quill and parchment. "Oh, Princess, we have rounded up the remaining townspeople. Thirty-six total." The pudgy man looked ahead to see the six Cerebrians still standing, armed and ready for death. "Will they be joining the lot, Princess?"

"Perhaps. Depends on what they do next," she replied. "And don't call me by my royal title. It is Blade Maiden out here!"

"My apologies, Blade Maiden. I will let you continue with your bidding." The large man trotted back toward the still-smoldering town.

"Now, on your knees before I do something terrible to each and every one of you," said Morrigan calmly.

The group begrudgingly threw their arms down, and one by one, they lowered themselves to their knees. Aloysius' fear of dying was not with him, but he did fear for Zavia, the rest of his friends, and even Tacitus. The army would easily stop him and the rest if an escape were attempted. All he could do was count the seconds until his and his friends' demise. He had never imagined such a barbaric ending lay in store for him, and he realized the weight of his decision to show off to these people was about to end their lives.

Morrigan gestured again to her archers. They advanced just steps from the group. There was no chance of escape now. Running would surely seal their fate. "This is much better. Thank you for complying. It would have been nasty to see your slim corpses litter the ground like trash." She sneered and moved closer. "All of you will get a chance to make up for what you have done today." Morrigan stepped in front of Zara and knelt down to meet her eyes. "Everyone here will serve a purpose, even you, darling."

"Get away from her!" shouted Zavia.

"Ah. Sisters. I can see the resemblance." Morrigan turned her attention to Zavia. "And what are you going to do to stop me from cutting her, from sending her to my soldiers as a plaything?"

Zavia spat in Morrigan's eye. "I like you," the Blade Maiden said, blinking and rubbing her eye clean. "You have fire. All of you have it. Is that why you call yourselves the Soldiers of Fire?" Morrigan looked around for responses. "No? Perhaps it is because you use fire as a weapon and a scare tactic, like cowards."

"We are not cowards!" shouted Aloysius. "And get away from them!"

Morrigan slipped her blades in an X pattern to Aloysius' throat. "You're right. Not cowards. Just stupid children then."

"Stop! If you are going to threaten anyone, threaten me, you bladed bitch!" cried Tacitus.

"Ah, yes! The leader of your little resistance." She removed the scissored blades from Aloysius' neck and traipsed happily over to Tacitus. "I almost forgot about you." She inched closer to Tacitus and leaned up to his ear. "Do you remember when I mentioned that everyone here was going to be used for something?"

"Yes," Tacitus said nervously.

"Do you know what your purpose will be?" she asked.

Tacitus shook his head. "No, madame."

"You will be my new pedestal," she said honestly.

Tacitus eyed her, confused. "I don't understand."

"You don't have to, boy," Morrigan said, gliding up and twirling away from Tacitus.

Tacitus' tan complexion drained from his face. Red leached from him. Two large cuts on either side of his tall neck split open. He attempted to stop the life from leaving him, but the volume was too much. Blood seeped between his fingers, dotted his knees, and stained his shirt red. Before he fell, he sent a look to Zavia, one of sorrow, and a glance to Aloysius, one of fear.

Cries of pain and sadness echoed through the group. Anger filled Aloysius—even more so than when he had seen the army at Brèdon, even more so than anything he had ever felt. His hatred for the Hydrarians began to burn through him hotter than the firestorm that had saved the tortured town. As his friends collapsed with grief, Aloysius rolled to his bow and quiver. His arms shaking with fury, he stood up and aimed for Morrigan. The Princess Blade Maiden merely smiled at him.

The whoosh of an arrow whistled, piercing Aloysius' left hand. He fell to the ground, loosening the arrow, making a stance in the ground next to him. Zavia ran to him, screaming at Morrigan, "You will die for this!" She held the wooden bolt with two hands and snapped the tail off. Then with a swift motion, she removed the object from Aloysius' bleeding hand. He held his wounded palm to his chest and rose with Zavia.

"The leader of the Soldiers of Fire is dead! With that, their resistance! Gather them up!" Morrigan ordered. "Log them in our manifest and throw them in the prisoner carriage."

The shuffling army did as they were told. The five remaining friends were dragged to the back side of the town. There, a gigantic carriage awaited. It was a monolithic structure atop dozens of axles attached to even more wheels, holding several levels of cages high in the air, all filled with prisoners from the army's travels. Aloysius, doing his best to press his hand against himself, looked back at Tacitus' body. Morrigan, Princess of Hydraria, the Blade Maiden of the Hydrarian army, stood over him, pouring out a familiar black liquid. With that, another soldier lit Tacitus' motionless body ablaze. Morrigan celebrated like a child winning her first game of cards.

Aloysius' eyes watered and tears cascaded down his face. Nothing could have allowed him to foresee this. At this moment, Aloysius regretted every decision he had made: convincing the Cerebrians to join him, separating from Aedan and Nestor, even simply arriving in Brèdon in the first place. He should have just stayed on his fishing vessel. Now Tacitus was dead, and he and four other innocent people would be put through unknown horrors.

A soldier signaled for the portable prison to halt its slow movement forward. The hydras that pulled it ceased, and the mammoth structure creaked to a stop. The group were led up a set of stairs and into a small hallway lined with cages of starving, dying, and dead prisoners. The smell of urine and feces permeated the enclosed space. Hope had been erased for anyone inside these iron bars.

The soldiers escorted Bas and Hagan into their own cell, and Zavia and Zara into another. Aloysius was privileged enough to be tossed into a cell with another, unknown Cerebrian. The cluster of five sat grieving in their new dwelling. Zavia and Zara held each other tightly. Zara sat in her sister's lap like a child. The other two stood silent, heads bowed, occasionally swearing and hitting the bars. Aloysius sat next to his new cellmate, still bleeding all over himself.

"I can't believe this is happening," Aloysius whispered to himself. "I mean...she just killed him, like he was nothing."

"If he was nothing, she wouldn't have killed your friend," said the bruised thin man sitting in the corner, knees to his chest and with his head down.

"What? How would you know?" asked Aloysius.

"Because I have been here since the start." He looked up to face Aloysius. "I was there when the Hydrarians attacked the first time." His thin face and sunken eyes showed a strong man who had been broken. "I was there when we set the bastards on fire and scared them away like frightened pigeons."

"Wait? What?" Aloysius asked. "I was there to! What is your name?"

"Magnus," he replied. "Magnus, town leader of Brèdon."

CHAPTER 37

SAVAGE HEATHENS

Uproarious cheers invaded Aedan's ears. His head was pounding from blood loss and the beatings he had received. His eyes closed now. He did not want to see the giant man swinging the swords of his demise. He could feel the large Cerebrian man change his stance, readying himself for the execution. The final moments of Aedan's life would be spent wishing for the end. *The last seconds will be the worst*, he thought. Aedan visualized the crowd screaming with glee for his decapitated head on display, like it was a melon in the marketplace. "Buy one, get a headless corpse free!" Death made him think strange thoughts.

"Stop!" ordered a voice. It was not that of the dignitary in charge. "Cerebrian, put down the sword!" the voice shouted. "If you disobey, it will be your end as well."

Aedan opened his eyes and shook as he breathed. As his eyes adjusted, he saw the giant, sword-wielding man obey the order from this newcomer, this savior from above. Someone was looking out for him. Perhaps he was worth more alive than dead. However, the same thought that comforted him also worried Aedan. He dared not move from fear, a potential beheading still firmly in his mind.

"Arise, Aedan of Dragonia!" shouted the voice.

Aedan slowly made a motion to stand and face his rescuer. As he rose, he patted himself to ensure nothing important fell out of him. How embarrassing it would be to lose one's entrails after just being saved. "Yes, sir," he replied. "And may I ask who has graciously saved me from a bloody death?"

"Do you not recognize him?" cried the dignitary, outraged and unworried over Aedan's condition.

"I do not," said Aedan, looking up toward the voice. "I cannot see you. My eyes are—"

"Silence dog!" shouted the dignitary who had announced the start of the match.

"It is quite all right, Aemilius. He is not from Hydraria. I sincerely doubt he could recognize his own king, let alone another's. You know their people are incredibly unintelligent."

Aedan's heart nearly fell to his feet. "King...King Ulysses?" he stuttered.

"I'm impressed the dog knows of you, my king," said Aemilius.

Ulysses stepped forward into the sunlight. His stern chin and the crown atop his head made him appear like he had just stepped out of a portrait. His jaw sat strong and his shoulders broad against the dark backdrop of the sun's shade. "You see, Aemilius, I believe this one is different from the other unworthy wits we have encountered so far. He may be the one we need to ensure victory." He raised his stone face upward and turned. "Clean him. Patch his wounds, and see to it that he is rested."

"What would you like us to do with him after, my king?" asked Aemilius.

"Once he wakes, bring him to me—no matter the hour."

"Yes, my liege," said the dignitary.

Aemilius clapped his hands and declared the match to be over. At once, guards entered the small arena to collect the two fighters. Aedan's mind swelled. He hoped it was due to Ulysses' arrival and not a fatal head wound. No matter the condition of his mind, he was whisked away into a private chamber. Inside, well-dressed, flowery-smelling attendants of Ulysses' choosing, Aedan assumed, dressed his wounds, bathed him in warm water, and provided him with new clothes. Aedan hadn't worn anything new in weeks. It felt incredible to be clean again. His skin was smooth and no longer covered in dirt and dried blood. His musky, tattered clothes were taken out with the bath water, the color of molded moss on removal.

Then as if in a dream of pure bliss and pleasure, he was led to another room with a bed—an actual mattress. Nothing special, but an improvement from the stones and cold earth. Aedan gratefully fell into the bed. He nearly forgot who had arranged these pleasantries. Thankfully, his body, depleted of energy, silenced his mind enough for him to descend into the tranquility and healing of a deep sleep. Aedan felt his body release the dread of fighting for his life and his worry for the rest of the continent. His burdens seemed to melt off him as his muscles and nerves completely relaxed for the first time since he had left home.

· · ·

Aedan woke many hours later. His head was hazy with the fog of sleep, his muscles heavy as iron. His eyes fluttered open to the dimly lit room. The warm glow of a candle reminded him of home, but only for a moment. His senses picked up the dull smell of flowers, the scent of the attendants from earlier. He rolled over and sat up. His stirring alerted the guard outside the door. An armored

Hydrarian man stepped in, hand on his sword, ready to unleash death if the duty called for it.

"I'm here to take you to the king," he said stiffly. "Move along."

Aedan briskly stepped out and into the hall. A second guard met and began leading him, while the first man followed as security. Aedan looked out a window; night had come. He had no idea how long he had slept, nor how he, a lowly Dragonian man who had started a resistance with two other men, could be of use alive to the tyrant they were fighting. His mind rattled with ideas, but none of them gave him any hope for his fate.

The guard in front approached a door with iron decorating the outside. Deafening knocking was followed by an "Enter" ordered by the king himself. Aedan stepped through the door and into the room. The quarters were humble for royalty. A large balcony over-looked the plains. Seats of varying size and comfort stood in rows, and ornate rugs and Hydrarian banners hung from the walls. King Ulysses was standing near the balcony, admiring the scenery.

"Aedan," Ulysses said. "You are rested, I hope."

"Yes. Thank you," said Aedan.

Ulysses waved off the guards. "Leave us. Don't wander far."

"Aye, my king," said the men in unison.

Ulysses walked over to a chair. "Please sit."

Aedan hesitated, but he finally succumbed to the king's offer. "What is it you want with me? Why did you spare my life? Your spy must have told you everything I've done."

"Wow. No introduction. No pandering. Straight to the point. I will admit I don't receive this type of kindness even from my own constituents," said Ulysses. "Yes, my informant revealed your past transgressions involving Brèdon and my first attack. He also informed me you and the resistance, aptly named the Soldiers of Fire, have taken up arms to stop any further advances."

"That is correct. Pointless violence will not be tolerated. Not by me and not by the rest of Ruxar," said Aedan.

"Wonderful. Absolutely wonderful. You see? Right here is the reason I spared your life. You, too, have conviction. You somehow led a group of townspeople—farmers, cerberus breeders—who had no right surviving that attack." Ulysses smiled at Aedan as if he were a child taking his first steps. "Boy, you do not understand the level of planning and conviction my crusade has yet required of me, and how much more help I will need."

"A crusade? Against what? Ruxar and all five kingdoms have lived in peace since the dawn of our history," said Aedan, outraged by the evil king's banter. "So why attack Cerebria? For what?" Aedan grew angrier by his own thoughts.

"I began my crusade because I had a realization. An epiphany." Ulysses smiled widely as he spoke. "I discovered something incredible, and I decided to dedicate my life to elevating myself to a standing that would allow everyone else in Ruxar to learn and appreciate it! But I have to execute my plans—to achieve those goals." Ulysses glanced out at the balcony. "I have to do terrible acts."

"What could you have discovered that would make you want to attack innocent people, burn down homes, and enslave men, women, and children? To fight for sport?" asked Aedan, trying to cool his temper. He knew if he tried to move on Ulysses, he would be down and dead before he hit the floor.

"Faith. I have discovered faith, young Aedan." Ulysses' smile grew like that of a child receiving a gift. Almost innocently. As if love, not evil, was the fuel that drove him to commit horrors against the people of Ruxar.

"Faith? I mean, I have faith in my family. In my friends, and until recently, I had faith in people of this world to be good to one another," said Aedan, unsure of the king's reasoning.

"Not that kind of faith that you have for people." Ulysses stood up with fervor. His arms pumped once in emphasis. "Faith in something beyond you and me, beyond all of our people. Faith in higher beings. Fate! Destiny!"

Aedan sat confused. "I don't understand. Higher beings? As in dragons and gargoyles? Those beasts fly, but to travel and hunt, not to rule over people."

"No, no. I have discovered them. Unearthed them." Ulysses raised his hands again in excitement.

"What?" asked Aedan, curious now.

"Gods," Ulysses said. The word hung in the air like blossoms leaving their tree and being cradled by breaths of wind.

"Gods? What are gods?" asked Aedan, now wrought with intrigue. Aedan recalled his dark dream after catching the arrow in the fight with the three men on the road. The shadows that swallowed and slaughtered others were still branded in his brain.

"Gods exist beyond us. They exist above, below, within, and all around our world. They dictate the world and how we live in it! They decide how we live, how we die, and most importantly, where we go after we fall dead." Ulysses' eyes became wild, his face contorted with reverence. "It must be hard to take in. I myself am still learning their greatness. Their purity transcends us, Aedan. They speak to us, but you don't even realize it."

Aedan's furrowed brow began to ache with confusion. "You're telling me you are destroying towns, invading countries, and murdering people, all for beings that cannot be seen or heard, but possess a mystical force that directs how we live our lives?"

"Essentially, yes!" shouted King Ulysses. He stepped forward like a dancer and held Aedan's hands in his.

"These deities told me—well, directed me to you." His smile was still prevalent. "They showed me that you are the one who can influence. You use fire, an element both of great danger and death, and a bringer of life and comfort. You use it to bring people to your side." He stood up again and walked over to a map of Ruxar on the wall. "What are the odds that a man, not of Cerebrian origin, be in Cerebria the same day my army attacks and that he pull together unworthy folk to defeat me?"

Aedan shook his head. "I don't know."

"Exactly! I believe you are here for a reason. A reason we will not understand until the events of today are long past. With that said, you are to become my harbinger, Aedan. My bringer of knowledge. My missionary." Ulysses looked back at him. "You will travel with my army to discuss terms of surrender. Teach them the ways of our new divinity. Lure them with your words, with fire of great joy or unspeakable danger."

"You want me to travel with you to convince everyone in Ruxar to give up everything they know to learn of and be ruled by gods? Or what? Be set ablaze for their noncompliance?" asked Aedan, hoping he was incorrect in his question.

Ulysses walked back to Aedan and flopped down in his seat. "That is precisely what I want you to do for me."

"You want everyone dead, don't you?"

"I don't wish to eliminate everyone, just those who resist. Those who disgrace our beliefs, my beliefs. Once everyone alive understands, then through the gods, I will tell them how to feel and what to believe."

Aedan could not believe what he was hearing. What Ulysses proposed was beyond maddening. Beyond insanity. He wanted Aedan's help in taking over Ruxar, one town and one person at a time. He stood up and began to walk away from the psychotic tyrant. "I can't. I won't," he said. "Do your people follow this faith of yours?"

"Oh, yes," said Ulysses. "Those who accept the teachings of Jormungand, our beloved Hydra god, are rewarded with lands and the homes of those who deny our faith."

Aedan started looking for an exit. He needed to leave. He needed to run. "I won't help you, King Ulysses! You are demented! You have lost yourself! You will lose your kingdom this way!"

Ulysses jumped to Aedan like a hungry cat at a wounded dove. "I will elevate our kingdom, you unworthy heathen! I will elevate all of Ruxar!" he shouted to the skies. "And I have already started. Brèdon has been taken by force, this time successfully. That will be the foothold we need to place our armies there to wipe out the Cerebrians."

Aedan was being held down by the king. He couldn't move. Ulysses' strength seemed twice that of Aedan's. Perhaps the king was mad, but Aedan felt like he was telling the truth—whether he was right was another matter. He felt it so much that he wanted to change how everyone felt in all of the land.

"You...are...going...to...have...to...kill...me," said Aedan, having trouble breathing now.

Ulysses released Aedan and stood up as smoothly as any animal after a kill. "Perhaps you don't fully understand the gravity of my discovery." Ulysses squatted back down to meet Aedan's eyes. "This faith I discovered has many gods. However, I and all of Hydraria will only be worshipping one of them: Jormungand. He is the almighty god. He is the creator of all others—of lesser gods and of people, and all other creatures that roam."

Aedan sat up and slid away from Ulysses. His back was up against a wall now. "So you want to worship this Jormungand? Make him happy?" asked Aedan.

"Yes! Elated. Proud. Everything. I want Jormungand to grant my people eternal joy after death, but his mission is to eradicate the other, lesser, unworthy gods, along with their people. Whether they understand or not."

"Lesser gods. Is there a Cerberus god?" asked Aedan, jesting now.

"Yes!" cried Ulysses.

"A dragon god?"

"Several! One for every element!" Ulysses said, even more excited than before. "You see, you do understand! That isn't even the most intriguing part, which may sway you."

"Okay, so there is at least one god for every kingdom and they all rule the world. How will this change my mind?" asked Aedan, growing so tired of this infernal talk. He almost wished Ulysses had let the man kill him in the arena.

"Because you have been lied to, Aedan. Lied to your whole life. We all have!" claimed Ulysses.

"Yes, you mentioned the faith. So what?"

"You must understand," said Ulysses. "I rediscovered our history. Older than any history we know of today, expressing and explaining in detail the lost faith of this land. And within that history ruled more gods than we have kingdoms."

"What are you saying?" asked Aedan.

"What I am saying is that many centuries ago, there existed a land here called by a different name that was not ruled by the five countries we know today." Ulysses paused to ensure Aedan was listening. "Instead, it was ten different nations."

Aedan's head swelled with awe and disbelief. "That is not true. That is more a lie than gods are!"

Ulysses lurched forward again. "You must see, Aedan. History was not kind to our ancestors. Something cataclysmic occurred to eradicate half of the world from existence, from history altogether!"

"You are truly mad, King Ulysses." Aedan stood up now. Ulysses mirrored. "I will not send people to their deaths for not believing in creatures that don't exist."

Ulysses slapped Aedan. "Do *not* talk ill of my god!" Ulysses ensnared Aedan in his arms, choking him fiercely. "If you do not submit to these beliefs, you will become just another savage heathen, used to fuel my war machine toward a brighter Ruxar, a purified Ruxar! And me at the pinnacle as its emperor!" Ulysses grabbed and threw Aedan to the floor, causing him to gasp for air. "You have until morning to decide. Join us or it's back to the arena with you, and this time, I will smile at your unworthy body as you breathe your last breath!"

With this ultimatum, Ulysses called for the guards to take Aedan back to his cell. Aedan, still seeing stars, felt many guards drag him through the doorway, down the hall, and back to the other captives. Aedan had to decide now whether to die an honest hero or to live as a liar and a mass murderer....

A SNEAK PEEK AT BOOK 2

FORGOTTEN FATHERS

If you enjoyed *Soldiers of Fire*, be sure to read the entire Beasts of Men and Gods series:

Book 1: Soldiers of Fire
Book 2: Forgotten Fathers
Book 3: Cataclysm
Book 4: Lost Sons
Book 5: Accursed Souls

For release dates and the latest updates on the
Beasts of Men and Gods series, visit:

www.BeastsofMenandGods.com
www.RyanMOliver.com

Here's a sneak peek into *Book 2: Forgotten Fathers.*

CHAPTER 1

WEIGHT OF WAR

Low grumblings thrummed the countryside. A smog of putrid death choked the trees and anyone still living. Screams of lost innocence and sadness echoed in the distance, atop the belching laughter of wickedness. Morrigan, the Blade Maiden, had led her forces deep into Cerebria. Its lands were bruised and burned, scarred from days of persistent pulverizing. Nothing would stop her from reaching the capital. Nothing would stop her from securing her army's foothold. She would prove herself as a commander, not only to herself, but to her father as well.

Morrigan stood at the head of a small town overlooking the aftermath. On orders, soldiers finished any resistance fighters, who were few. She found it interesting that most inhabitants of the strongest nation were stunned rather than furious over the surprise incursion. Those who fought back were dealt with swiftly and mercilessly, to be used as an example to the others. One zealous Hydrarian soldier went so far as to decapitate a man's head for the fun of it. All others fell into line after that, and eventually, chains would fall upon them.

"Madame of Blades," said a squirming, soft-bellied man.

"Blade Maiden. It's Blade Maiden. How many times do I have to tell you?" Morrigan replied.

"I'm so sorry, my princess. I am not accustomed to such violence. I'm afraid I may be losing myself." The man whimpered.

"Then how about you do yourself and me a favor? Find yourself and lose the fear, because we are not yet through."

"Yes, Commander," he answered. "And what of these Cerebrians? Are we to capture them as well? The prison is getting full."

Morrigan grinned at the thought of such large people cramming into the rolling cages like meat in a basket. 'Yes. We take them all. I have plans for them."

"What plans, my princess?"

Morrigan scoffed at the royal title again. "You shall see. If what I suspect is happening truly develops, then we all will see. Just be patient."

• • •

With each town, city, and insignificant settlement they passed through, Morrigan and her army acquired more and more prisoners of war, squeezing the rolling building of iron cages to beyond its capacity. The hydra pulling her mobile prison lurched forward against the outcropping of rocks and debris, following another successful invasion, only to endure a loud and sudden crack. An axle of the gigantic holding chamber came to a terrible, grinding halt.

The massive, two-headed beast, a fairly young hydra, growled and cried loudly as the machine's wheels ceased to roll. The crows and other fowl of the skies hovered overhead like an ominous cloud as impending meals raced through their small bird minds. They saw a fresh meat wagon filled to the brim, waiting to be cracked open for them to land. The squawking and chatter sounded like bothersome gossiping to Morrigan, who now felt the weight of this setback.

"Damn! We are but a few days' march from the capital. How did this happen?"

"Too much weight for the machine to handle, Commander," said a soldier, inspecting the damage.

"Well, can you fix it?"

The soldier crawled out from under the platform and cringed at the conclusion he had arrived at. "Yes, we can repair it."

"Excellent! Do it. Make the repairs as soon as possible."

"The problem is we have to take all of the weight off the axle to repair it. And the repair will only get us to Ansgar, no farther."

"That's just fine. I will only need it until that point, anyway."

"So do we have your permission then, Commander?" asked the soldier.

"To fix the axle? Of course! Make it so!"

"Okay, then where do you want us to place the prisoners?"

"Excuse me?"

The soldier sighed nervously. "We have to take all of the prisoners out of their cells. They weigh too much. That, along with the rocky and uneven terrain, caused the break."

Morrigan closed her eyes, wrinkled her face, and let out a burst of air, frustrated by the solution. "Then make it so. We will gather our forces to surround the prisoners, outside here in the fields."

"How will the soldiers prevent them from running, or worse, attacking us?"

"That is simple, sweet soldier," Morrigan said with a sinister smile. "We will make the cost of defying our orders too steep a price to pay."

"But how?"

"Follow me; we must find the Cerebrian children."

About the Author

Ryan Oliver is the author of the new fantasy adventure series *Beasts of Men and Gods*. *Soldiers of Fire* is the first story within this grand fable. Ryan's inspiration for writing and storytelling originated in years of studying history and reading great works of fiction. He aspires to improving his craft and bringing wonderful new tales to the world.

Ryan works for the Department of the Navy, while aspiring to developing into an author, speaker, and coach. Prior to his days within the civil service, Ryan worked as a substitute teacher for several years. Ryan hopes to continue teaching in other formats throughout his career.

Born and raised in Kitsap County in Washington State, Ryan graduated from Bremerton High School. In 2011, he earned a bachelor's degree in elementary education from Central Washington University.

Ryan and his wife, Ashleigh, live with their two sons, Lucas and Jackson, in Bremerton, Washington.